One Summer In Montmartre

TEAGAN KEARNEY

ISBN: 9780993028144

DEDICATION

To the one and only Tim—where would
I be without you?

And to every single one of my
readers—a genuine heartfelt thank you!

CONTENTS

ACKNOWLEDGMENT

Grateful thanks to my editor, Sarah Watts.

Chapter One

Life is unfathomable in its infinite variety. People come and go, loving, hating, making babies, laughing, crying their tears, caring and not caring as they live their lives till death arrives. On the whole, we view our own lives as the most important.

London, May 2007

Anna was indifferent to the clamorous sounds of the city, focusing on the click of her heels as she walked. She kept her head down and her attention fixed on the pavement, diverted on occasion as a pair of flamboyant shoes flashed past. Even the smell of freshly ground coffee failed to tempt as it teased its way through the air, chasing a flirting drift of newly baked bread. From time to time, she looked up to check her direction, trying at the same time to ignore the hurrying passers-by. She avoided looking at shop windows—she did not want to catch sight of herself.

Anna did stop once when a window display caught her eye. She was mesmerized by the long swathes of pure white cloth before noticing her reflection in an oversized gilt-edged mirror in the center. The black jacket and skirt she wore did her no favors. Her hair, bright auburn in her youth, now fading and tired, was scraped back in a bun, although several strands had escaped and fluttered around her face. Her pallor, the dark shadows under her eyes, made her look wraithlike and ghostly. She wanted to retreat into her inner world, away from the noisy bustle of pedestrian and motor traffic.

Anna had postponed this trip after the sudden, shocking death of her son, Jeremy, in a car accident six months ago, until she surrendered to the fatalistic realization that each day would be no different from any other. Jeremy had loved spring. Today chubby white clouds scudded across a blue sky and the air was apple crisp with promise. A shame it wasn't raining, because then no one would have noticed a tear or two. She would just have to work harder at maintaining the pretense of normality.

The old-fashioned bell tinkled as she opened the narrow door of the art restoration shop tucked away in a corner off Belmont Mews. Sighing with relief, she gratefully accepted the peaceful respite offered by the dark comforting interior. She had come here for a purpose. The world reconfigured itself back into an identifiable place where she could function.

Mr. Bentonly popped out from between the faded purple velvet curtains which separated the front of the shop from his workspace. He adjusted his glasses, his careworn face creasing into a smile when he saw his customer. "Ah! Mrs. Seeger. How good to see you! I hope you and the family are well?"

A sliver of panic edged itself into her awareness. What should she say? The truth? She didn't need to hear the same respectfully polite phrases trotted out where they ran needle-like along well-worn grooves, rasping at her grief. People were sometimes uncomfortable when a truth they were unprepared for was laid out too bluntly. She and Greg had used this particular framing shop for many years, but this was a business relationship.

"We're fine, thank you." She hoped her clipped tone would discourage conversation.

"And the children? I expect they're grown up and flown the nest?" His mild politeness hurt.

"Oh yes, off doing their own thing." She pushed down on the emotional wave swelling in her gut. For a second she was back in the church, standing at the end of the pew next to Jeremy's wreath covered coffin. She'd been so medicated she hardly managed to stand—Greg's hand under her elbow held her upright—and the one image haunting her mind, impossible to eradicate, of Jeremy's broken remains in the coffin. Her prayer, then and ever since, was that his guardian angel had taken away his pain and eased the last few minutes of his life. Please God, she begged, no more questions. "Does the frame do justice to the painting?"

Mr. Bentonly gave no indication that her change of topic came as a rebuttal. Remorse flitted briefly across her mind. He'd never been anything else other than courteousness personified.

"Please, come through. You can check for yourself and if the work is satisfactory, we'll arrange a delivery date." Mr. Bentonly led the way, cautiously threading a path through stacks of frames of various shapes and sizes on one side and paintings in stages of re-framing on the other. Anna's painting, illuminated by glistening shafts of sunlight, stood at the rear of the crammed workshop. He stood attentively to one side as Anna examined the frame. The doorbell chimed.

"Take your time, Mrs. Seeger." Mr. Bentonly left to attend to his customer.

Anna turned from her scrutiny of the frame to the picture itself which depicted a large bunch of flowers in a vase on a windowsill. A few strokes and dabs of paint indicated a rural landscape outside the window. But the flowers drew the eye in, dominating the picture; a glorious riot of chrysanthemums, forget-me-nots, cornflowers, daisies, poppies, lilies and roses with every line, shape and shade giving visual delight.

The years melted away and she could hear Greg's voice, dizzyingly full with eagerness and love.

"No," Greg insisted, laughing. "I'm carrying my beautiful adorable bride over this threshold too!" He'd lifted her up, and doing his best to ignore the abundant creamy white silk and chiffon tangling around his legs, staggered across the room until they collapsed on the bed, arms and legs flailing wildly in the air and laughing hysterically. "I love you," he said, his blue eyes dancing with happiness.

The ebullient mixture of champagne and youth meant it didn't take Greg long to shed his wedding apparel, while Anna struggled to extricate the elaborate pearl and gold clips out of her thick, copper hair. When the mass of curls tumbled down her back, he'd paused for a moment, his breath caught in his throat and, overawed with the beauty of her, he hardly dared speak.

But they'd fallen back into hysterics as Greg struggled with the thirty tiny silver hooks tucked behind a seam at the back of her dress, cursing the fact his fingers were blunt spades and unsuitable for such tasks. When at last she escaped her wedding finery, they made urgent, passionate love.

They were ready to leave, with the taxi waiting outside to take them to the airport for their honeymoon in Monaco, when Anna spotted a big, rectangular object wrapped in brown paper leaning against the wall. Curiosity took precedence and she'd imperiously made him wait, a humble servitor, as she searched for a pair of scissors and cut the string binding the paper in place.

"I bet it's a mirror, with a gorgeously elaborate frame," she speculated aloud, ignoring Greg's playfully piteous pleas about times and airplanes.

Tearing the covering off, she'd been silenced by the blaze of color leaping out from the painting, and startled at the generosity of such a gift. "Oh Greg,

It's beautiful. I adore it." She ran her fingers along the intricately carved border. "Gold leaf," she murmured. "Is this the original frame, because it's a work of art too?" Turning to Greg, she reached up impulsively, planting a carmine kiss on his cheek.

"Of course it is, and we've got the rest of our lives to gaze at it when we get back, but we have a plane to catch. Come on!" He grabbed her hand, pulling her out of the room and down the stairs.

Their youth and passion had made them invincible; they were confident and secure in their exacting demand of joyous fulfillment from life. Somehow, in that time and in that place, they'd been untouchable.

The gilded memory receded, and Anna moved further back to view the painting, momentarily lost in delight.

Lucas Marteille, a less renowned artist associated with the French Impressionist movement, had painted the picture, and it was, without a doubt, one of his finer works. Gregory's father had inherited it, and he, in turn, had given it to them as a wedding present twenty-five years ago. The painting with its vivid colors encapsulated life itself, and she'd placed it in their bedroom, wanting to contemplate it at her leisure.

It had been a while since she'd noticed the gold leaf on the frame flaking off around the edges and contacted the framer for his services, but she hadn't been ready to come and view the new frame until today. Seeing the painting once more, she recognized how much it meant to her.

"Is everything satisfactory, Mrs. Seeger?" Mr. Bentonly inquired softly at her shoulder.

"It's perfect. How soon can you have it delivered? I've missed this painting. It really is my favorite possession."

Back out at the counter, Anna paid and made arrangements for delivery.

"Ah, I have one more thing." Mr. Bentonly's voice wobbled with a faint tremor. "This." He took out a faded envelope from under the counter. "We came across this attached to the inside back of the frame." He handed it to her.

Anna took the thin yellowed envelope, turning it over and inspecting the back. She opened the unsealed flap with care, removing one sheet of folded paper.

"I believe you're the first one to open that letter since it was placed there."

She paused momentarily as her heart skipped a beat. A fleeting presentiment flickered into life but fled before she grasped its intent. She read the letter before passing it to Bentonly, who waited with patient interest.

He glanced at the page but ruefully returned it. "I'm afraid, Mrs. Seeger, I don't speak French. Would you be so kind...?"

"I'll try." She knew a little French and was proficient in the little she remembered, but her vocabulary was limited. She scanned the letter. "The signature says Luc Marteille, but I need a French dictionary to translate the whole thing. I'll read you what I can if that's okay with you?"

"Oh, more than satisfactory," Mr. Bentonly replied.

Anna cleared her throat. "My dear Hélène... we have parted... remember this... shall keep... I know you love me..." She broke off and stopped reading. "I'm sorry but there are too many words here I don't know. What I'll do is I'll send you a copy after I complete a translation. Would that be okay?"

"Oh, yes. That's very considerate of you. A fascinating find don't you think?" he said as Anna replaced the letter in the envelope where it had lain cocooned for over a century, before slipping it into in her handbag.

"Yes, indeed, and my thanks for this intriguing letter, and of course, for the work on the frame. It's a pleasure doing business with you. I'll be in touch."

"Goodbye, Mrs. Seeger." The doorbell tinkled as Anna left.

Taking a deep breath and plunging into the pulsing streets, she encountered the strangest of feelings. The unforeseen discovery of the artist's letter, and knowing her painting would soon be home, offered space for a gleam of hope to slip in, lifting the despondency of her earlier mood. Walking briskly back through the lunch time crowd, she realized she was experiencing anticipation and something else recently absent from her life, optimism.

Chapter Two

The space surrounding an artist is, of necessity, an arena of chaos because a sterile environment does not nourish creativity. Seeds are sown, nurtured and burgeon in apparent anarchy, and whether the turmoil is internal or external is irrelevant.

Paris, June 1873

Luc Marteille's attic studio was ideal for painting. There were two skylights in the roof so that light flooded the space even on the dreariest of winter days, and a window gave a limited view of Montmartre's wooded hill. The room was a generous size, but that wasn't the first impression visitors received upon entering the room after climbing four flights of narrow stairs, as they were usually too out of breath to notice.

In pride of place was the canvas currently being worked on; nearby stood a number of battered wooden tables littered with brushes, clean and dirty mixing palettes, glass jars, rags and paraphernalia needed for painting. Canvases in various stages of preparation and paintings at different levels of completion were ranged along the walls, filling the available space. The odors of oil paint, linseed oil and turpentine permeated the room further bewildering the senses and the impression was one of chaos to the untrained eye.

A battered brown couch for friends or prospective buyers was positioned at one end of the room. At the opposite end was a chaise longue, where his current model, Hélène, lay stretched out on one side, elbow bent, chin resting on her hand, her shawl and dress draped just so.

Luc stepped back from his canvas thoughtfully studying his model for a minute and, without a word, resumed working with unwavering concentration. Moving back after a while to take another measured look, his face contorted. "No!" he shouted, slamming his brush on the table then rushing over to the young woman.

She in turn dropped the pose she'd been holding, clutching the shawl around her body and pressing as far back into the couch as was possible.

"No, no, no!" he fumed. "For goodness sake, girl! What's wrong with you? Stay where I put you and stop being so frightened. What do you think I'm going to do to you?"

"I'm, I'm sorry," she stammered in alarm at his outburst. "I'm sorry M'sieur Marteille. I will try harder not to move. This is my first job as a—"

"I know, I know. You're standing in for Louise because she's pregnant and about to drop her baby. I know. You've told me ten times already."

She blinked rapidly as unexpected tears appeared at the corners of her eyes.

"Oh, merde! You're not going to cry are you?"

She swallowed hard, managing to avoid an embarrassing flood.

"There, there." Luc patted her on the shoulder in much the same way as he would have patted a cat or a dog if he'd had one, but his art absorbed him far too deeply to consider the value of a pet in any shape or form. "Let's have another try." He gently but firmly repositioned Hélène exactly as he wanted her, with a little turn of the shoulder here, a raising of the chin there, before standing back a step or two to check her posture. Finally satisfied, he returned to work, checking for one last time before starting to paint. "Good, and don't move a centimeter until I give you permission." His sharp tone left no room for anything but absolute submission.

Half an hour later Luc stopped and examined his work in detail, a frown creasing his forehead as his eyes flicked back and forth between Hélène and the painting. Satisfied, he gave her a brilliant smile, turning the full charm of his looks and personality on her. "The light isn't going to last much longer, so we're finished for today."

Hélène stretched as much as was possible in front of someone she felt was a complete stranger before swinging her legs onto the floor and standing up. She smoothed her skirts as her body adjusted to the pleasure of being able to move.

"Tell me about yourself. Héléna isn't it?" Luc asked her as he began to clean his brushes.

"Hélène, M'sieur."

"Well Héléna, are you from Paris?" Luc dipped his brushes into in a glass jar filled with pungent mud-colored liquid, swilling them around in little circles before wiping them on a scrap of cloth, then placing them in another fractionally less dirty glass jar, filled with the same sharp smelling solution.

"I'm from a small village near Bordeaux, M'sieur. Louise is my second cousin. This is the first time I'll be an aunt." She smiled at the thought.

Luc studied her. "Come here." He took her by the arm, leading her over to the window where he examined her face.

She was far too intimidated by such a celebrated artist to return his gaze. Instead, she stared out over the roofs of the houses. The fields and woods glittering in the distance reminded her of home. Paris was new, big, and different. Luc was standing so close it was hard to ignore his breath on her cheek.

Louise had spent time—at least half a dozen conversations—impressing upon her how popular Luc Marteille's work was at the moment among people who bought art. Before Hélène left that morning, she'd repeated her warning. "He's passed the up and coming stage and is considered to have arrived. He showed several paintings in the Salon des Refusés exhibition last year that were the talk of the town. You don't know how lucky you are to be in Paris and sitting for Luc Marteille!" And as an afterthought, she added "And don't, whatever you do, fall in love with him. An artist's mistress has a very short life. Besides, your parents and Claude would kill me!"

Hélène had laughed. "I'm betrothed to Claude, and everyone knows how I feel about him. Anyway, when you've had the baby," she cast a critical eye on Louise's bulging bump, "which I think will happen soon, I'll be gone because I have a wedding to attend. So stop teasing."

Louise's lips had tightened, and Hélène guessed this wasn't the last time she would hear of the subject. Louise was determined to open her cousin's country bumpkin eyes to the realities of city life—especially to the truth concerning good-looking young artists in Paris.

"You have a wonderful tone of skin," Luc said, "and the color of your eyes is remarkable. When I finish this painting, I'll hire you for another, as I have an idea I want to pursue."

Hélène blushed.

Luc released her arm but continued to stare, observing the rosy flush spread across her cheeks. "But don't worry. I'm sure Louise will have told you, and she knows from experience, you won't find me less than professional with my models. Besides, my wife is very beautiful and I adore my children."

Hélène breathed out in relief as he moved away from her.

He fished a couple of coins out from

his pocket and checked the amount before dropping them into her opened palm. "At the same time tomorrow, Mam'selle Hélèna?" he asked as she moved toward the door.

"Yes, and thank you. Au revoir, M'sieur Marteille."

Luc followed her out onto the landing and watched as she headed down the narrow twisting staircase. He waited till she'd disappeared before he returned to his work, whistling a jolly tune he'd heard the night before.

Hélène floated along Rue Gabrielle, her thoughts a peculiar jumble of gratification and chaos. Before the sitting Louise's advice had left her apprehensive and jittery, but after four hours of posing she felt elated that she'd been able to satisfy the artist—in spite of her difficulties in maintaining the position he required.

Luc Marteille was different from what she'd expected. He was older, and she'd found his closed expression, fierce concentration, and eruptions of temper intimidating, but his smile was infectious and the playful twinkle in his brown eyes captivating. She pushed away the thought of his touch on her skin as he'd positioned her and the memory of his face as he scrutinized her by the window. Casual intimacy with unfamiliar men was not part of her experience and thinking of him left her bewildered and unsure. Yes, she was beginning to understand the reason for Louise's warning.

She would have to let Louise know she'd pleased him and he wanted her for another painting. The money would be useful. The shout of an old farmer as he urged his horse forward, and the noise of his cart rumbling past, pulled her back into the present, and she put aside the day's new experiences. It's natural for a lass from the country to be overwhelmed by a famous person like him, she thought, recognizing one of the street names her cousin had made her memorize.

Louise and her husband Pierre lived in a second-floor apartment on Rue Theloze, in one of the new gray stone apartment blocks recently built in Montmartre. Pierre, a tailor, had lately been promoted to the position of assistant head at the select shop where he worked in Rue St. Honoré in the center of Paris.

As she climbed the stairs wondering if Louise would mind if she rested for a bit before helping her with the evening meal, a piercing shriek startled her. Louise! It must be the baby, but it wasn't due yet. She picked up her skirts, and in an adrenaline fueled dash, sprinted up the stairs.

Rushing in, she saw Louise doubled over in the middle of the sitting room, supported by the midwife, Collette.

Louise's neighbor from upstairs, Irene, bustled into the room. Irene was a veteran, her figure round and plump after giving birth six times. One had been stillborn and another died within six months, but four offspring had survived for her to boss around. She had taken Louise under her wing in the absence of the young woman's mother. Irene fired off instructions at Hélène, taking Louise's other arm to support her. "Ah, thank God you're here. Into the kitchen. Quick. When the water's boiled, bring it into the bedroom and get the next lot on."

"That's fine," Collette soothed Louise. "You're fine. The baby will be fine."

After the contraction had passed, the two older experienced women continued to walk the sweating trembling Louise slowly around the room.

"Don't stand there gawping, girl," Irene commanded. "You're going to be an aunt soon. Get on with it."

An aunt! Hélène grinned back at the women.

"And fetch more sheets," Irene added as Hélène shed her jacket and hat, flinging them on the nearest chair before hurrying into the kitchen.

She checked the water in the pot on the stove and did a little dance. "Has the baby turned?" she called from the kitchen.

A month ago, after ascertaining that it wasn't in the correct position, Collette had given Louise a strict daily regime of simple exercises aimed at turning the baby. But so far the baby had ignored the cajoling and the threats. Babies could turn at the last moment, but if this one didn't get a move on, they'd find out the truth of the midwife's assurances that she'd never lost a baby during a breech birth. This had allayed everyone's fears right up till this moment. Pierre's running joke was that this child was obviously as stubborn as its mother.

Hélène had listened to her mother and countless village women recount their childbirth experiences when somebody was in labor and helped plenty of cows, sheep and goats give birth, so she knew the risks of a breech delivery. She remembered seeing a stillborn lamb when she was very young. It had lain with its eyes closed in death, curled up pale and lifeless in its caul. She had cried herself to sleep that night.

However, this was the first time she was attending a woman giving birth. One second she wanted to jump and shout with happiness at the thought of seeing Louise's baby coming into the world, and the next she wanted to fall on her knees and pray no complications would occur.

"No!" Louise screamed as she convulsed with another contraction.

Hélène made the sign of the cross and sent a quick prayer to St. Gerard and a second to St. Collette for Louise and the baby before rushing back out to see if there was anything she could do to help.

"This baby is going to kill me!"

"Shush, there," Collette said, "this is nothing. You've got years of worry about this child ahead of you."

Louise continued to groan till the contraction was over.

"On your knees," Collette instructed, wiping the sweat from Louise's forehead and helping settle her into position. "There, get your bottom further up. Here," she looked at Hélène, "you can do this," she said, showing her how to massage the small of Louise's back.

"I need to make certain that oaf, Henri, has fed everyone," said Irene. "I won't be long." And she was out the door to check everything was under control with her brood upstairs.

Around six thirty Pierre returned home. Louise lay on the sofa between contractions, with Hélène wiping her forehead with a dampened cloth. He rushed over to Louise his eyes filled with concern. Taking the cloth Hélène handed him, he knelt down and began to soothe his wife.

"Ma chérie," he murmured.

Collette bustled in. "Oh, M'sieur Lefeuvre," she exclaimed, deftly removing the cloth. "She's fine and I believe," she said, placing her hand under his elbow to make sure he understood, "M'sieur Durrence is going to keep you company till the baby arrives. So off you go." Ignoring his protests, she hustled the anxious Pierre to his feet and dispatched him upstairs. "Tell Irene, we're moving Louise into the bedroom and we'll be needing her soon," she called out after him.

Irene's husband, the gregarious Henri welcomed Pierre, giving him a glass of wine, and commenced a detailed retelling of his personal experiences during the births of his offspring.

Irene left, with strict instructions for

the children to stay in bed and for Henri to stop frightening Pierre.

Henri drank copious amounts of wine, but Pierre was so wound up he couldn't touch a drop. He was completely unable to follow the expert's well-intentioned advice to drink up and forget what was going on until he was called to admire the newborn. Unable to stop worrying, Pierre periodically left the increasingly intoxicated Henri, tiptoeing down the stairs to stand outside his apartment listening to Louise's outraged cries. He would wait till Louise had stopped screaming and knock timidly on the door. Departing after reassurances from Hélène, he would return within half an hour or so, pleading to be told everything was going as expected.

"But she is suffering so," he complained miserably to Henri.

"It is the same for all women, is it not?" said the older man. "That is how our mothers suffered. It is how women will continue to suffer as they give birth. It's part of life, is it not?"

Pierre, wracked with worry, could do nothing but nod in agreement.

Hélène's main duty was to apply more cooling damp cloths to Louise's heated forehead. This was the easy part—not screaming as Louise excruciatingly crushed her hand when the contractions came was more challenging. From time to time, Irene and Collette would go outside to confer, and she could hear their guarded whispers. Was it feet or buttocks first? Was the labor taking too long? Should the doctor be fetched?

Louise, pale and sweating, was becoming too exhausted to care.

During the contractions, Hélène

would repeat, over and over, "Louise will be fine. The baby will be fine." Then, in an agony of uncertainty for her cousin, she appealed first to Our Lady, followed by prayers to St. Nicholas, St. Germain Cousin, St. Guinefort, and her favorite, St. Teresa of Avila, and ended with an entreaty to any saint whose name she could remember.

As midnight approached, Collette urged. "Push. Come on. More effort. Your baby's coming,"

"I can't," Louise whispered her voice barely audible. Her dark curls stuck wetly around her face, her eyes a stark contrast to the whiteness of her complexion.

"Yes, you can," Hélène insisted.

"Any minute," Irene murmured, holding towels ready, and winking at Hélène. "You'll see."

"Keep trying, Louise." Collette

commanded." I can see the baby's back. Come on, you don't want your baby stuck, do you? So when the next contraction comes, use every bit of strength you've got left. Ready?"

Louise looked up at Hélène, who smiled at her, then squeezed her eyes shut as the contraction began and she pushed.

Hélène bit her lip to stop the yelp of pain as Louise mashed her fingers together.

"Baby's out! Your baby's out," cried Collette.

"And it's a fine-looking boy," said Irene, a big grin on her face, as she held the newborn while Collette cut the umbilical cord.

"You've done it!" Hélène bent and kissed Louise's forehead. "I'll go tell Pierre."

Hélène, exhilarated and exhausted,

climbed up to Irene's apartment to give the nerve torn husband the good news. She hadn't raised her hand to knock when the door opened and Pierre was out on the landing, his face cracking into the broadest grin when she told him.

He grabbed her shoulders, kissing her on both cheeks, before turning to Henri, who had blearily followed him out, and kissing him too. He ran down the stairs with his intoxicated neighbor staggering behind him. Pierre cried when he saw his baby son in his wife's arms, a smile of joy on her face.

"Oh! What an adorable babe," Henri said, approaching the bed from the other side, bending and swaying over Louise in an alarming fashion.

Irene grabbed his arm and dragged him out. "I think you've celebrated for Paris," she said hustling him out the door.

"Don't you want another lovely kid yourself, ma chérie?" was the last they heard before the front door banged shut.

Collette settled Louise and the newborn for the night, giving Pierre and Hélène strict instructions what to do and what not to do, promising to return and check on both of them first thing in the morning.

Looking in on the new mother before going to bed, Hélène saw Louise had drifted off to sleep with the babe in her arms, and Pierre sat on a chair by the side of the bed, gazing at his sleeping son with such a look of love that it brought tears to her eyes.

Hélène lay on her narrow cot, in the room that would be the baby's when he was old enough, staring up at the ceiling; she needed to sleep as she was due at Luc's studio by ten o'clock but her emotions were running too high. She was an aunt, and would soon be married and having babies. There was no doubt in her mind she would have several; she wanted three boys and two girls. Would her first labor be difficult? Would she take after her mother who'd given birth to five babies with ease, although she and her elder brother were the only two who had lived past their first year? Who would her children look like, her or Claude? Wasn't that what life consisted of? What more could she want? The thoughts spiraled around and around.

When sleep finally arrived, the last thing which came to mind had nothing to do with the momentous events of the evening, nor was it of Claude, her betrothed. The final image lingering before her inner eye was the sharp calculating look on Luc Marteille's face as he dropped the coins into her hand at the end of the session.

Chapter Three

We are never aware that a specific moment in our life is pivotal. When we make and/or agree to decisions, we can never be completely certain of what the outcome will be. The one point we can be sure of is at that instant, it is as if we are blindly impelled toward a particular choice.

Pennwood, Bath, May 2007

Anna sat on the edge of her bed, with the letter in her lap and a French dictionary by her side, gazing at the painting. Greg had wanted to place it in the living room or dining room so others could see and appreciate its vibrant intensity. Anna hadn't wanted to be so generous, and she kept the picture in their private space. Today she had changed its position, moving it from where they could both see it to the wall facing her side of the bed.

Tearing her attention away, she extracted the letter from the envelope. Holding the delicate, less faded, sheet of paper with careful fingers, she re-read the letter. Taking up her dictionary and pad, with a pen to hand, she set to work, intent on gratifying her curiosity through a more accurate and fuller translation than the one she'd offered Mr. Bentonly.

My dear Hélène,

I realize we have parted for the last time, but I must tell you that knowing you has changed me. My golden hearted Hélène, I would have given you everything that I possibly could, though we are both aware it is not enough to win you. But remember this, I did, and still do, love you. With every beat of my heart. You have shown me my world afresh. I know you love me because I have seen it in your eyes.

I am broken into a thousand hard useless pieces and my days will be empty without you. I cannot ask you to be with me, but I shall keep my sweet love for you locked away in a secret place deep inside my soul where I shall cherish it. When dark clouds descend, for my life will become bleak without your presence, I will take out these precious memories of our time together and they will comfort me.

Your distraught admirer,

Luc.

Anna wiped away the tears rolling down her face. The writer's poignant cry of longing for an absent love resonated with her own unhealed wound. She was well acquainted with the misery expressed in the letter, although she no longer broke down, her loss bleeding from her eyes, at the slightest allusion to anything associated with her son. Three months before his death he'd turned twenty-two years old. Her first born wasn't meant to die at twenty-two.

At first she shut off her emotions, retreating from the pain, unable to sleep or eat, let alone run a house and care for a husband and daughter. She'd strayed into a disjointed emotional landscape of anguish and pain, where there was no favorable path to follow, and spent long melancholy hours lying inert, staring at the painting's burgeoning flowers. Transient, yet vibrant with energy and life, they grew to symbolize Jeremy's life, and the picture became, for her, an archetypal representation of how fleeting life was for humans.

And there were the dreams. Jeremy visited her often in her dreams. One birthday he'd presented her with a bunch of flowers—identical to the ones in the painting—offering them to her with a grin.

"Look familiar?" he'd said, his brown eyes twinkling and an impudent grin on his face. "They're for you."

Not till after a clinical psychologist had given a diagnosis of grief-induced depression, with Gregory making sure she took her prescribed medication, had she slowly and reluctantly resumed her customary routines of daily life. Going up to London to view the picture in its re-gilded frame was the first trip she'd had the courage to make since they buried Jeremy six months ago.

Her attention was split between the painting of flowers in front of her and the letter in her hand, turning questions about Luc Marteille over in her mind. What role did this Hélène have in the artist's life? Why 'aspiring'? Toward what goal did he strive? It piqued her that she didn't know. Gregory's father had researched the artist and the information he'd come across made for dull reading; a good husband, good father, and no sniff of any scandal. Despite her familiarity with every stroke and daub of paint on the canvas, the letter plucked a dissonant chord in her preconceived view of its painter as a model family man.

Rapid footsteps up the stairs and the door flew open.

"Hey, Mum." Ingrid, now her only child, whirled into the room and threw herself on the bed. Eighteen going on twenty-four, with burnished copper red hair coiled on top, curls tumbling out, proclaiming to the world that they, like her, refused to be restrained,

"Two more days... and freedom." She flung a hand out dramatically, knocking the dictionary onto the floor. "Oh, sorry, Mum," she mumbled as her mother retrieved it. "What's that?" She pointed at the pad, covered with scribbled writing, balanced on her mother's lap and the envelope clutched in her hand. "And, pray tell, what are you doing with my French dictionary?" Sitting up, she eyed the writing on her mother's pad, trying to disguise the calculating look in her eyes with mock innocence.

"Ingrid, do you have to fling yourself on my bed in that way?"

"Relax, Mum. This room is so spotless it needs something like me to...

you know...."

"What? Provide color?"

This was an old conversation between them. Anna and Greg's bedroom was decorated in shades of white. The redwood floors, laid when the house was built 200 years ago and magnificently restored, provided the one color alleviating the severity. This room had become her refuge in recent months. An absence of objects, other than the antique dresser and an original, bright turquoise Bauhaus plastic chair positioned by the window, made it easy to slide into a state of blank nothingness where she didn't have to feel.

But Ingrid was already pushing open one of the doors along the wall of built-in wardrobes. It slid smoothly into a recess revealing a collection of expensive clothes.

"Mum, you need a little chaos." Ingrid pointed to where Anna had arranged her clothes according to garment and color, with one section devoted to jumpers and another section for underwear, gloves, scarves etc., etc. Every piece of clothing was folded meticulously in piles of perfect alignment. "This is ridiculous."

An idea was forming in Anna's mind—disparate thoughts coming together and beginning to flow in a certain direction.

"Do you fancy going to France?"

"Er, Mum, we are going to France as soon as Dad finishes his conference."

Anna resisted the urge to spit out a comeback at her smart-mouthed daughter. Ingrid's teenage touchiness and her own fragility meant that conversations degenerated into verbal sparring between them far too often.

"No, darling not the trip to Biarritz. Before that. To Paris."

Ingrid stared at her mother as if she'd gone mad. "Mum, I'm going to the concert with Matt. Remember? I'm not going anywhere else. There's no way I'm missing *The Spirits Unborn*. Sorry, Mum."

"Come here." Anna patted the space next to her, "what's your opinion on this?" She showed Ingrid Luc Marteille's letter, along with her translation. "What do you think?"

Ingrid skimmed the translation. "Mmm. Interesting, I suppose."

Ignoring Ingrid's less than enthusiastic response, Anna continued. "How about you and I do a bit of research? Be detectives and find out who this Hélène is?"

The concept was crystallizing. It offered something different, something new. Her present existence offered no freedom to explore. It was fixed and constricted by routine, and going back to how it was before wasn't an option.

"Mum, I told you. I can't."

"But this is something we could do together." She paused trying to come up with a reason more powerful than the latest pop group. "I would love to spend time alone with you...." she trailed off.

Arrangements with Ingrid required negotiation. Jeremy would have... but she blocked that sequence of thoughts. She didn't want to plead with her daughter because that might reveal her nervousness or lack of courage at the thought of going alone. But the more her mind tracked back around this imaginative fancy, the more attractive it grew. "It'll be a challenge. Just the two of us."

Ingrid looked for a moment as if she might consider the idea, but shook her head. "Mmm. Let me see. Matt and the concert? Or haring around Paris with my mother playing Sherlock?" Her sing-song voice told Anna the answer.

"It's not as if you're going to marry him, is it?"

Anna could have bitten her tongue off as Ingrid shot to her feet, her face flaming almost as red as her hair, her eyes sparking fire at her mother. "You don't want me to have any life of my own. You can't let go, can you?"

Before Anna could muster an apology, Ingrid was slamming the door behind her.

Anna didn't move. *I'm the adult. I'm the adult,* she repeated. She tried to remember what she'd been like as a teenager. Not many images came to mind. A few stray memories: a scratchy school uniform; trying cigarettes with school friends; her first real kiss at fifteen—Frank, her best friend's brother had given her a quick peck on the lips one evening when her friend disappeared into the bathroom—she remembered the spots on his forehead.

Her parents certainly wouldn't have tolerated these outbursts. But the grief counselor advised patience; people showed their grief in different ways. Better to allow the grieving process to achieve resolution, the woman had advised, otherwise, it might emerge at a future date as a serious issue.

Anna found it hard to not feel as if she'd been emotionally slapped when these confrontations took place. She glanced at the letter and back at the still life. The desire to find out more about Luc Marteille was growing. For the first time since Jeremy's death, she wanted to go somewhere and do something different; something which could lift her spirits. Perhaps part of resolving your grief meant finding things to occupy your mind while you learned how to cope without the loved one?

She decided to discuss the plan with Greg at dinner although after dinner was better when he would be more relaxed.

Nowadays they rarely ate in the dining room, a habit they'd given up since none of them needed to be reminded of happier times. The large round breakfast table at the far end of the kitchen accommodated them in comfort and the view, through the French doors into the garden, encouraged daydreaming.

"Thank you, darling. I enjoyed that." Greg pushed his half-eaten meal away.

"I'm full."

Anna thought he looked gaunt; he'd lost weight over the past few months, but discussing it with him was out of the question. Conversations between them were minimal; polite questions and stock grunted answers. Their interactions these days fell into the 'Pass the salt' category.

Since Jeremy's death, an invisible screen separated her from Greg and Ingrid, and no matter what she said or did she felt unable to reach them.

"Are you going anywhere this evening?" Anna asked Ingrid.

Her daughter usually ate and left as soon as possible. With exams finished and no homework, she spent her evenings with friends, most of whom Anna hadn't had the pleasure of meeting.

"Not sure."

Anna couldn't tell whether she'd earned Ingrid's forgiveness for her earlier remark.

"Well, don't forget to stack the dishes in the dishwasher." She made an effort to make the reminder casual, not a nag, before turning her attention back to Greg. "Do you have much work tonight?"

For the past few months, Greg had increased the amount of work he brought home. After dinner he retired to his study, working till late. Leaving him alone to work presented no problem as he required nothing from her. They coped in different ways.

"Yes. We have a lot of new cases at the moment." He finished the last of his wine, a sure sign he was ready to leave.

Anna took a deep breath and told him about the Luc Marteille letter.

"Imagine what value the picture will gain as a work of art if he painted it for a mistress. I'm thinking," she spoke hesitantly, "of going to Paris and doing some research on the story."

Greg stared at her, his gaze critical. "Google it and I'm sure you'll come up with the same results," he said, settling back in his chair and helping himself to more wine.

"Yes, I could take that approach to the subject," Anna said quietly, "but your father's research never came across any references to this woman."

"It's a good proposition, but you can't go alone."

She heard Ingrid's indrawn breath. It was rare for them to display their disagreements in front of the children. Anna frowned at her husband. You're not my keeper, she thought. He hadn't always been so unadventurous. She could easily accuse him of being dull these days when his work appeared to be the sole activity that enlivened him. Jeremy's death revealed how much they'd grown apart over the years, but she thought she understood his heart. Had he withdrawn that from her too? Or was she the problem? Was she the one who'd withdrawn? She couldn't say, but the reality of their marriage was that she and Greg were strangers; neither of them revealing matters of any import to the other anymore.

"I'll go with Mum." Ingrid stared at her plate, not looking at her father as she talked. "I saw the letter earlier. Listen, Dad, when you're away on that summer conference before our Biarritz trip, Mum and I will visit Paris for a few days and check out where he lived and painted. Maybe we can learn what happened between Luc and Hélène?"

Anna hardly dared raise her eyes. She didn't bother to ask why Ingrid had changed her mind. That she had was enough. Her heart quickened, and she experienced the slim breaching of an inner door, the other side of which lay— she couldn't see what, but it beckoned. The tantalizing possibilities of what she might discover captivated her. Resistance was useless; the battle to hear the voice of reason was lost to this new cause.

"Well, it's late for booking flights." Greg's voice sounded flat.

"You can't assume that." Anna's combative spirit, dormant the last few months, twitched awake. She addressed her daughter. "If we're lucky, we might be able to squeeze in some shopping." She threw the carrot at Ingrid knowing she'd catch it.

Ingrid's face lit up. "Oh Mum, that's

a brilliant plan. Wow! Paris in summer!"

Anna turned to Greg and without missing a beat moved in, pressing home her advantage. "We can easily meet you in the transit lounge after the conference and fly south together. You won't have to take one step outside the airport."

"Won't you miss what's his name?" Greg asked his daughter, trying a new angle.

As far as Anna knew, he'd not ever given a single indication that he was acquainted with any of Ingrid's fleeting infatuations with the opposite sex.

"Who? Matt? That's not serious. It's not as if we're getting married, is it?" Ingrid shot a conspiratorial glance at her mother, who smothered the smile threatening to break.

Oh, Greg, Anna thought, don't you know how much your daughter takes after you when it comes to winning an argument?

"And I won't be seeing much of him after the hols 'cos he's going to Exeter. No, I'd much rather be in Paris and do proper historical detective work. Sounds much more fun. Right, Mum?"

Anna nodded, a sudden rush of gratitude to her daughter surging through her. The irritation with Greg dissipated as they made plans.

"Yes. We can stay in Montmartre and do the research from there. Walk the very streets that Luc and Hélène walked."

She didn't need Greg's money. Income from her freelance graphic art jobs gave her enough independence, but the habit of deferral to her husband's wishes, built over a lifetime of marriage, was a constraint not easily discarded.

Greg finished the rest of his wine in one gulp and shoved his chair back. He never accepted defeat gracefully. "I'll be in the study if you need me. I've got a pile of papers to check over for tomorrow. Let me know what you decide," he threw over his shoulder as he left, his tone suggesting he didn't much care either way.

Anna stared at his back. What was up with him? Couldn't he show more support? What was wrong with flying off to Paris? Was it because she hadn't included him? He should be pleased she had a project, an interest in something that might drag her out of the apathy she was drowning in. Wasn't it what the psychiatrist prescribed?

"I'll do the dishes." Anna hoped her peace offering to Ingrid would achieve two goals: make amends for the earlier squabble and make sure her daughter didn't have another change of mind. It had been too long since she and Ingrid ganged up in opposition to Greg, and the thought of their alliance gratified her.

Ingrid accepted the offer with alacrity.

After finishing his work, Greg went straight to the bedroom from his study, bypassing the snug where she sat watching TV. Anna wondered whether his work absorbed him to the extent that he hadn't noticed she was downstairs. Or did he think the cold treatment would affect her decision?

*

Anna slid into bed, turning away from him.

He reached for her.

She remained silent, not moving, not

responding. His hand felt heavy as he stroked her back. She knew he was trying to gauge if this aspect of their lives had undergone any change.

He stopped stroking her back, moving his arm to encircle her waist and snuggling into her curved back, aligning his body with hers.

She stood it for as long as possible until she could no longer bear the heat of him warming her as he encroached closer. Stiffening, she took hold of his hand, lifting it carefully off her.

"For Christ's sake, Anna! When? When are you going to be a real wife again?"

The same old argument. The last time he'd used that phrase, they'd had a titanic humdinger when she'd gone from silent depression to manic rage in the blink of an eye. She threw back the duvet. "I'm going to get a drink of water. Do you want one too?" Anna used her submissive voice. She didn't want to hurt him but this was about her, not him.

Silence.

She padded to the bathroom and ran the tap. Using softness as a deceit wasn't calculated, but sometimes it was the most efficient and least painful method of dealing with people, including Greg. First a dominating father, then a husband with a prominent position had shaped the way she interfaced with others. To avoid confrontation, she cultivated a pliant facade. Nonetheless, she did possess a harder core, and rarely did something after having decided against it.

When she returned, Greg lay on his back staring at the ceiling. Anna lay staring at the painting. At two years old, Jeremy had big eyes, dark curls, and she'd hold him in her arms, and point at the flowers. She'd tried to teach him to say chrysanthemum, but the only bit he managed was the last syllable—mum. A tear trickled from the corner of her eye onto the pillow.

The gold of the frame glistened in the moonlight. What was it that drew her in? Even in this monochrome light, the flowers possessed a vitality which made it easy to imagine them swaying in the summer breeze of a southern French summer. She wondered about Hélène.

"This is very difficult for me, Anna. Can't you understand?" Greg's voice, harsh with demand, intruded.

"Is this your 'a man has his needs' speech?" Her voice was ice.

He closed his eyes, turning away from her.

"I'm sorry." She spoke the truth.

They were drifting apart; both incapable of putting themselves in the other's position and unwilling to move from their entrenched corners.

Greg didn't answer.

Tomorrow she would book the tickets.

Chapter Four

Relationships are fluid, not static, and have to be worked at constantly. The give and take between two people, the subtle flow of reciprocal emotion and energy, needs attention from both parties. Compromise is the name of the game.

Paris, July 1873

The sky was deep blue, cloudless, and the sun, a disc of hazed gold, battered the city. Luc had opened the windows, but there was no respite from the afternoon's heat.

Hélène's footsteps receded down the stairs.

"It's very good, Luc. You've captured the essence of her nature," Guiseppe De Nittis moved back from studying the almost completed painting of Hélène. De Nittis was a young Italian artist new to the group and he and Luc had quickly formed a close friendship.

Luc lay sprawled on the battered brown couch. "And what is her essence?" Luc asked. "I mean, how do you see someone's essence?"

"In the face, the eyes, the posture. In their demeanor. Everything about a person indicates something of their inner self. A wholesome country girl like Hélène is an uncomplicated character; she has no need to mask or dissemble, unlike our Parisian sophisticates. She epitomizes the wholesomeness of country life, don't you think?"

Luc considered Hélène's portrait. He'd painted her lying on her side on the couch, her head propped on her hand, turning to one side as if she were conversing with someone out of sight. The bright light falling from the skylights illuminated the details of her fresh complexion, glossy curling hair, and slim figure

"Hey, Luc! This is a conversation!"

"I'm sorry." Luc dragged his eyes away from her image. "What did you say?"

"I'm saying that painting says that you're in love with her."

"Don't be ridiculous." Luc laughed. "I'm a faithful husband."

"Open your eyes and look. Your work says otherwise. Faithfulness is in the heart as well as the loins." Guiseppe stood. "I have to go. Keeping M'sieur Verizon waiting isn't going to improve his generosity."

"He's looking to buy?"

"It's a possibility. When I spoke with him last, he said something about commissioning a portrait of his family." He paused at the door. "If I can't satisfy him, I'll put in a good word for you. Will you be at the cafe tonight?"

"Probably." The door shut, and De Nittis clattered down the stairs. "Good luck," Luc shouted after his friend.

After studying Hélène's portrait for a bit longer, Luc took the canvas off the easel, placing it at the back of the room where it wouldn't disturb him. He tried to work on a smaller canvas but couldn't settle. He made an effort to work on a couple of other pieces which needed finishing, including one of his children playing in the garden, but in the end replaced the painting of Hélène back on the easel.

She'd started modeling for him at the beginning of the week, and already there were times, after she'd left a sitting, when her expression as she looked at him, the way her breasts, hips, and thighs curved under her clothing, consumed him; all he thought of was making love to her, possessing her and making her his.

The fact she was returning home at the end of the month, to marry some uncouth farmer, constantly niggled, worming away at his peace of mind, filling him with desperation at the thought of losing her. He knew he was becoming more obsessed with her; happy and elated when she sat for him, morose and unable to paint when she wasn't there. This yearning for her was becoming a compulsion over which he had no control and was beginning to dominate his life.

He found himself attempting to engage with her; something he'd never had any interest in doing with other models. Flirting, coy smiles, and flattery were behaviors he despised when he saw other artists seducing their models. Despite his best efforts, her responses were polite, submissive, distant; those of employee to employer. Luc wiped his forehead with his arm. Looking at the painting of Hélène was driving him mad. He had to get out of the studio.

The route from Montmartre to his house on Rue Murillo took him through the Parc de Monceau. Families sitting on the grass under the welcome shade of the great oaks lining the lake reminded him that he had a wife, a beautiful rich one, who loved him deeply, and two children he adored. His mind glossed over the tragedy of their last, stillborn child. He was well on the way to success in his chosen field, achieving everything he'd set his heart on. Nevertheless, he felt tormented at the sight of love-struck couples strolling in the park. He blamed Hélène.

"Papa! Papa! You're early!" Six-year-old Guy, sturdy, thick brown hair, and on his heels four-year-old Giselle, her golden curls flying, threw themselves at him with abandon. They had been picking flowers from the small front garden and dashed toward him the instant he opened the gate.

Their maid, Marie, huffed after them.

"Look, papa. What I picked for maman." Giselle thrust a full-blown red rose up at him.

First, he admired the rose, holding it to his nose and exclaiming over its perfume. Next, he picked her up and swung her around. She screamed in delight and he gave her a loud kiss on the cheek before putting her down. He pulled his son close, ruffling his hair with affection. "How is Madame?" Luc asked Marie who stood watching the three of them with an indulgent smile.

"She's resting, M'sieur."

Luc stood looking at his children for a moment. Guy had his mother's fine features, his father's darker coloring and possessed a serious nature. Giselle had his bone structure, mercurial temperament and her mother's fair skin and hair. Both of them adored their father. From out of nowhere, Hélène's smile flashed before him, shadowed by a twinge of guilt. He brushed both aside. "Tell Annette I'll have lemon tea on the veranda."

Marie bobbed her head and trotted off.

"Bring lemonade for Guy and Giselle," he called after her. "We'll sit together, eh?" He smiled as they raced off around to the back of the house, their exuberant squeals filling the air.

*

Luc stood in the doorway of the bedroom observing his wife. She was asleep, her chest rising and falling, her breathing shallow. Despite her poor health, Émilie remained a strikingly beautiful woman. Her blonde hair, combed and arranged earlier in the day, now fell in disheveled curls framing her finely chiseled features. Luc thought she was like a delicate flower in the midst of the pile of green satin pillows. A subtle touch of color on her lips and cheeks hid her pallor, and asleep, he couldn't see the exhaustion in her eyes.

"I knew you were there." She opened her eyes and smiled at him. Her voice was a whisper.

"How are you?" He crossed the room and bent down to kiss her forehead.

"A bit better," she said.

"Fibber," he answered, his tone softening the word. He helped her sit up, feeling her bones through the flimsy gown and noticing how frail she'd become as he propped the fat goose down pillows behind her. He sat carefully on the edge of the bed.

"I had a letter from papa this morning."

Luc hid his irritation, his customary reaction to the mention of his father-in-law. Émilie was wealthy, being the sole beneficiary of both sets of grandparents, but her father had never approved of, or been able to thwart, her choice of a penniless artist for a husband. Luc's distinguished ancestry was his one saving grace.

"He insists we must visit with him and maman at Le Conquet. It would be good for the children to get out of the city in this heat. You know the sea air is good for all of us."

Luc said nothing but sat listening to the birds chattering in the garden as evening drew on.

"You can visit Boudin in Camaret, and Monet will probably be in Le Havre." Émilie continued her cajoling. "Papa wrote that it's fine with him if you want to paint. He said you can have the garden house as a studio."

Yes, he accepts my art these days because I'm becoming successful. Nonetheless, he'll take the opportunity to acquaint me with the fact he thinks I'm a parasite. "Yes, of course," Luc responded, "that's a wonderful idea. You go ahead and I'll join you after the academy lists are up."

Émilie covered her disappointment at his answer with a quick smile.

He raised her hand to his lips, turned it over and gently kissed her limp, damp palm before continuing. "Check with the good doctor that you're allowed to travel before you start Annette and Marie flustering around and packing everything up."

"Dr. Brasson is coming tomorrow at midday. You could wait and hear what he says for yourself. If he agrees to the idea, we could be in Capelle by the weekend."

"I've got three paintings to finish before the submission date."

Émilie paused before answering. "Of course. As long as you're not putting off visiting my father?"

Luc laughed. "You see right through me don't you?"

"Please, Luc. For me," she sweet-talked, making sad eyes at him.

"I surrender, I surrender. I'll do my best to come at the end of next week but I can't promise. Does that satisfy you?"

The sound of a gong chimed softly from downstairs, followed by Marie's voice calling the children.

"Go and eat, darling. You don't want to make Annette cross with you by letting your meal get cold."

"Sleep and get well, chérie."

"Close the drapes for me before you go. The light's bothering my eyes."

He kissed her forehead. Her skin felt hotter than when he'd arrived. Even a few minutes conversation took a toll. He closed the drapes and walked quietly to the door, turning to look at her before he left. The light penetrating the green voile drapes coated the walls, furniture, and Émilie in shades of leafy green. She had closed her eyes, and her skin looked translucent in the ethereal light.

*

The whole of Paris appeared to be out that evening, relishing the relative coolness of the air that came at the day's end. Luc threaded his way through the group clustered outside the entrance to the Café de Nouvelle Athènes and pushed open the glass door. He nodded and waved to several acquaintances further back in the main part of the crowded smoke-filled café reverberating to the noise and laughter of courtesans, artists, and writers. His friends sat at the two round marble tables that were customarily reserved for them in the front section of the café. Manet was holding forth. The intimate group of artists listened with attention, for he was clever and entertaining when he spoke, and there was often a hidden barb behind his wit.

"Bonsoir," Manet sang out to Luc as he spotted him "A chair. Bring a chair for our newest recruit—our quiet serious painter!"

Luc greeted the others around the table as a waiter hurried forward with a seat for him, and he sat down amidst the welcoming laughter. This was where Luc needed to be. The association of these artists, who wanted to change the status quo of the art establishment, kept his enthusiasm strong. They painted what they observed in front of them, and their visions were different from the staid, proscribed pictures so beloved by the academic elite makers and shakers of the Paris art world.

The laughter subsided as Manet continued to argue with Degas. The two men were on opposite sides politically, but both had served in the army when the Prussians had laid siege to Paris three years ago.

"We need peace, not a republic," Manet said, tossing back his dark blond hair.

"Ah, my dear socially advantaged friend that is where you're misguided. You must understand that without a republic, there can be no peace." More laughter as the two bantered back and forth.

"It doesn't matter what government we have. If we can't exhibit our paintings, how can we make a living? Why should we—well, most of us anyway, have to endure such poverty?" said Pissarro. There were nods of agreement around the table.

Luc had been lucky. He'd already spent most of the small inheritance left to him by his father when he'd met Émilie. Marrying her had made it possible for him to continue as a painter. She believed in him, and it was she who'd initiated the move to Paris, insisting that if he was serious, the capital was where they must live. Émilie's money had bought their house and paid the monthly fees for his attendance at the Académie Suisse for three years. Nonetheless, even though his work was beginning to sell for a satisfactory sum, it was Émilie's money that paid for his studio.

A waiter approached the table with a tray of drinks. "From Dr. Gachet," he told them placing the drinks on the table.

Manet nodded at the thin-faced mustached gentleman who stood inside the bar. The artist lifted his glass, and in unison, everyone copied him, turning toward the café's interior. "To our good doctor's continued health," Manet toasted. A round of cheers ensued, and they downed the drinks.

Monet cleared his throat. "Frederick and I had an idea." A look of pain crossed the lean face of the new speaker as he remembered the tragic death of his closest friend. Frederick Bazille had been an artist of great promise who had died during the Prussian retreat at the end of the war.

"Well, spit out this brilliant idea. Don't keep it to yourself," Manet interrupted.

Monet continued as if the other man hadn't spoken. "It's very simple. We have our own exhibition. Not a Salon des Refusés," he emphasized the last three words, "but a group exhibition of our best work."

"The realist movement exists. It is. It has to show itself separately. I agree; we absolutely have to have a realist Salon." Degas's enthusiastic voice boomed across the room.

There was silence for three seconds before pandemonium broke out among the artists as they argued the pros and cons of Monet's idea. Most of the artists were a good bit older than Luc and had struggled for many more years than he had. They were ambitious to attain success in a world that refused to consider anything new, except to reject it.

"Do you think Corot, Courbet or Daubigny would be interested?" asked Renoir, clouds of smoke rising from his pipe, a sure sign of his interest.

"Tissot and Legros are in London. I'll write to them," put in Degas.

"What of Cezanne?" Luc spoke tentatively.

Heads turned to where the tall bearded man sat alone, hunched over a small side table morosely nursing his drink, oblivious to the raucous laughter and gaiety around him.

"No!" For once Manet and Degas spoke in agreement.

Pissarro joined the argument on Cezanne's side. The two artists had recently struck up a friendship and Cezanne listened to Pissarro, seeing him as a mentor.

By the end of the evening, a decision had been made. They would canvass supporters, patrons, and friends, and find a salon where an independent exhibition could be held. They were determined to take themselves out of the realm of academic arguments and petty jealousies rife at the Salon des

Beaux Arts. They wanted to display their art where the public could view it and make up their minds for themselves.

When the group broke for the night, Luc decided it was too late for him to return home. He said his goodbyes and headed for his studio. As he walked through the cobbled streets, he ignored the sultry siren voices calling from the shadowed doorways. He no longer had any interest in Brigitte or any of the other women.

Besides, he was intoxicated with the ideas buzzing around his head. The decision to mount a separate exhibition was, so far, purely the talk of discontented artists and might never materialize, yet he was busy assessing which paintings he could show. He pushed the thought of leaving Paris and staying at Brest for the summer out of his mind, dismissing the memory of Émilie looking at him that afternoon, her eyes filled with love. She would be well taken care of by her parents and she understood how important his work was to him.

When he opened the door to the studio, the first thing he saw, illuminated by the dull yellow light from the stairs, was the painting of Hélène. Her fresh innocence captivated him. He knew, aside from the fact they had no venue or date set, this painting, or the next one of her, would be one of those he exhibited.

Chapter Five

You never stop loving someone after they die, but time teaches you the lesson of living without them. Time dulls the knife-edged pain of loss, blurs and fades memories. The love for someone who is no longer with us has a different, though no less important, quality to the love for someone living. In the present, life is forever changing, whereas the past is fixed.

Paris, July 2007

The soul of France animates Paris making it a charismatic magical city. In Paris, you feel the heartbeat of a nation, and every year millions of visitors come to experience its charm.

The air-conditioned Charles de Gaulle airport hummed as excited or exhausted passengers entered and departed.

"I think that one's mine, Mum," Ingrid fretfully shoved her sunglasses further back on her head. "Or maybe not," she mumbled, eyeing the suitcase in question as it rumbled past.

Anna waited with the stoicism born of experience, ignoring her disheveled hair and crumpled linen suit; she should have known it would resemble a dish rag if she wore it for traveling. Within minutes both had their suitcases off the ramp and trundling behind them as they headed for the exit.

One hour later, and ten degrees warmer, a taxi deposited them outside the Hotel des Artistes, Place de Tertre, Montmartre. After registering, a polite young porter took them up in the lift to their room. Anna couldn't help but notice his fascination with Ingrid's mass of wild curls

Dumping her luggage, Ingrid crossed the room and flung open the French windows, stepping out onto a small balcony.

Anna joined her daughter, and they stood listening to the distant thrumming of the city.

Voices from the street below floated up, the unfamiliar words and cadences of the French language sounding exotic.

"Please, Mum. Let's go out and explore. We can unpack later. We're right here. Paris, where Manet, Gauguin, Renoir, Monet, Degas and those fabulous artists lived and painted. It's historic. Oh, and look! I can see an artist selling paintings along there, to the left where the road bends."

Anna looked where Ingrid pointed,

and sure enough, she saw a dark tousled head bent over a canvas, talking animatedly to a prospective buyer. "He's selling to a tourist," said Anna. "See that camera slung around the man's neck and those bags he's holding?"

"Yes, and he's doing what you and I, who are also tourists, by the way, should be doing." Ingrid adopted a pleading hands together pose, stuck out her bottom lip and made goo-goo eyes at her mother. The gesture evoked the image of two small children, who used the exact same movements when begging for some indulgence. "Come on, Mum. Didn't you say this is a famous square? Can't we go and check it out? It'll be good to stretch our legs and let's face it, the suitcases aren't going anywhere."

Anna smiled at her daughter. She

hadn't asked Ingrid why she'd changed her mind about coming, but she was glad of her current high-spirited mood and wanted to keep it that way. Despair had consumed Anna after Jeremy's death, leaving little space for the needs of her youngest. Guilt over her neglect was another shadow that haunted her.

Recently she'd attempted to place her memories of Jeremy in a separate compartment of her mind. She thought of it as a retreat, a haven where she revisited the joys he'd given her in his short life. The trouble was, these memories didn't live in isolation. They were intimately connected to other people.

Let it go; another mantra she was trying put into practice. Today I'm in Paris with Ingrid. She shook her head as if to dislodge the past. This was a chance to spend time with her daughter and she was determined to make the most of it. "Ok. Let me freshen up, and we'll go."

The sights and sounds of Montmartre entranced Anna and Ingrid as they exited the hotel and sauntered toward the artist displaying his wares on the corner. Four o'clock in the afternoon saw the square crowded with curious tourists, attentive to everything they saw; in contrast, the locals continued with their daily business, nonchalant about where they lived.

Arm in arm, mother, and daughter strolled along, pointing at the gray tiled roofs, whitewashed buildings with their painted wooden shutters and red awnings above the shops. Everything bewitched them. Even the gray-bricked road and pavement drew admiring comments.

The artist they'd seen from the hotel balcony had no customers by the time they drew level with him.

"Mesdames. Please look, and if there's any picture you like, we can discuss a special price for you." He gestured at his paintings.

The artist was younger than Anna expected. In fact, the clear gray eyes and angular face topped by hair which needed a good trim belonged to a young man not much older than Ingrid.

"Thank you." Anna began examining his work.

Ingrid dallied by the artist. "How could you tell we're English?"

"Oh, that's easy. I can tell by your shoes."

Ingrid gave him a puzzled stare.

"Italians wear elegant sandals, Germans wear sensible sandals and Americans wear sneakers." The painter laughed as Ingrid looked at her sandals.

"But ours are elegant and sensible," she retorted, "and it's too hot for trainers."

"Well, there you 'ave it. Elegant and sensible; that's the English for sure, eh?" His joke made them both laugh. He held out his hand. "Hi, I'm Jean-Paul."

"Hi, I'm Ingrid, from near Bath, and I'm with my mother, also from near Bath. How long did it take you to paint these?" Ingrid's gaze flicked over the ten or so paintings on display.

"Most of the year. I don't live in Paris, but I'm 'ere for the summer, and 'oping to sell these paintings. I 'ave more at home but they are too large and it's difficult to bring them on the train, and there's not enough space 'ere to display them. So, there. You 'ave my life story." He displayed his best salesman's smile. "How long are you and your mother 'ere visiting Montmartre?" Jean-Paul spoke English well, but he talked fast, and with a noticeable accent.

Ingrid had to listen carefully to catch everything. "Oh, for a few days, after that we'll be joining my father near Biarritz for the rest of the summer."

"How much is this one?" Anna called out, interrupting their tête-à-tête, and pointing to a small canvas with a vivid red rose.

Jean-Paul nodded to Ingrid and moved over to Anna. "That one is 40 euros, Madame. But for you, I make a special price, 35 euros."

"I'll give you 30 euros." Anna pulled out her wallet and took out three 10 euro notes, holding them out toward him.

"Madame, you drive a hard bargain with a poor struggling artist, but I accept." Jean-Paul ceased bargaining and pocketed the money with surprising speed. He gave her a charming smile before unhooking the painting. Within minutes he had it expertly wrapped in brown paper and string. "Thank you, Madame and Demoiselle Ingrid."

Ingrid's eyes filled with laughter and she smiled sweetly at him, "Au revoir, Jean-Paul."

As Anna and Ingrid sat drinking coffee at one of the outdoor restaurants nearby, Anna quizzed her daughter. "And may I ask where did that 'au revoir, Jean-Paul' come from?"

Ingrid smiled with deliberate innocence at her mother. "Yes, you may and he was being friendly. We were chatting while you looked at his paintings. That's it. He probably has a sales patter for tourists like us."

"Well, I wouldn't have said he was old enough to be so calculating." Anna looked appraisingly at Ingrid. Greg's sky-blue eyes, her own delicate coloring, down to the same summer sprinkle of freckles across a nose that was neither too short nor too long, and the slender figure of an eighteen-year-old who can wear sackcloth and make it look gorgeous.

Anyone could tell the two women were mother and daughter. They had the same thick curly hair but Anna kept hers shoulder length so she could wear it loose or up, and Ingrid's insistence on a visit to the hairdresser had temporarily banished the effects of time on her hair. Ingrid's hair was that rare deep copper shade and fell almost to her waist. It was hair any pre-

Raphaelite artist would have died to have on a model and caused heads to turn wherever she went.

"Makes me appreciate you're a young woman and not a child anymore." Anna's voice caught in her throat as she looked at Ingrid's bright beautiful face.

Ingrid affectionately patted her mother's arm. "I'll always be your little girl. You know that don't you?"

"Yes, of course. But I can't boss you around anymore, can I?" And they laughed. "I'd like to take a walk and stretch my legs a bit before going back to the hotel." Anna looked at the crowded street. "What do you think?"

Ingrid followed Anna's gaze. "Actually, I want to use the internet. I saw a computer in the lobby." Ingrid played with her hands before looking up through her eyelashes

"The internet? Whatever for?"

"Mum, don't be dense! I want to talk to Matt."

"Oh." Anna hid her disappointment. This was supposed to be their time together. But she didn't press the matter. "We're in the home of the Impressionist movement, the stomping ground of many famous artists, not to mention Luc Marteille," she rolled her eyes, "and you're thinking of Matt and the internet. What's wrong with texting?"

"I need to charge my mobile, and the hotel has Skype."

"Oh, go on then. You remember where we're staying?"

"Yes, Mum, and I'll unpack your suitcase if you're not back when I finish." Ingrid was gracious in victory. She gave her mother a kiss on the cheek. "See you soon."

"I'll wander about for an hour or so. Will that be long enough for you?"

"Whatever works for you, Mum."

They were in Paris, and Anna couldn't remember the last time she'd experienced this sensation of lightness and freedom. It was impossible to stay cross with Ingrid for long, and her momentary irritation dissipated as she watched her daughter stride off toward the hotel. Men, and women, turned to look as she passed. Ingrid was striking, even in a sophisticated city like Paris, thought Anna, with a flash of pride.

She searched for the small map of Montmartre she'd put in her bag. Damn! It wasn't there. She pushed aside her annoyance, determined that nothing was going to spoil her mood today. Looking around she spotted the white half-moon dome of Sacre Coeur rising above the far end of the square.

Ah! There's a reference point if ever I saw one, she thought; *that must be visible from everywhere in Montmartre. Figuring out how to get back to the hotel will be easy.*

Anna set off in the opposite direction from the hotel, filled with the sense of adventure, a real explorer. Reaching the end of the block, she paused, her attention caught by a frazzled mother arguing with a screaming five-year-old boy in the midst of a full-blown tantrum.

At that moment the memory hit her.

The day at the supermarket. Ingrid was teething and intermittently crying—a painful high noise that grated on her nerves and made it impossible to think of anything but how to silence that sound. Nothing she tried–baby Aspirin, homeopathic tablets–worked. She ended up carrying her most of the time as holding her close and being patted calmed her enough to stop other women shooting her those 'what kind of mother are you' looks.

Jeremy, a handsome lively four-year-old, who usually enjoyed fetching items within his reach, kept running off. She'd placed Ingrid in the trolley, paying no attention to her screams, and plonked Jeremy in the second front seat, where he persisted in attempting to grab items and throw them out.

She wanted to scream and slap him but did neither. Eventually, with most of the shopping piled as far away from Jeremy as possible, she managed to get through the check-out and unload everything into the boot of the car before giving Jeremy a sharp telling off. He sulked the whole way home and sat with his chin pressed to his chest.

When she got home, he continued

sulking. She tried everything, including bribery, to get him out of the car—until something in her voice told him she was running out of patience. Nonetheless, he delayed retrieving the final X-men figures as long as possible and was standing by the door clutching them as Anna took her morning frustrations out on the door by slamming it shut.

At that instant, Jeremy spotted one last figure hidden by the side of his seat and stuck his hand into the closing gap. Then he began screaming. A gush of blood spilled dark red splashes onto the garage floor, and she saw the deep slashes in two of his fingers.

What happened afterward remained a blur. Somehow she'd had the sense to run into the kitchen and grab a towel. Jeremy stood, stiff and traumatized as she bound his hand.

Lifting him into the car, she deposited a bawling Ingrid with a neighbor and drove to the emergency room at the local hospital as if the hounds of hell were yapping at the wheels of the car.

A surgeon reattached the tops of his fingers without any difficulty. The hospital staff informed her she'd done the right thing to wrap them as she had. A small sop to her increasing guilt.

Jeremy hadn't said a word the whole time.

It wasn't until much later after she carried him up and laid him on his bed, with the painkillers leaving him sleepy, that he spoke. "I'm sorry, Mum."

She had sat by his bed, holding his good hand till he slept. Afterward, she went to the bathroom and cried. She'd never been so full of remorse. No matter how unwittingly, she had hurt her own child. Could that have been an early warning sign that he and cars would have a fatal relationship? No, that was a ridiculous idea. She remembered the way his child's smile lit up his face. It had broken her heart with love then and it broke her heart with loss now.

The memories returned often at first, but as days, weeks and months passed, they resurfaced less often. However, she could still be taken by surprise, as it remained impossible to anticipate what and when something would trigger the past intruding into the present. She looked around, but one woman, frozen for a moment with her mind adrift, hadn't raised any eyebrows on a busy street. Digging a tissue from her bag, she dabbed at her face. Not today. Today everything was new. She left the Place du Tertre, with its perky red café umbrellas reminding her of so many poppies, and headed up Rue Norvins.

Time opened out, and it was as if she had all the freedom in the world. To think that Luc Marteille had walked these streets, conceivably going to visit Hélène, or after a secret liaison. How had she become a model for him? How long had their affair lasted? It couldn't have been serious as the research she'd done hadn't mentioned any extra-marital flings.

She looked around considering how different it would have been. Of course, no tourist shops, but surely some of the buildings with their small louvered windows would have been here? The little boulangeries where people bought their bread—although the shelves were empty at this time of day; the patisseries, the cobbled streets. For sure Luc Marteille would have gazed upon some of the same sights.

Anna delighted in the abandonment of her daily routine. She was falling in love with this city; its otherness, the lure of discovery, of adventure was irresistible. Sauntering along, she relished the unfamiliar smells, while her attention jumped from one sight to another, registering a detail of architecture here, a splash of color there, before another novelty grabbed her attention.

She stopped and bought a postcard for Greg. They had a custom between them that whenever one of them was away—mostly Greg—they sent the other a postcard. Her third scrapbook was full, and it tickled her that, for a change, it was her turn to send one to him. The acrimony between them, almost unbearable during the last few days, was diminishing with distance.

Anna meandered on, not sticking to the main road, but intrigued by the smaller streets with their narrow roads and tall buildings leaning toward each other as if exchanging confidences. She remembered Australian Bushmen went walkabout and figured this was as close to it as she was ever going to get as she explored whatever road or turning she fancied.

An hour or so had passed before she noticed the pale orb of Sacre Coeur was no longer visible above the tops of the houses. The street lights had come on, and the light had taken on that particular clarity heralding the onset of twilight. Anna checked her watch thinking she should head back, or at least phone Ingrid. She rummaged in her handbag, but the phone wasn't there. Damn, and damn; she must have left it with the map.

She checked the street. Left, then right. Her earlier sense of liberty had gone, and she was struggling not to panic; *you'll see the Basilica's dome wherever you are in Montmartre,* she reminded herself. It wasn't possible to have walked so far that it was no longer visible. She simply had to keep going, and she would spot it soon, peeping out behind one building or another.

She walked faster, doing her best to ignore the flood of uncontrolled feelings waiting to drown her. Breathe in, let it go. Breathe out, let it go. It was one thing to focus on your breath sitting in an armchair in your living room, but when you were lost in a strange city and night was creeping in, it was far harder to accomplish. She emerged from the short road she'd taken and there was the iconic landmark looming over the landscape at the end of another small narrow street. Anna didn't understand how she'd gotten so near without noticing it. She could have sworn she was heading in the opposite direction from the church and not toward it.

Should she continue or try to retrace her steps? She stopped, trying to think logically. The twilight deepened, and for a second no one was in sight. She was alone on a deserted street.

A group of laughing youths came around the corner.

As they neared, their loud brash voices and unintelligible words startled her, and suddenly she was frightened. She couldn't think. Darkness rimmed the edge of her vision, and her heart started pounding. She spun on her heel and began walking away from them as fast as she could; she didn't care where she went, she had to get away.

Anna raced along, her imagination lurching from one awful scenario to another until she'd left them far behind, but the need to keep moving propelled her onward, well after their voices had faded.

How had she managed to be so careless as to leave both her phone and the map behind? She was the one in charge of this trip, the one who was expected to know what to do. Yet look at her. It hadn't taken long for her blithely undertaken walkabout to turn into a disaster. She was tired, and she'd left Ingrid alone. What if her naïve young daughter left the hotel in search of her? Her thoughts rioted, abandoning that calm safe space she'd found so difficult to create. If Greg saw the state she was in, he'd feel justified in saying she shouldn't be trusted out alone.

Without warning, as if a guardian angel had been looking out for her, she turned a corner and was back in a crowded tourist area. Families with children and couples, arm in arm, strolled along; everything looked normal with people window-shopping, laughing and talking as they went about their business. She took a deep breath. Everything was going to be fine. She simply had to find her way back to the hotel. Anna searched her bag again, realizing she'd also forgotten to bring the phrase book. She suspected it was piled neatly on the bedside table together with the other two items.

At that second, as she was craning her head this way and that, seeking the dome to anchor her in this alien territory, her right foot came down between two uneven cobbles. The next thing she was toppling sideways, a ten-pin bowling ball about to hit the skittles. But it wasn't the ground she hit, it was the startled pedestrian next to her whom she crashed into, and who mercifully broke her fall. They both staggered a step or two before a strong arm pulled her upright, and she was looking into her rescuer's concerned face.

"Oh, I'm so sorry," she gasped. "Are you all right?"

"Excusez-moi?"

Anna couldn't help but note that he was rather good looking, of the older, distinguished variety. She leaned back as the man bent toward her. "I'm sorry," she repeated, feeling both grateful and foolish. "I wasn't looking where I was going."

"Are you hurt?" he inquired, his eyes

full of concern. His English was fluent.

"No, I'm okay." She brushed at her skirt. "I lost my balance when I twisted my foot on the..." she pointed to the cobblestones.

"Well, as long as you're not drunk," he said. "Don't you have those in England?"

Anna couldn't believe her ears. Did he honestly think she was drunk? How rude. "Which way do I take for the Place du Tertre?" She snapped at him, her gratitude disappearing in a huff of resentment. What a comment! She'd get the directions and be gone.

"Place du Tertre? This way." He pointed off to his left. "You are quite close. I'm heading that way myself."

To her dismay, instead of completing the directions, he started walking alongside her.

"I'm François Gibran," he said

introducing himself, and making a little bow in her direction. "It's no trouble to accompany you and reassure myself you get there in one piece."

Anna wondered if he was attempting to make amends for his ill-mannered remark because if that was his intention, he'd failed. He'd given her his name as if he were conferring an honor for which she should be grateful. She ignored the sharp comment she was about to make as the 'please' and 'thank you' politeness her mother had impressed upon her as a necessary quality for success surfaced. "Thank you. I'm Anna Seeger."

As they walked along, Anna realized it had been a long time since she'd met anyone new. Everyone she dealt with, either family or friend, she'd known for a long time. There were times in life, mostly when you were young and exploring new situations and had new jobs, where you met new people and established networks of support. As the years went by, social and emotional needs were met through family, friends and colleagues; and as you aged, you went into reverse until immediate family—if you were lucky—and caretakers were the few people with whom you communicated. She wondered when the body was failing and enjoyment of the physical side of things dwindled, would the powerful emotions—hate, revenge, love—run as strong?

"Where in the UK are you from?"

She glanced at him realizing, by the irritated look he gave her that he was repeating the question. What had he said his name was? She had a moment of paranoia, thoughts of abduction flitted through her mind, but she decided that aside from his superciliousness, there was something safe about him and being kidnapped wasn't a likely option.

"Near Bath, in the West Country," she answered but his attention had shifted as they reached a junction.

"And are you staying here long?"

"A few days."

"Oh, what a pity. Paris is a wonderful city." He clearly thought giving a brief couple of days to Paris indicated that whatever priorities she had, they were radically wrong.

"Yes, it is" she agreed, unable to think of an observant or witty remark in response.

They strode along in silence. Her ankle began to throb, but there was no way she was going to ask him to walk more slowly. Anna shot a glance at him and had the impression he was preoccupied with his own thoughts. She was evidently someone not worth the effort of conversation. Yes, a patronizing Frenchman, Anna thought, is essential to round off this exploratory outing.

She was thankful he'd been there to prevent an accident, but she certainly hadn't requested an escort, and it showed precisely how wrong first impressions could be. The atmosphere between them was decidedly polar in spite of the sweltering heat.

They turned onto Rue Norvins, and she brightened with relief at recognizing the shop fronts and the café with its outdoor seating next to the hotel.

"I know where I am. You've been very kind. Thank you." She spoke with exaggerated politeness.

"Good. Are you sure? It is no

problem for me to take you further." The frostiness in his tone indicated otherwise.

"No, I'm fine," she reassured him fervently, glad of the opportunity to be rid of him. They said goodbye and he strode off. She stood watching him disappear into the crowd, his height making him appear like a liner surrounded by smaller tugs.

Relief at his departure was mixed with the tiniest twinge of regret. A little voice inside acknowledged if he'd been more polite, she'd have considered the encounter quite pleasing, but she dismissed such a whimsical thought. What did they mean to each other? Two straws floating down a stream, side by side for a very short time, before the current separated them. There was nothing more to tell.

She resolved to say nothing to Ingrid

about her panic attack, near broken ankle and encounter with a stranger. Besides, there was nothing of importance to relate. As she approached the hotel, her fears melted away, and she admitted they'd been no more than that—fears, not reality. She should remember that next time something happened and not surrender to every suggestion her overactive mind tossed her way.

The lobby was empty when she entered the hotel. Ingrid would have finished talking with Matt ages ago, but the familiar niggle of worry didn't let up until she opened the door to their room, and saw Ingrid lying on the bed reading; only then did the tightness in her chest ease.

Ingrid was as good as her word and had unpacked both of their suitcases, hanging their clothes in the wardrobe in an orderly un-Ingrid manner.

"Why don't you change, Mum, and we'll go and find somewhere to have dinner?"

The cheery words and smile on her daughter's face brought tears to her eyes. She blinked them away. "Good idea. You do have your father's character, don't you?"

"If you mean organizational skills, yes. Tomorrow we'll begin our detective work on the mystery of Hélène and Luc Marteille but tonight, it's us and marvelous Montmartre."

"Whatever did I do to deserve you?"

"A lot of pious activity in your last life!" Ingrid tartly responded as she straightened her dress. "I'll wait for you downstairs. That lobby is a great place to people watch, you know."

After her daughter left, Anna put the afternoon's events out of her mind. She decided to wear one of the new dresses Ingrid had chosen for her. Ingrid had insisted they both have a few new outfits before they left and shrewdly negotiated a promise for one designer shopping trip in Paris.

Anna chose a three-quarter length, light blue turquoise cotton dress with pencil straps, and a shape that skimmed the waist and hips before flaring out into a mass of flounces near the hem. She would never have bought such a dress, but Ingrid's delight with how she looked in it, and her insistence she buy it, overcame her resistance.

Studying her reflection, she admitted Ingrid's choice was faultless. She styled her hair up in a chic French pleat, and dug out the matching pashmina shawl, draping the silky smooth material over her shoulders.

Ingrid wasn't in sight when Anna

entered the lobby, and she assumed she'd popped to the loo. While waiting, she wandered through to the bar. On impulse she ordered a glass of white wine, letting the bartender choose for her. As she relaxed in a comfortable brown leather armchair, taking small sips of her drink, she had to admit, coming to Paris was a brilliant idea.

When Anna thought about her life, who she was, what she was doing, she pictured herself in relation to others. Her identity as an adult had mostly been as Gregory's wife, and Jeremy and Ingrid's mother. Before that, she'd been her parents' only child.

These days her life was divided into pre and post Jeremy. Today the stimulation of new unfamiliar surroundings was prompting a paradigm shift in her perceptions. Anna felt strangely liberated as if she were floating; the possibilities for new experiences were so tangible, she could almost taste them.

As soon as she acknowledged the novelty of this feeling, guilt overwhelmed her. This was a particular guilt that hadn't appeared immediately after Jeremy's death, but one which insinuated itself, making its subtle presence known step by step. This dark guilt stood stealthily at her shoulder and whispered in her ear, asking how it was possible for her to enjoy living when her beloved first-born lay with his beauty rotting to dust beneath the earth.

Ingrid's laughter disrupted her melancholy spiral of thoughts, and she was surprised to see her daughter and the young artist from the afternoon enter the bar, engaged in lively conversation.

"You remember Jean-Paul, don't you? Well, it turns out he's staying at this hotel too."

"Madame." The young man gave Anna a deferential nod.

"Hello. For the second time." Anna smiled at the young artist, registering the engaging way Ingrid gazed at him. The past year or so, Ingrid had dallied with two or three boyfriends, but nothing serious until Matt arrived on the scene. Anna had watched as her daughter discovered the attraction of the opposite sex, wondering when the day would come when she moved from mild infatuation and friendship to her first love.

"I've invited him to have a drink with us. Ok, Mum?"

Jean-Paul waited with a polite, but unsure, look on his face.

Feeling somewhat back footed, and

with little choice in the matter, Anna agreed. She understood that in the unfolding scenario, 'us' meant Ingrid. "That's fine."

Sure enough, as Anna watched, Ingrid and Jean-Paul walked over to order drinks at the bar looking as if they'd been together for years. They chatted comfortably, and Anna saw nothing of the shy awkwardness that generally accompanies the first stage of getting to know someone.

She suppressed a grin as she observed her daughter flirt unashamedly. Anna was conscious of what her beautiful, clever daughter was doing. You instinctively accepted Ingrid's manipulations were without malice, and you accepted you'd benefit from going along with her; in the same way, you instinctively understood there was no point in not doing what she wanted. Ingrid took after her father. No beating around the bush; if she made a decision, she went straight for the jugular.

As the couple returned, Anna felt instant sympathy for Jean-Paul. To be honest, he didn't stand a chance. In true Ingrid style, one minute she was introducing Jean-Paul, and the next had Anna agreeing it was a good idea for him to join them for dinner. As they exited through the lobby, Ingrid informed her that Jean-Paul knew a chic restaurant nearby. Anna nodded, resigned to the fact that there was no resisting the spirit of impulse which had invaded her world today.

The streets of Montmartre were magic. Old-fashioned street lamps and lights placed halfway up the front of buildings combined with brightly lit restaurants to generate a festive mood.

Red canopies stretched over elegantly set tables on the pavement. Most of the eateries had seating both inside and out, leaving the road for pedestrians. Intuitively Anna searched for the Basilica. She was fascinated by the way the pale orbs, lit up by the lights from the district below, dominated the skyline—day and night.

When they arrived at the restaurant, Jean-Paul secured them a table outside where they could watch people wandering by and enjoying the nightlife. Anna let the two youngsters' chatter float over her as Ingrid enlightened Jean-Paul as to why he should give up meat. She had no inclination to participate. For the moment she was content to do nothing but be an observer.

"Mum, you look fantastic in that dress," Ingrid complimented her as they waited for the menu to arrive.

"Merci beaucoup. And what is it you're after?"

"Am I that obvious?" Ingrid's eyes looked particularly mischievous. "Jean-Paul's uncle is going to join us. Is that all right?"

"Yes, I'm sure it'll be okay." Anna swallowed her reluctance. After what happened earlier, she'd decided to take everything in her stride. Be calm. What was another stranger?

"He will be 'ere soon," Jean-Paul told them, putting his phone away and anxiously scanning the crowd. "Ah, 'ere he comes."

Anna suppressed a smile. He was trying so hard to please. She turned to inspect the approaching uncle. This was the third new person she was meeting that day. She hoped he would turn out to be more sociable than the one she'd bumped into earlier.

"Oncle! Ici!" Jean-Paul stood and waved both his arms as if guiding a plane onto the landing strip. He turned to the two women. "Please, Ingrid, Anna, meet my uncle François."

Chapter Six

Seeing what the future holds is beyond our control. The one thing we can decide is our response to events. Nevertheless, we must be aware our reactions will have ramifications that echo down through time—for ourselves as well as for others.

Paris, July 1873

Since Émilie's illness, she'd needed to sleep undisturbed, so a bed had been made up for Luc in a guest room on the other side of the house. Up early, Luc decided to absent himself from the house before anyone woke. Telling himself he didn't want to disturb anyone, he slipped out without looking in on his wife.

Yesterday had been pandemonium with Émilie, enlivened by the upcoming visit to her family home, instructing Marie and Annette in what to pack. Preparations for leaving would continue today, with the maidservants rushing around, and the children shouting with excitement. The fuss entailed for these journeys exasperated him, but today he wanted to avoid answering awkward questions about his plans for joining his family in Brittany.

Setting off at a good pace, he breathed in the early morning air still laced with night's coolness. The heat would come later. The faint gray mist layering the dew-wet grass among the trees in the park captured his attention; he studied the scene for a moment, thinking he must make a plan to come out and paint here one morning.

When he began a new work, he experienced a certain excitement, a particular keenness of purpose. The painting lived already in his imagination, and he would add details, needing merely brush, paint and canvas for the image to become concrete.

Today he was starting the new portrait of Hélène. One minute he was hot and jittery, the next cold and shivering, sure he was running a fever. Three days ago, overwhelmed by his chaotic emotions, and not needing her to finish off his current painting, he'd given Hélène time off. The thought of seeing her again exhilarated and petrified him. He had to keep a tight rein on himself.

*

Hélène walked along, feeling like a true Parisienne. Louise had given her a pretty straw hat adorned with a jaunty red silk flower. Lifting her chin high, she enjoyed the bright morning sunshine, eager to model for Luc's new painting. She had spent the last couple of days with Louise and baby Benoît, who was no longer a blood and mucus covered squalling newborn but had transformed into a creamy complexioned infant.

Hélène took in the smartly dressed gentlemen hurrying along the streets as if their business was of the utmost importance, the laundresses loaded with huge bundles, market sellers pulling carts with a variety of goods, and the usual scruffy gang of urchins looking either to beg or steal. Soon she would be home, and the wooded hill of Montmartre with its windmills, famous artists and Luc would be no more than a memory. She drank in the sights, fixing them in her mind.

Luc lifted his prepared canvas onto the easel and fussed about organizing his paints. Trying not to think of Hélène was pointless. Of necessity, communication between them was minimal, and they'd never had a real conversation in the normal social manner, yet they spent hours together while she sat and he painted. Whilst he studied her in detail, and there was without doubt an intimacy in the situation, the relationship wasn't one of familiarity or friendship. He'd given a great deal of consideration as to how he wished her to pose today.

As Hélène turned onto Rue Gabrielle, she determined to make the most of the days she had left. Her stomach started to churn as she climbed the stairs, and by the time she reached the top, she couldn't control the trembling in her legs. She paused outside the studio door, taking a few deep breaths before knocking. Making sure her hat hadn't shifted from where Louise had carefully positioned it, she smoothed back the stray strands of hair sticking to her forehead. As she raised her hand to knock, the door swung open.

"Come in, Mam'selle." Luc waved her in. "Over there, if you will." He rattled off his instructions, pointing to a chair placed halfway between the chaise longue and his easel. "No, no," he said agitated, "Take your hat off first." He waved at the chair again. "Please, sit."

He was using his painting voice, as Hélène called it, the one he employed when instructing her how to position herself for the pose. She had confided to Louise how flattered she was that

Luc wanted to paint her portrait. The local boys at festivals, where she'd never lacked partners for dancing, weren't in the same league as a Parisian artist. She perched on the edge of the chair.

"Yes, sitting up straight is good, but further back on the chair, I don't want you falling on the floor."

She looked up at him. No, it wasn't a joke.

"Look straight ahead. Yes, that's good." There was silence for a minute. He cleared his throat. "Please loosen your hair."

Hélène sat motionless.

"Mam'selle Hélèna, I need your hair loose for the picture. It's for art." He punctuated his words with impatience at what he obviously perceived as her rural backward attitude. "Please, your hair."

Hélène slowly raised her hands and reluctantly began pulling out the pins keeping her hair in place.

"Arrange it on one side. Like this." He demonstrated, arranging a head of imaginary hair, pulling it forward over one shoulder.

He looked so funny, she giggled.

"I'm glad you find me amusing, Mam'selle."

She wiped the smile from her face.

He pointed. "Your hair. Please."

Hélène took out the rest of her hairpins, and her hair, a mass of wheat-gold curls, fell down her back. Following his instructions, she lifted it off her neck, rearranging the bulk of it so that it fell over the front of her right shoulder. She started as he picked up a handful of hair.

"Your skin is perfect and your hair— how it glints in the sun. Ripened grain.

That's what color it is."

Hélène kept her eyes fixed on the easel directly in front of her, doing her best to ignore how close he was. This morning, he seemed unlike his usual self and generated an air of unpredictability. He made her nervous. When he touched her neck, heat from his fingers warmed her skin. The tingling wasn't an unpleasant sensation. She didn't reply to his comment, not sure what she could say, as he lightly smoothed and arranged her hair.

Touching her hair and skin was almost too much for Luc, and he sensed his control slipping. The fine silk of her hair slid through his fingers, and he moved away, clenching his hands as they began to shake. He busied himself, checking his brushes till his heart stopped thumping, his breathing slowed, and he could present some appearance of normality. "That's excellent, Mam'selle," he snapped. Not trusting himself to say another word, he started work.

Louise's advice to occupy her mind when posing was to picture something pleasant. She said it made you feel better, and then time passed before you realized it. Today that was easy because yesterday Louise had walked into the kitchen with Benoît swaddled in blankets asleep in her arms and waved a white envelope at her.

Hélène stopped cleaning, dried her hands and snatched it off her cousin. "It's Suzette's writing," she said stifling a shriek. "This is from Claude." She clutched the envelope to her chest, an enthusiastic grin lighting up her face.

"His younger sister writes his love letters for him?" Louise's astonishment made her opinion clear.

Hélène's smile disappeared as she went on the defense. No one was going to think badly of Claude for any reason. "Claude can write, but not well, and he asks Suzette to write for him because he feels it's important. He wants things, such as this letter, to be proper."

"Men!" snorted Louise. "Come," she patted the seat next to her. "Read it out to me. I'm your older cousin, and it's my responsibility to act as a chaperone in your parents' absence. They expect me to see that you two lovebirds behave appropriately, even in your letters."

"Well, not the whole letter," replied Hélène playfully as they settled themselves on the couch. She opened the letter with care. Yes, there it was— a rose. A sigh of contentment escaped her lips as she tipped it out onto her hand. The rose was small, its dark red leaves veined with pink, and flattened through drying and pressing. She raised it to her nose and inhaled, closing her eyes so she could picture Claude–the safe, secure Claude that she loved–searching for the right flower.

"Does she pick and dry the flower for him?"

"Louise! Stop it. No she doesn't. He's my betrothed and I love him. Stop making fun of him. He's clever in his own way. With the land, with animals."

"And he's so strong and handsome" interrupted Louise laughing. "Oh, forgive me, cousin. You are so easy to tease. Look at you! You'll be the prettiest blushing bride in the whole of Bordeaux!"

"Oh shut up," Hélène said. "Listen. Here's what he says."

My darling Hélène,

How are you? I hope you are well and the flower pleases you. I picked it from the bushes in maman's flower garden. She and papa are in good health as is Suzette.

At present, the young lambs are fat and plump. We have had good weather and the crops are growing well.

I eagerly await your return. I miss you so much.

Much love,

Your fiancé

Claude.

He is missing you very much. Maman and papa nag him the whole day to do his work as he's mooning about the place quite love sick without you.

Your soon-to-be sister, much love, and hugs.

Suzette.

"Suzette sounds sweet. Tell me how do his maman and papa treat you?"

Benoît opened his eyes, his little mouth pursed into an o shape, and a healthy high-pitched wail burst forth.

Louise opened her blouse straight away, positioning him at her left breast.

His tiny rosebud of a mouth latched onto her nipple and he started feeding.

Hélène tried not to be envious as she watched her cousin. Motherhood suited her.

"Well, tell me. Are they ogres who'll make you work day and night?" Louise joked as Benoît suckled with quiet satisfaction.

They laughed as Hélène related tales of how her prospective father-in-law was overly partial to his home-brewed brandy, continually hiding his weakness from his wife. But he'd get drunk and leave bottles lying around. Next, she'd throw out all the bottles she could find, including those with liquor left in them. After he sobered up, he'd go looking for the thrown out bottles.

"Apparently she was a beauty when she was young, but you know what farm work does to a woman's looks." She remembered how pleased they'd been when she and Claude told them they wanted to get married. The whole family had welcomed her.

Louise had made plans for her own little family—if Pierre could get away. She hoped to visit her parents and simultaneously accomplish several objectives; attend Hélène's wedding, meet her cousin's new extended family, and introduce Benoît to his grandparents. "I'm looking forward to meeting them."

"Your mother will adore Benoît."

The object of their attention was

satiated and his eyelids opened and closed as he drifted in and out of sleep.

Louise handed him to Hélène. "Walk him so I can clean up, will you?"

Hélène took the half-asleep infant, and settling him in her arms, walked around the room crooning a lullaby to him. He was the most beautiful thing she'd ever seen. She loved holding the baby: he was so small a bundle to be the source of these warm, soft feelings which welled up when she held him.

"Hélèna!" Luc's voice was sharp. "Stop smiling." He put down the brush. What was she thinking of that put such an expression on her face? He experienced a stab of jealousy at the thought that it was probably her fiancé. "Take a break. Try not to touch your hair," he said irritably, "and tell me when you're ready to continue."

Hélène winced at the sharp remark

but held her tongue as she stood up, stiff from sitting. She paced back and forth till the stiffness in her body and legs eased. She tried to keep her head still so as not to muss her hair. "I'm ready, M'sieur."

Rearranging her dress wasn't a problem–the portrait was of her head and shoulders–but the aggravated expression on his face as he strode over told her something had annoyed him. She remained completely still as his hands twitched and fiddled with her hair.

The only sound was his ragged breathing. "Mam'selle Hélèna, I find you most attractive. Surely you know what feelings I have for you," he continued, his voice breaking.

She recoiled. Anger started deep in her gut and swept through her. Suddenly she was on her feet, pushing him hard in the chest.

He stumbled back, his gaze following her as she marched over, collected her hat and headed for the door. The push shook him, snapping him back to reality. He ran after her and grabbed her arm; she attempted to shake him off but couldn't loosen his grip. "Hélèna! Hélèna! I'm sorry. I'm sorry."

"Monsieur Marteille. You are hurting my arm. Please let go."

He dropped her arm as if his hand was burning, stepping away from her. "I apologize for my outburst." He bowed his head. "I don't know what came over me. Please, please come and take your seat. I promise, I give you my word, this will never happen again." He gestured at the chair. "Please, I would like to continue with the painting."

"I'm from a respectable family,

Monsieur Marteille. Not from Paris." Her voice was stern. "But you must also understand I'm engaged to be married, and I love my fiancé."

He looked genuinely distressed and abjectly apologetic.

Her anger retreated, and she relented. With her back straight, she walked over to the chair, carefully resuming the pose. "So if it is necessary for the painting, you may arrange my hair, but please, let us be absolutely correct with each other."

He bobbed his head in agreement looking so comical she suppressed a smile.

He was far more appealing when she had the upper hand, and he was submissive and repentant. "And speaking of correctness, my name is Hélène, not Hélèna!"

"Of course, Mam'selle Hélèna, I

mean Mam'selle Hélène."

As he returned to painting, she tried to put his inexplicable behavior out of her mind. She'd never met anyone who so puzzled her. From where she was sitting she looked directly at him, and had plenty of time to observe the way his eyes creased as he looked from her to the portrait, the fleeting irritation when he wasn't satisfied, and the light of pleasure when he was. She couldn't help but be aware of his changing moods, his face was so expressive.

During the rest of the sitting, Luc clamped down on his errant thoughts, focusing entirely on transferring what he saw onto the canvas in front of him. He was determined to be professional. There would be no repeat of his earlier inappropriate explosion.

"Au revoir, Mam'selle Hélène," he said, courteous and distant at the end of the session, dropping the coins into her palm and making sure he didn't touch her outstretched fingers.

As soon as she left, he put away his brushes with painstaking care, staggered over and collapsed on the couch. He lay there staring up at the skylight, his words and actions replaying themselves over and over. The relief that she'd not walked out was overwhelming, the painting was not nearly advanced enough that he could dismiss his model, and he didn't know how he would manage without her.

*

In her room late that night, Hélène re-read her reply to Claude.

My darling Claude,

Thank you for your letter. It was wonderful to receive it with the token of your affection. I love the color of the rose. I am keeping every single one of the flowers you send.

Louise gave birth to a healthy baby boy, and they have named him Benoît after Pierre's father and her grandfather on her mother's side. He is adorable. I am well and look forward to when we meet.

Your most affectionate and loving Hélène.

She would post the letter tomorrow. If Claude knew the situation, he wouldn't be pleased with her returning to the studio to sit for Luc. In the country, no one considered an unmarried woman being alone with a married man proper behavior. At large family or local gatherings if such a situation occurred–even with a family member–a young woman was taught to leave. You had to be far more deceitful to do anything illicit in a small community like hers. She pushed those thoughts to the back of her mind.

Hélène pulled off her blouse and stared at the emerging bruise where Luc had held her arm to stop her leaving. She covered the place where his fingers had been with her hand, remembering the hard squeeze of his fingers on her skin.

Chapter Seven

People are either on their best or their worst behavior on holiday. An exotic, different location can bring out our finest qualities, or it can remove the normal restraints and barriers.

Paris, July 2007

"Uncle François, this is Ingrid, and her mother, Anna." Jean-Paul gave a big grin.

Anna couldn't believe her eyes. It was the rude Frenchman she'd met that afternoon. He looked her up and down, and for the briefest of seconds, she registered his flash of approval before a mask of conventional courtesy dropped.

The coincidence of tripping and

falling on top of a strange man, and later the same day being introduced to him as a relative of her daughter's latest captive, left Anna speechless. They stared at each other in an embarrassed silence. She was conscious of Ingrid and Jean-Paul watching them.

"Pleased to meet you," François murmured taking Anna's hand and bringing it briefly to his mouth.

The softness of his lips surprised her as they touched the back of her hand. She couldn't remember the last time anyone had treated her with genuine old-fashioned civility. A welcome change from his earlier behavior.

As he sat down next to her, she leaned toward him.

"I've said nothing to my daughter about, you know, my... um... accident. Please, can you not mention it?"

"My lips are sealed. I shall keep your secret," he murmured.

But the second she saw the spark of indulgent amusement in his eyes, she regretted her decision. What on earth had possessed her to ask that of him? She should have explained straight away to Ingrid and Jean-Paul how she and François had met. The trouble was, having suggested the charade, she felt obliged to continue with it. She would appear somewhat ridiculous if she now came out with "Oh, didn't we meet earlier this afternoon? Oh yes, that's right we did. How silly of me not to recognize you."

Of all the people she could have bumped into, she'd managed to choose one whose condescending attitude had riled her. Furthermore, without any hesitation, she'd foolishly proposed and was now trapped into propagating a lie with him. She swallowed her pride, deciding her best course of action was to be as gracious as possible under the circumstances.

"Please call me François, and may I call you Anna?"

She nodded her agreement, thinking the loud voice, obviously for Ingrid and Jean-Paul's benefit, was a little exaggerated.

"Have you ordered?" François asked Jean-Paul. He hadn't. Needless to say, Jean-Paul had eyes solely for Ingrid.

"So you see," Ingrid glanced around the table, but zoned in on Jean-Paul to finish explaining her recent conversion to vegetarianism, "that's why it's better not to eat dead rotting animal flesh."

Jean-Paul nodded enthusiastically.

Anna thought he'd eat cyanide pie if Ingrid told him it would improve his health.

"For you," François told her, his face alive with humor, "we shall order vegetarian. French cuisine can easily accommodate these habits," he said, subtly emphasizing the word 'habits'.

Anna's spine prickled at his tone, but she couldn't decide if he was being patronizing or hadn't a clue as to how he sounded.

As François beckoned the waiter over and ordered, she looked around wanting to pinch herself. This morning she had sat at the breakfast table with Greg discussing how many times they needed the gardener to come during the summer. Despite twenty-five years of marriage, she couldn't remember the decision they'd made. It had been one of those necessary conversations that take place in daily life where words are exchanged but nothing is said. Their goodbyes that morning had been polite, distant as if they were strangers.

Barely twelve hours later, here she was sipping wine, ready to enjoy a meal out in the romantic quarter of Montmartre with her daughter and, if she made a few mental adjustments, some pleasant company.

Jeremy, with his appetite for adventure, would have loved this. The thought of his mother meeting and dining with strange men wouldn't have fazed him in the least. Thinking of how he would have enjoyed this situation eased the chronic pain of his absence.

"So how is your foot?" François asked Anna in an undertone.

"It's fine," Anna replied, her tone sharper than she intended. She felt churlish, but she was irritated at the evening's unexpected development. "Are you from Paris?" She spoke loudly; two could play at this game, she thought.

François gave her a surprised glance. "No, I'm looking after my nephew for a month so he can try out life in Paris."

"Will he be moving here?"

"Yes, he'll be studying art at the École des Beaux-Arts."

"That's impressive." This topic was surely safe territory. "His work is good. I bought one earlier."

François smiled, obviously fond of his nephew. "Yes, his sales patter is charming. And you? Tell me something about yourself," he said, dropping his voice, "and please, nothing of the West Country."

The arrogance of the man. What could she say that was honest? I'm grieving over the loss of my son and hoping this visit will help by researching why an artist from the past wrote a love letter. "Freelance graphic artist, one child sitting opposite, one husband who'll be joining us shortly. Not much to know. Yourself?" There, that should shut him up.

"I started my career as a stockbroker—after that became an estate agent. Currently retired." He was as cryptic as she'd been.

No mention of a wife? Probably divorced several times she concluded and wanted to conceal his philandering.

"And what do you do when you're not chaperoning your nephew?" She wasn't very interested in his answer as the hors d'oeuvres the waiter placed on the table looked far more appealing.

"My ambition is to sail around the world. Since my wife, Lucie, died two years ago, I've needed something serious to occupy my interest, and my time." He looked away.

The intimacy of his revelation

startled her. For once the shoe was on the other foot, and she was unprepared for how awkward she felt. "Oh, I'm sorry to hear that." Repeating the same words she'd heard many times over the past few months, when she'd disconcerted people by telling them about Jeremy, felt trite. Revealing something tragic to an unprepared listener opened opportunities for intimacy, for empathy, but she could think of nothing else to say.

"Thank you. I have had time to accept what was a tragedy for me...." François trailed off.

There was an uncomfortable pause. She wondered whose loss was greater. Could you compare levels of grief? Would she, in a couple of years, be trotting out her loss of Jeremy in a similar matter-of-fact voice at a dinner with strangers? She didn't know where to take the conversation next, so she gratefully accepted the plate of grilled goat's cheese bruschetta he offered, as he indicated she should help herself to the different types of olives and hummus spread before them on the table.

They started eating and, amidst the general chatter around the table, she surreptitiously studied François's face. She saw a definite family likeness to Jean-Paul, but he wasn't as attractive as she'd initially thought when he saved her from an ungainly fall. Yes, he had good cheekbones and a firm jaw line, but his nose was a bit too big and slightly longer than perfection demanded. Fine age lines decorated the skin above and below his deep-set eyes, and his hair had more than a sprinkling of gray. Knights in shining armor shouldn't stick around, she decided.

As they ate their way through a delicious tarte à la oignon, salade nicoise, aubergine et fromage, pain d'épices, and drank their way through a bottle of wine, which slid smoothly down her throat, she revised her opinion of François. Whether it was the wine, the atmosphere, the company, the location or a combination of all four, she began to relax, responding to his efforts at entertainment. In a couple of hours, he'd gone from being a handy landing pad and irritating tourist guide to an amusing dinner companion. Tonight François was clearly making an effort to be polite, and instead of being exasperating, she found him funny. His tales of learning to sail his boat made her laugh out loud; she was enjoying his company, and that surprised her.

Ingrid appeared far too absorbed in

Jean-Paul to notice anything until François asked the reason for their visit. Anna hadn't even blinked when Ingrid jumped in, hardly missing a beat as she caught the question, and filled François in on the details of their quest.

"Mon oncle is something of an expert on the Impressionists," Jean-Paul said.

"Would you be interested in helping us?" Ingrid asked.

"It does sound a fascinating mystery," he said, sipping his drink, and deliberately not looking in Anna's direction. "I would love to help."

"Oh, that's brilliant," Ingrid enthused, shooting a sideways glance at Jean-Paul. "We're going to the Musée des Impressionists. You wouldn't happen to know how to get there, would you?" She batted her eyelashes at François.

Anna's bubble of pleasure

evaporated, a stab of disappointment puncturing her mood. This mission was hers and Ingrid's: bonding and building memories because one day her daughter would inherit the painting. She knew Ingrid was angling to spend the day with Jean-Paul. The thought that her mother might not want to spend a single moment more than she had to with this stranger didn't occur to her. Ingrid blatantly ignored the pained expression on her mother's face, continuing to bestow her full attention on François.

"Why yes, I do, and it would be my pleasure to take you." He cast a quick glance at Anna, but she ignored him and played at folding her napkin.

"That is very, very kind of you." Ingrid gazed at François, the look in her eyes telling him he was her savior, and she'd be forever grateful.

By the time they finished the meal, a decision had been made. Tomorrow François would take them to see the Basilica, and later to the museum. He told them it was devoted to the Impressionists and the best place to start researching. Jean-Paul said he'd come along too, informing them with a smile that a day with the Impressionists was a master class for any artist.

To Anna's dismay, and the young couple's delight, though they didn't gloat, Ingrid's scheming had succeeded. Once she'd recovered from the shock of meeting François, for the second time that day, the evening had been pleasant enough, but after he inveigled himself onto their search, conversation with him became increasingly onerous for her.

They left the restaurant with François and Jean-Paul accompanying them back to their hotel because, what a coincidence, they were staying at the same one.

Anna ignored François as they walked, trying not to be upset by the sound of Ingrid and Jean-Paul's laughter behind them. By the time they reached the hotel, she was so eager to be rid of him she barely had enough patience left to utter a respectable polite goodnight.

"It's been a long day," she said.

"Of course," he replied. "We'll meet here tomorrow morning at ten o'clock."

His company no longer appeared quite so charming as at dinner as his former condescending self resurfaced. Anna suppressed her anger at his dictatorial tone. "Yes, that'll be fine. Good night," she muttered, trying to muster a shred or two of gratitude. "Ingrid, don't be late," she said as

Ingrid and Jean-Paul looked set to linger in the lobby for some time.

Back in the hotel room, strangely deserted without Ingrid, Anna removed her make-up, cleaned her teeth and climbed into bed. Finding it impossible to settle, she got out of bed and sat in the armchair waiting for Ingrid. She picked up the book she'd brought for holiday reading, but her mind was stuck in a groove playing a record that said this trip was for family. Nobody else.

When Ingrid came in an hour later, she wore the smug expression of a cat that had eaten a tasty bowl of cream. She'd hardly closed the door when Anna's anger boiled over.

"How could you?" Anna couldn't keep the harsh resentment out of her voice.

"How could I what?" Ingrid's dreamy expression vanished. She marched over to the bathroom.

Anna followed, remaining in the doorway, waiting to talk.

But Ingrid deliberately ignored her mother and rooted through the drawer for her hairbrush. After energetically brushing her hair for a minute, Ingrid looked balefully at her mother. "Mum! What's got into you?"

"What's gotten into me?" Two spots of color appeared high on Anna's cheeks. "We—you and I—came here to spend time together."

"Mum, I'm not your property. You can't keep me to yourself." Ingrid stared at her mother, her expression tight with defiance.

"I want to be with you. How..." she stopped. Her shoulders were shaking, and the tears began.

Ingrid crumbled. "Mum." She came over and put her arms around Anna, pulling her close. She stroked Anna's back. "We're here for such a short time. There's the rest of the summer to spend together before..." She didn't finish the sentence, not wanting to upset her mother more.

"I know, I know." Anna pulled away and wiped her face. She wanted to explain that this trip was more than doing research on Luc Marteille's history. This was also about the two of them being together, creating memories.

Spending time alone with Ingrid had always been difficult, except when she was a newborn with Greg at work and Jeremy at nursery. After a few months, the demands of husband and son had made inroads into her time with the new baby. In a couple of days when Greg joined them and they headed for Biarritz, she'd have to share her daughter again. But it wasn't purely assuaging guilt for lost opportunities— Jeremy's death left her sensitive to the urgency of the present.

"François will help us get around much more easily. He knows Paris and Montmartre and the Impressionists and..."

Anna raised her hand, gently covering Ingrid's mouth. "Sssh. Yes, I know, I know. I'm sorry Ingrid. I'm just a bit disappointed."

"But you'll see, mum, everything's going to be okay. I mean, you do like Jean-Paul don't you?"

"Well, from the little I've seen of him, I suppose he has my approval."

"That's generous of you! So I can continue to see him because he has your approval eh?" Ingrid rolled her eyes. "And you'll be fine with François. He's nice too." And with that, Ingrid shut the bathroom door.

Thoughts jumping feverishly, Anna walked out onto the balcony. Ingrid had jettisoned their plans with remarkable speed, and there was no doubt she wanted to explore the possibilities that Jean-Paul presented. That she preferred to be with him rather than her mother hurt. It shouldn't, but it did.

Losing Jeremy had been the single most painful experience of her life, and she was losing Ingrid too fast. Not to the ultimate finality of death but to life; to her own life where time would unveil the paths and journeys she'd take. Most of which would be without her mother. Anna wondered if her role as a mother, giving birth and raising her children, was over. The thought that this might be the case in the near future, if it wasn't already, was hard to accept.

She stared down at the square. The night atmosphere was different. Gone were the bustling daytime workers and eager tourists; it was the turn of a different crowd—out to dine and see the sights by night. People sauntered along in dribs and drabs. Laughter rose carelessly into the air.

Anna watched an old woman with an empty basket hobble along, thinking how she shouldn't have dumped her sour feelings into Ingrid's lap. Unlike before Jeremy's death, when she hid behind propriety, pretending something was okay when it wasn't, these days she kept little or nothing back. She had to or otherwise she couldn't cope; even now, when she was calming down, her emotions were too near the surface.

Her thoughts circled back to the evening with the Frenchman and his nephew, and how the unexpected change of plan had thrown her. She must try harder; she needed to learn how to be adaptable, flexible.

When she re-entered the room Ingrid had fallen asleep, her long hair, a loose plait of gleaming copper, spread out behind her as she lay on her side. God, she was beautiful. Anna came around and gently kissed her daughter's smooth cheek.

Restless and not wanting to sleep, Anna went to the bathroom. She examined her reflection, deciding her age didn't show too much, especially if she tilted her head back. At that angle, the bags under her eyes didn't show. She was lucky and her figure remained slim; carrying and giving birth to two children didn't show. It had been a long time since she'd thought of how others perceived her as a woman in her own right, not as an appendage of Greg's.

She thought of Greg with a flush of guilt, but as she recalled their most recent argument, bitterness laced her mood. Greg had sought release from his grief over Jeremy by burying himself in his work, which had left each of them coping with their sorrow alone.

She felt unsettled and out of sorts. On the one hand, she'd banked on enjoying this time with her daughter, but it was becoming apparent she was going to spend her visit to Montmartre in the company of a man whom she thought vain and exasperating, and about whom she knew nothing.

On the other hand, what had Ingrid meant when she said You'll be fine with François? Was it her imagination or had his gaze been frankly appraising when they'd been introduced? He'd been caught off balance, but she would swear he'd been pleased. She pushed

her misgivings to one side, finally
deciding she'd at least be able to keep
an eye on her daughter and that young
Frenchman. There was no way she
would allow the pair of them to go off
by themselves. Who would trust a
charming and talented artist?

When Anna opened her eyes the
next morning, she was disoriented, and
gazing at the unfamiliar ceiling, couldn't
think for a minute where she was.
Turning her head, she saw a patch of
clear blue sky out of the window and
heard the muted sounds of traffic in the
distance. Then she remembered and
relaxed, relishing the promise of the
day ahead.

She stretched with anticipation.
Abruptly it came. The memory. Since
his death, thoughts of Jeremy were
never far away, and when she woke,
the first topic that always came to mind

was a scene from his life. Sometimes the memories were fresh and bright as if happening right there in front of her as if she were in a cinema watching a film on a screen; other times the memories were shrouded, vague images, and she'd have to work at the details of when and where the episode had taken place.

And no two memories were of the same event. This time, he was smiling as a friend dropped him off on his first visit home for Christmas after starting uni. She'd been watching out for him from an upstairs window, expecting him at any moment. He leaned into the car to get his bag out and said something to his friend. They'd both laughed before Jeremy turned and walked toward the house, hoisting his bag on his shoulder, his face expectant, his walk confident. The familiar ache of loss, a permanent companion, lessened a fraction as she sent him a soft kiss.

Anna took more time and care than usual getting ready, gathering her hair up into a large clip, and picking out another of the new dresses chosen for her by Ingrid.

"Paris is making you glow," Ingrid teased as they entered the lift on their way to meet François and Jean-Paul. "That shade of blue suits you."

The four of them met in the foyer after breakfast. Ingrid gravitated toward Jean-Paul, who carried a large satchel over his shoulder; they were two magnets unable to resist the pull. They immediately fell into an animated conversation that excluded everyone else.

"We must first visit the Basilica of Sacre Coeur," François informed her as they stepped out into the sunshine and busy streets of the Place de Tertre.

"We must?" She wasn't going to pass judgment this early in the day, but if he thought he was going to take over her time without any consultation whatsoever, he was in for a shock.

"From there, the whole of Montmartre, and Paris is laid out before you. It's a magnificent view."

Okay, maybe he did know the city better than she did. As they waited for Ingrid and Jean-Paul to catch up, Anna studied François's profile. His looks weren't classical by any means, but his strong nose, jaw and full lips would make him an interesting subject to sketch.

He took her elbow as they crossed the road.

His touch was warm and dry, his hands strong. She flushed as her body reacted with pleasure to the contact and his close presence. She'd never been unfaithful to Greg, never had any inclination to, and almost sniffed out loud as the thought of indulging in an affair at this stage of her life flickered through her mind. As they reached the other side of the road, she wrenched her arm out of his grip.

Surprised by her sharp movement, he looked at her, his eyebrows rising.

She looked away to hide her annoyance at the fact that, as well as not being able to talk with Ingrid because she was so wrapped up in Jean-Paul's every utterance, she had to contend with a letch of a Frenchman.

The pavements were narrow, and it was impossible to create any distance from him. As they walked, the aftershave he used kept tickling her nose. She actually liked the perfume, a pleasant musky smell, which annoyed her even more. How could you enjoy something and reject the source of that enjoyment at the same time?

François insisted that as they weren't invalids the funicular route was out, and they were to go by foot. In no time at all, Ingrid and Jean-Paul were well ahead. As she and François climbed the wide flights of steps up to the church, the dome of the Basilica rose up in front of them, an ever larger luminous half-moon, and more of the two side domes, like bridesmaids flanking the bride, became visible.

Anna took several rest stops on the way up under the pretext of enjoying the view. She paid no attention to the many tourists chatting in different languages as they strode up the steps past her, enduring the heat and climbing far faster than she did. She hung onto the handrail hoping it wasn't obvious how much she needed it. But when they reached the top, the effort of getting there was forgotten as she stood stunned by the beauty of the church. The idea of being an architect was one of several career ideas she'd explored at school, but she hadn't attained the grades needed in mathematics. She stared up at the intricate embellishments and the statues of saints gazing down on supplicants with compassion; the sheer size and scale overwhelmed her.

"Impressive, don't you think?" François's voice in her ear made her jump.

She spun around to find him standing so close she breathed in his scent. Why couldn't the damned man stand further away? Did he think there was something wrong with her hearing? "Where's Ingrid?" she snapped at him.

She checked the area, searching for Ingrid and Jean-Paul, her gaze flicking here and there, her heart rate increasing, the distressingly familiar rush of panic. "They were right in front of us. Where have they gone?"

Chapter Eight

All cultures welcome and adore babies. When we see them, we are reassured of our individual continuation, as well as that of our species. A man who presents a tough hardened exterior can croon and melt at the sight of a beautiful healthy baby, whereas a woman whose physicality, by nature is more delicate, can–if her child is threatened–transform into a fiery dragoness.

Paris, July 1873

Most sessions Luc hardly spoke to Hélène for the three or four hours other than a formal 'Bonjour' when she arrived, 'Take a break' and 'Fine' during the sitting, with a final 'I'll see you tomorrow' as she departed. Yesterday he'd not pointed out her late arrival— something he would have previously pulled her up on with a sarcastic comment.

How he could be so different from her first sittings for him was bewildering. Then he'd been chatty and silent in turns, punctuating his work with lively conversation. She'd learned a lot about other artists who influenced him–Manet in particular–and of his opinions on the artists in his circle. Cezanne, Renoir, and Degas were names, among others, he discussed frequently, and regardless of her ignorance of art in general or their work in particular, she knew Luc's opinions of them.

These days he conducted himself

with polite reserve. She understood his silence and absorption in his work was his way of being professional with her, but she missed the other Luc, preferring the friendlier chatty, if moodier, artist she'd met when she first sat for him. The man who at present painted her showed a different personality. Which Luc was real and which one was a facade?

As she sat facing him today, she couldn't help but compare him with Claude. Two different men. One was tall, muscular with physical work, fair-haired, ruddy complexioned, and wore his thoughts openly on his face. The other was smaller, wiry and leaner with dark permanently unruly hair because he constantly ran his hands through it when thinking. One had clear, bright blue eyes and was honest as a summer's day; the other had brown eyes, often dark with mischief, but whose expression changed, like his moods, from lively humor to inscrutable in the blink of an eye. They were opposites. One had a life where the body moved with the rhythms of the earth, the other appeared ruled by his emotions and a dedication to his art.

Hélène had tried but couldn't forget Luc's declaration. She wondered if he would deny his words if she had the courage to bring up the subject. But what would be the point of that? Her stay in Paris was nearly at its end, and the sittings for Luc would finish as soon as the portrait was complete. Louise and Benoît were healthy, and the date of her wedding moved closer. In a few days, she'd be on her way home to Claude and this would be history.

"I'll see you tomorrow, Mam'selle Hélène," he said as the session ended.

"Au revoir, M'sieur Marteille," she said, accepting the daily payment.

As she climbed the stairs to the apartment, she could hear Benoît's plaintive crying. She quickened her steps. Inside, Louise was walking around the room, shushing Benoît as she rocked and attempted to soothe his fretful cries.

"Thank God you're home. He's been crying for ages. It doesn't matter what I do or what I try. I've changed him, I tried to feed him, but he keeps crying." Louise struggled to keep her tears back as the words tumbled out. "I have to get Pierre's dinner and I have to clean the place but I was so tired after going out this morning, I fell asleep. Until Benoît woke me."

Hélène stroked the baby's forehead. His soft skin felt too hot.

"I'll fetch Irene and after that, I'll

take him."

Louise smiled, relief on her face. "Of course, of course. But don't be long."

Irene was in the middle of preparing a meal for Henri and her brood, but she immediately handed the wooden spoon she was stirring the stew with to her eldest. Shouting instructions behind her as she banged the door shut, she hurried downstairs behind Hélène.

Irene's concern when she held Benoît, feeling his forehead with the back of her hand, was apparent. "He's very hot. It may be nothing but a small fever." She unwound the blankets Louise had swaddled him in, looking from one to the other. "Babies often get them. They come and go quickly. But," she paused and lowered her voice, "get Collette, or better, if it's possible, a doctor. A baby's health isn't something you want to take any risks with, is it?"

Tears trickled down Louise's face.

"Tell me where to go and I'll get whoever you want," Hélène said. She'd had experience with newborn lambs and kids. They could appear fine at first but die for no apparent reason in the days and weeks after birth.

Leaving Irene holding the squalling infant, Louise took Hélène aside. "Do you know if Luc was planning to stay at the studio?" she asked.

Hélène looked blankly at her.

"Hélène, do you know if Luc was planning to stay at the studio? How far along with the painting was he?"

"It's nearly finished." Hélène couldn't understand what Luc had to do with any of this.

Louise kept her voice low. She shot a glance at Irene, obviously not wanting her to hear.

Irene had opened Benoit's vest and was dabbing his face and chest with a damp cloth, making soothing noises. His cries had quietened but not stopped.

"Look," Louise hissed impatiently, "Luc paid for Collette. I'm sure he'll do this for me. If Irene's saying we should fetch a doctor..." She left the rest unsaid.

Hélène finished the sentence off in her head: it must be serious.

"I'll go to the studio first." She picked up her shawl and threw it around her shoulders, preparing to leave. Luc was full of contradictions. He had generously given money for her cousin's midwife, but she'd never have known if Benoît hadn't gotten sick.

"Here," Louise rummaged in a drawer for pen and paper and wrote down an address "is his home address in case he's left the studio." She scribbled a bit more. "And these are the directions to his house, but please God, you won't need them."

"I won't be long, you'll see. I shan't stop till I find him," she promised her cousin. She tucked the piece of paper into her blouse and gave Louise a quick hug.

"Tell him it's urgent," Louise called after her as she ran down the stairs.

Evening was coming on and the light deepened as Hélène left. She walked to and from Luc's studio by herself regularly but had never been out alone this late in the day. Ignoring her anxiety, and with the incentive of Benoît's piteous cries echoing in her ears, she ran back through the same streets she'd already walked twice that day. She ignored the looks people gave her and prayed that Luc would be at the studio. Louise was depending on her.

Hélène hurried along the road, disturbing thoughts buzzing in her head. Louise had never said one word about Luc paying for Collette's services. Why not? Pierre must know. It wasn't a secret, was it? And how usual was it for artists to help out their models? Her cousin had modeled for Luc for at least two years. She didn't know if it was usual for artists to keep the same model for such a long time.

The roads were filled mostly with workers who were hurrying home to families and hot meals. Hélène envied them the comfort that awaited them; she too had been in the same situation not long ago. How frail everything is, she thought. One sentence, one word, one moment, and your life changes forever; instead of peace and comfort, you had pain and loss. No, she wouldn't think in that way. She'd tell Luc the problem and he would get the doctor. It would turn out to be nothing but a small fever, and as Irene said, Benoît would soon be fine.

She ran up the stairs to Luc's studio at the top of the building. Knocking loudly, and putting her ear to the door, she listened for any sound of movement inside, but only heard her own loud breathing. Answer the door, she prayed, but after knocking hard several more times her heart sank as she realized the studio was empty.

She dug out the crumpled bit of paper with the directions to Luc's house. But what if he'd gone out to the cafes he frequented before returning home? Perhaps he'd said something to the landlady, Madame LaGrange, an old woman who often hovered about spying on her tenants.

"I have to make sure everything's in order," she'd told Hélène one day when she caught the woman standing halfway up the stairs near his studio.

Hélène hurried downstairs and knocked on her door. After a minute or two of impatient waiting, the door opened a crack.

"Oui?" The landlady peered at Hélène sourly. "What do you want?"

"I'm looking for M'sieur Marteille, the artist who has the studio upstairs. Do you know where he is?"

"You're one of his models, aren't you?"

"Yes, but it's really urgent. I have to find him. I need a doctor."

"Oh, what's wrong? You don't look sick." An acquisitive gleam flashed in her eye at the thought of obtaining a juicy piece of gossip about her artist tenant.

"It's my nephew. He's newborn, and he's fallen ill with a fever."

Sympathy must have softened the old woman's heart as she opened the door wider. "He left not long ago. You've not missed him by much."

"Oh, thank you. Do you know which direction he took?" Hélène hoped he'd gone home, and she wouldn't have to go searching through Montmartre's numerous cafes. She'd heard tales of the riotous Parisian nightlife from Louise.

"He headed home." The old woman looked at her with sympathy. "You should go before it gets too dark," she said. "If you cut through the park, it'll take you half the time than if you go by the main roads. Enter through the main entrance, walk straight on, and you'll see the signs for Rue Murillo. It'll be on the right, and will bring you out near his house."

"You've been so helpful." Hélène leaned forward and surprised the woman by giving her a quick peck on the cheek. "Thank you."

When she came out of Luc's building the sun was setting in a blaze of crimson across the sky and there were fewer people on the streets. She walked fast, keeping to the main road, but didn't run. Benoit's health was at stake, and she wanted to be sure she didn't get lost. The built-up quarter of Montmartre was soon behind her, and she could see the park ahead on the left, trees and bushes clumping together in the dusky twilight. Large houses set in residential gardens spread along the other side of the road into the distance.

She paused under the grand arch

above the main gates. Following Louise's directions would take her half an hour longer than cutting through the park. Claude would have chosen the longer safer route rather than the shorter riskier one. He was dependable, never giving into impulse, doing everything with careful attention. Claude did make mistakes, but it wasn't because he'd not thought things through—it was one the qualities she loved in him.

She thought of the extra time needed for fetching the doctor and returning to Louise's apartment, then hurried through the main gates. There were a few gas lights here and there providing enough light to spot the sign for Rue Murillo, and her shortcut, without any trouble. She hesitated, glancing nervously around.

A narrow band of pale blue, the last

of the daylight, was fading fast over toward the west, and above, the first stars appeared.

The shadows were lengthening, but Hélène didn't have the luxury of time. If the encroaching darkness appeared more menacing, she'd have to remember it was her nerves. Shadows didn't hurt you. Taking a deep breath, and thinking of Louise and Benoît, she offered a fleeting prayer to St. Leonard and set off, her footsteps echoing along the darkening path.

Chapter Nine

In this world, it is said there is danger at every step, but no one can go through life thinking in this manner. Instead, we have to trust that when our foot touches the earth, it will be there to hold us. Nonetheless, tragedies and accidents, big and small, do happen.

Paris, July 2007

Anna sensed the panic, waiting, poised, ready to slice through her sanity.

"Over by the entrance." François took her arm and pointed at the Basilica. "Look, there."

Ingrid and Jean-Paul were deep in conversation, standing in the warm shadows of a decorated stone archway. She felt stupid she hadn't seen them. One minute she was fine, a tourist on a quaint quest, the next, a neurotic middle-aged female having a full-blown fit of hysterics. In public. She really needed to get a grip on her fears.

"Of course. Sorry, I—"

"Anna," he smiled at her. "You must relax. This is Paris."

She said nothing, allowing him to hold her arm and guide her over to the cathedral. He let go as they followed Ingrid and Jean-Paul into the dim coolness. The interior of the church with its ceiling paintings, stained glass windows, and statues offering benediction from their niches surpassed her expectations. She looked around in wonderment and awe. Centuries of worship had imbued the sacred space with stillness and tranquility.

The silence soothed her, and she appreciated François following her lead as she meandered toward the front altar. She stopped, François close behind her, as a line of nuns emerged from a side door, walked out in front of them and proceeded to arrange themselves for choir practice. Anna slid into a nearby pew; François followed suit.

As the pure sound of the nuns' harmonies filled the church, her mundane concerns dropped away and her heart filled with the beauty of their adoration of the Divine. If only life were this straightforward, she reflected, feeling for a moment the pull of a life free from hankering and lamenting for material desires, with the promise of eternal bliss after death.

After the choir finished and filed out, their cheeks flushed with effort, and silence ruled once more, she went over to one of the black metal candlestands adorned with stalactites of wax. Lighting a candle, she placed it in an empty candle holder and knelt on the green padded step.

After she'd left home for uni, Anna had ceased attending church altogether. In fact, she hadn't thought much about life and death until the foundations of her protected world shattered with unexpected tragedy. Since then, she hadn't found spirituality, or comfort, in the formal religion of her childhood. But she had learned how precious hope is, no matter how small or ephemeral, when you thought the world a hopeless place. She offered the candle with a prayer for Jeremy's soul.

François didn't kneel, but took a candle, lighting and placing it next to hers. He remained standing, lost in his own thoughts.

Half an hour later, as they stepped out onto the forecourt of the Basilica, they were unexpectedly blinded by the sunlight.

As their eyesight adjusted, the noise from the city, unheard inside, reminded Anna that life flowed on unremittingly around them. She headed over to a look-out point enjoying the light breeze cooling her skin. The deep green of the squares and parks below stood out like oases in the concrete and stone desert of the city. Viewed from above, people bustling through the importance of their daily lives appeared as tiny moving dots.

"Believe it or not, much of Paris, as you see it today, was rebuilt a mere two hundred years ago." François indicated the city beyond Montmartre to where the Paris rooftops, sizzling in the summer heat, marched geometrically into the distance. "Your London burnt in the 1600's, we burnt our Paris in the 1800's."

She imagined searing flames engulfing houses, people running for their lives.

"At the end of the Franco-Prussian War, the people of Paris decided they didn't want the old government and set up their own in its place."

She half listened as François mellow voice continued, letting her thoughts drift as he spoke.

"The government objected and the two sides battled for days. But before the Communards lost, they set the city alight. So the Paris laid out before you is an architecturally elegant city—but has a hidden violent past."

He was the perfect tourist guide,

babbling on and full of interesting facts, but not requiring any spoken contribution. Nodding and making the occasional appropriate sounds were enough. She knew Jeremy would have loved this; the architecture, the magnificence, the history, and the people of the city. But no matter how many times they'd holidayed in France, they'd never had the urge to bring the children to the capital.

The first time they visited France they'd hired a mobile home and gone touring for the summer holidays; Jeremy and Ingrid had been ecstatic as they let the road or their fancy, lead them. They'd fallen in love with the west coast with its wide beaches, high domed skies and the wonderful feeling of freedom. At night they made bonfires on empty beaches, watching driftwood burn, talking, laughing and fantasizing about a journey that had no end.

Late one evening as they motored through a forested stretch of the coast along a minor road, Greg spotted a track wide enough to explore in the mobile home. They hadn't gone far when they saw a parking space, far enough away from the road for them to be secluded, but not so far as to prevent a quick start the next day.

Next morning, they awoke to birdsong, and the forest looked so beguiling with the sun filtering through the green canopied shade, they decided to stop there for a day. In the cool of the late afternoon, when shadows had stretched long fingers along the ground, they went exploring. Jeremy begged them to play hide and seek. Night had fallen by the time they found him. Until the news of his death, those five hours had been the worst of her life. Anna's throat was hoarse with shouting when Jeremy finally heard her.

He'd cried, putting his arms around her, and burying his head in the folds of her blouse, saying between sobs, he thought they'd left him. The next morning, they headed south for the sun and sand of the open beaches.

A lump formed in her throat. As a distraction she pulled out her camera, not caring if she looked like a typical tourist. Pointing the camera, she clicked away, thinking she might be able to use these for paintings when she returned home, and realized it was the second time that day she'd had an idea for her work. Jeremy's death had frozen her desire to paint, but here, in Paris, the urge to create was re-surfacing.

"The Musée de Montmartre, the Impressionists, and your Luc Marteille await. Shall we?"

"Yes," Anna agreed absentmindedly as her eye considered angles and shades of light and darkness.

"The walk is a pleasant one."

She'd been so absorbed in her private thoughts at the same time as trying to listen to François's account of Paris's turbulent past, that they'd descended several steps before she realized Ingrid and Jean-Paul weren't with them.

"I have to go back for her," she told François, turning to go back up. "I can't leave her." Her voice shook.

"Why not? She's with Jean-Paul." He stated this as if teaching a dull pupil an obvious fact. "He's probably sketching." He dismissed her worry with a wave of his hand

Anna recalled the satchel Jean-Paul had been carrying and paused before answering. Her tense worry, this constant need for reassurance regarding Ingrid's safety was verging on obsessive. It had been bearable at home, where she knew where Ingrid was and what she was doing, and if needed, could pick her up at a moment's notice. But here, in unfamiliar territory, fearful thoughts conjured themselves into existence, invading, upsetting her balance.

"It's that...,"

"Jean-Paul is a reliable boy."

Anna heard him sigh as he took out his mobile and dialed

"Don't worry. They'll be fine, you'll see." François fired off a barrage of French down the phone. When Jean-Paul answered, their hands touched as he passed her the phone.

"Mum," Ingrid's voice, confident, happy, sounded in her ear. "I'm going to stay and keep Jean-Paul company. He's sketching. The views are fantastic. We'll meet up later. Love you. Bye."

And the phone went dead. Ingrid had abandoned her. She could feel the emotional umbilical ties to her daughter stretching. She handed François his phone, and their hands touched again.

"After the Musée I know a suitable place for lunch." He took her hand and tucked it under his arm.

Why he thought it was acceptable to assume this intimacy with her, she didn't know. Probably it was a French thing. But without the anchor of Ingrid's presence, his physical touch was comforting, because it made her feel less alone. She let him take charge, and, as if they were a couple or a pair of old friends, they began their descent from the calm heights of Sacre Coeur.

"So tell me something about Luc Marteille," François said when they were taking a short rest half way down the long flight of steps. "Isn't he a minor Impressionist artist?"

Anna did her best to disregard the burning in her calves. She would have a relaxing soak in the tub when she returned to the hotel. "That's the thing. I thought I did have the major facts of his life." She looked out over the streets of Montmartre getting closer, noisier. "Luc was born in Rennes, brought up by his mother. They had to move to Brest and live with her brother's family after Luc's father died. He had a small inheritance and fell in love with Émilie de Soubignon, who had enough personal wealth to support his painting. They married and moved to

Paris where they had three children, two boys, and a girl. He also had a studio in Montmartre and exhibited his paintings along with many other artists at the first Impressionists' exhibition."

"So what changed when the letter came to light?"

"The letter's very intense, and he was obviously having, or had recently finished, a love affair with a woman called Hélène. It made me want to find out more. I'm not sure what my opinion of him as a man is anymore. Don't get me wrong, I'll always love my painting." She stopped, and dug her phone from the depths of her bag, and spent a minute finding the photo she'd taken.

He studied the painting. "It's beautiful," he said.

"This is Luc Marteille, that's his wife, Émilie, son, Guy, daughter Giselle, and the baby's name was Gustave." Anna scrolled down and showed him another photo, pointing to each individual as she spoke.

Luc stared out, from the faded sepia photo, his expression intense, one hand resting possessively on his wife's shoulder as she sat holding the baby; the children stood, straight-backed, either side of their mother. They looked the epitome of a respectable middle-class family.

"May I?"

Anna handed him the phone for a closer look, his fingers brushing hers as he took the phone.

He peered at the screen. "A handsome family."

"I'm not a prude, don't get me wrong, but I had this picture of a dedicated artist, good husband, and father, and I have to say that my view of him, well, it's changed."

François appeared amused by her comment. "Because he made love with another woman? And what is a prude?"

From what she'd gleaned from films and books, people in France viewed extra-marital relationships with a different attitude from her more conservative standards.

"A prude is someone who behaves strictly according to a moral code, and who thinks they are superior to those who don't follow the same rules."

François looked quizzically at her. "Are you a prude?"

"Please. Don't make fun of me." She gazed out over the city not far below; she could hear cars honking.

"I wouldn't dare." He raised his arms as if in surrender.

Oh! He was laughing at her! The quaint English woman with her outdated views.

"And how many affairs did you have?" She regretted the words as soon as they left her mouth.

"None. I was never unfaithful. I loved my wife too much." He stared at her coldly. "But I don't judge. You cannot pass judgment if you have not marched in another's place. Yes?"

"I'm sorry." Embarrassed at her lack of control, she stared out at the city, unable to meet his gaze. They had managed a brief cordial détente, and she'd gone and put her foot in it; the barricades were up once more. He didn't look at her or reply, but set off at a sharp pace down the steps, and back into the hot bustling streets.

The Musée De Montmartre bore no resemblance to the grand Musée d'Orsay which housed the most important and well-known

Impressionist paintings. The museum was small, set in cobbled streets bordered with trees and shrubs, and they entered through a curved stone archway. The museum's focus was mostly on records of Montmartre's history, but it did possess an interesting collection of artworks.

François followed her at a distance as she studied the works of Toulouse Lautrec, Utrillo, and Kupka and finally came across three of Luc's pictures hung in the far corner of the last room.

The largest was a portrait of a young girl, fresh complexioned with thick honey blonde curls falling loosely over one shoulder. She looked directly at the viewer; her wide blue eyes frankly assessing what she saw, her expression a tad quizzical as if she couldn't understand why there was any fuss. The frills of a white blouse revealed her shoulders. The backdrop was a lush dark red.

Anna bent close, examining the title of the picture. One word. *Hélène.*

Her face alight with excitement, she beckoned him over. "I've seen photos of this painting in books but titled *The Country Girl.* This is her, the woman Luc wrote the letter to. But standing here and looking right at her—whew! It's exhilarating."

François moved closer studying the information below the portrait. "Donated to the museum by Giselle Collet. Do you think that's his daughter?"

"Mmm, more things to find out."

"Why do you think he never posted it?" he queried.

"I'd love to know because when you read the letter, you're sure he's in love with Hélène, but he was married.

Maybe his wife suspected he was having an affair? Maybe it was one step too much for her and she forced him to choose. Your mistress or me?"

François laughed.

She flushed. Yet again he was mocking her.

"You have a vivid imagination. Possibly he wrote other letters which might tell us more. Many of Manet's letters, and letters from other Impressionist artists have been published."

Anna chose to ignore him. How had she managed to end up being stuck with a Frenchman who had no imagination?

After a while, he walked away.

She studied Hélène for a long time before moving onto the other two paintings. The larger one, of a garden with two children playing, focused on the bright-colored flowers splashed across the foreground. These attracted the eye first. The children, placed in the background with heads bowed as they examined an object in the grass, hadn't been painted in much detail. Below, the title said *L'Ete en Brest*. Second was a rural scene: a high open sky with clouds in thunderous colors dominated the farm tracks and peasants at work in the fields below. This was titled, *Normandy*. She loved the way Luc painted; his fresh and immediate style brought her in and made her feel part of the scene.

"Ah," said François returning, "I have news."

"I bet you they're Luc's children." Anna nodded at the painting.

"There are several letters but we will have to make an appointment and come back later. The library archives open at special times. What do you say to having lunch and returning later?"

Instinct told her to reject any offer from this objectionable man, but what option did she have? What could she say? *No. I'd prefer to be by myself as my daughter falls in love with your nephew, and the pair of them disappear to goodness knows where*. She wasn't finding François the easiest man to get on with, but without being asked he'd gone off and efficiently communicated with the curator. His translation skills would be very useful this afternoon. Why did he make her feel so defensive? "Yes, that sounds good," she said. His mention of food reminded her she was hungry. "But I'd like to speak to the curator about my letter first."

"Of course. Follow me."

He strode off, Anna trotting behind him. A group of tourists surrounded the curator, and they waited till he'd finished. Before she could say a word, François and the little round man with a shiny badge proclaiming him as Monsieur Battingnon, Le Curator, were chatting volubly in French.

Everything was going well, breathe, let it pass, but she clenched her jaw as François held his hand out.

"Have you the letter?"

"I brought a photocopy with me," Anna told the curator, ignoring François. This was her project, hers alone. Not his, nor anyone else's. She took a brown envelope from her handbag and carefully pulled out the photocopy.

M'sieur Battingnon's eyes widened with pleasure as he skimmed the letter. "This way, please. We should conduct this business in my office."

In the tiny overcrowded space that

passed for his office, the curator shifted a pile of papers off his desk and took some minutes scrutinizing the photocopy of Luc's letter. "I'll write you a receipt for this and will see what I can do about having it verified." He pulled a pad toward him and scribbled on it. "I understand you're here for a short time, so I'll do what I can. You're coming back this afternoon, so we can speak later." The little man glowed with pleasure as he handed her a receipt.

Anna smiled back. She was making progress.

Outside the museum, François took hold of her elbow.

This time, her enjoyment of the new familiarity of his skin touching hers was a surprise; under the influence of an impulse she didn't understand, or recognize, she allowed this small intimacy. The sane, level-headed side of her disregarded the idea she was exploring something out of the ordinary, and possibly dangerous, with somebody new. She knew Greg would be taken aback if he saw how relaxed she was in the company of another man, one she hardly knew, guiding her in this way through the labyrinthine back streets of a foreign city.

François took her to a busy bistro tucked away on a side street and chose a table near the edge of the outside seating area. He held a chair out for her.

Greg wouldn't have cared where she sat, and he certainly wouldn't have pulled out a chair for her. Was this normal behavior for a French man? she wondered. It was different but pleasant and relaxing. She experienced a certain gratification in surrendering, in allowing someone to make this small decision for her.

He sat opposite. "Vegetarian?" he inquired.

She looked up sharply but didn't catch even the tiniest of smirks. "Yes, I'd better," she gave an embarrassed laugh. "I promised Ingrid. When she became a vegetarian, she insisted we promise to try it for a year."

"And you don't want to break your promise. That's good and not a problem." He looked at her.

She looked away, his direct gaze unsettling her.

"Shall I order?" he asked.

"Please. It would make things easier."

And they laughed.

A companionable laugh, thought Anna, noting how his eyes lit up when he smiled. He became another person.

"So how many of you have made this

promise to the charming, and obviously irresistible, Ingrid?"

She wavered before answering. "Oh, my husband, Greg, and myself."

"Do you have any other children other than Ingrid?"

Anna's expression changed.

He picked up on it immediately. "I apologize. It's a casual question. I don't mean to intrude. Have you been to Paris before?"

Anna took a deep breath. In and out. Focus on the breath, on the lilt and rhythm of the French language around her. Even if you'd never learned a single word of the language, the sound was more expressive, and somehow more sensual, than English. What did they say about French? Wasn't it called the language of love?

Everything is fine. She repeated the mantra silently over and over. People.

Normality. She was handling the situation; she just hadn't mastered the turmoil that assaulted her when she told someone for the first time. "No, no. It's okay. It's...." and the words fell, tumbling out of her mouth. "It's that my son Jeremy died six months ago in a car accident. So there were four of us, now there are three."

The chatter of conversation and laughter from a noisy group at a nearby table continued as if she had said I have an Uncle Fred or some other words of little meaning.

"I'm very sorry." François leaned forward and placed his hand over hers covering it completely; his palm was slightly rough, his touch warm. He squeezed her hand.

"Thank you," she said, making no effort to shift her hand from under his. "I'm still adjusting."

"Loss is hard. Whether it's sudden or you watch them eaten day by day by a disease you can do nothing to stop." His voice wobbled. "I know what it means to lose someone." For a moment his face softened with memory. "Life does go on. Yes, that's a cliché, but one that's true."

Ah, she thought, and an infinitesimal paradigm shift occurred. We have something in common. He understands grief. "Yes," Anna sighed, "but does it get easier?"

"It does, and, yes, you do learn to live with it. You have to. It's not possible to go to your bed and stop living, is it?"

"M'sieur? Madame?" A waiter appeared at the table.

François moved his hand away, and the moment was gone.

Over plates of delicately flavored

salad and spiced tagine, accompanied by a fine white wine, which she appreciated but was imbibing more than she was accustomed to, especially at this time of day, they began to share parts of their life stories.

She discovered an interesting fact about him; he wasn't French. He came from a Lebanese Christian Maronite family, which intrigued her as she'd never heard of the sect. This explained his exotic looks. His family had been prominent, and his uncle, an up and coming politician, was assassinated early on in the conflicts which tore Lebanon apart in the seventies and eighties.

"My father took the decision to leave for a safer country to bring up his children in, so my parents left Lebanon and we came to France when I was seven."

"That must have been hard," she said, hoping he didn't think her comment trite.

"Yes, it was." He didn't speak for a moment. "A few memories of a different life remain but not many. However, France still remains a more secure place to live and raise children."

She learned he was retired. First, he'd been a successful stockbroker who after marrying had given up city life to start a family in the south of France. Using his business skills, he'd built up a prosperous business in real estate. He'd recently visited his daughter, living in America, and seen his two grandchildren for the first time. His son, a doctor, of whom he was immensely proud, and constantly worried about, worked with Médecins Sans Frontières at a refugee camp in Kenya. Jean-Paul's mother was his younger sister.

He'd been so open she told him stories she'd not shared with anyone for a long time. She talked about her passion for art and mad art student days in Glasgow, but talking about her younger self felt like discussing a stranger. As they waited for coffee, she wondered where that adventurous young woman had gone. She believed she had channeled her passions into being a mother, bringing up two wonderful children and looking after a husband. She'd kept her art alive in a part-time job that Greg viewed as a hobby because they didn't need the money. But she was starting to understand that she'd neglected an important aspect of herself, regardless of being able to justify her choice.

François glanced at his watch. "We should get going if we're to catch the archives." He looked around for the waiter. "I'll get this," he said, point blank refusing to let her contribute.

She fished her phone out of her bag, and put it on the table wondering whether to call Ingrid or not? She finished her coffee, watching François through the window as he paid, and thought about Greg. Was she in love with her husband? Or had he become a habit—a dependable but well-worn armchair you were reluctant to dispose of because it had become so comfortable? Did relationships have a sell-by date? Would an affair be such a bad thing? Would she be an awful person if she cheated on the man she'd married and lived with for twenty-odd years? She wondered idly where these notions were coming from. Were the barriers she'd installed with such deliberation and care over the years disintegrating? Or was the intoxication of being in Paris revealing a side to her nature she'd hidden from everyone—a side she'd never acknowledged, even to herself?

Her chair jerked and she spun around in time to see a young man racing away. In stunned bewilderment she recognized the object swinging from his hand was her handbag. "François! François!" she shouted, her voice rising. "Help! Thief! Thief!"

Chapter Ten

When you think you may lose something or someone, that object or person increases in value. However, sometimes you do lose something precious, after which, life is never the same.

Paris, July 1873

The night closing in didn't bother Hélène; she was a country girl used to going out into the fields at night to search for lost animals. But this wasn't the countryside. The area around the Parc de Monceau was where some of the richest men in the country lived, but which also harbored the worst criminals. Her mother had filled her head with dire stories of what happened to young girls on the streets of Paris.

She heard a noise, turned, scanning the path. Nobody. I'm simply imagining things, she thought; it's a squirrel, or an owl, or some creature settling itself for the night. Nonetheless, she increased her pace, repeatedly checking the path behind her.

Once, after a bitter winter, when she must have been about twelve years old, local farmers had started losing animals, and the story spread that a pack of wolves had been sighted in the hills. Her father had decided to spend a few nights protecting his flock of sheep and was taking her older brother. She'd begged and pleaded to go with them, and her father agreed, overriding her mother's protests. That night the three of them sat in his shepherds' hut overlooking the flock. Her father gave them a couple of old metal dishes and spoons, instructing them to bang hard and yell at the tops of their voices if any wolves appeared.

Around two o'clock in the morning, she jolted awake, roused by her father's shouting as he ran out the door firing his old shotgun into the dark. She and her brother ignored his command to remain in the hut and dashed out to see what was happening. A flicker of movement caught her attention, and there, right up at the edge of the pasture, she saw two wolves disappear. Excitedly retelling the story later, this flash of two tails transformed into a horde of ravening beasts that she, her brother and her father had boldly routed.

As a couple of figures appeared out of the dark walking toward her, her pulse began to race. If she was able to face wild wolves, she thought, surely she could deal with anything she might meet tonight. As the men came closer, she saw they were young lads. Nothing to be afeared of. One thing her father had impressed on his children was that showing your fear didn't help.

"Bonsoir, Mademoiselle." The shorter of the two, a stocky youth, stood directly in her path, blocking her passage and forcing her to stop.

She didn't like the way he was looking her over and balled her hands into fists. Her brother had taught her to fight a good few years ago when he'd become interested in the sport of boxing and needed someone to practice with; that is until he gave her a bruised eye and their mother realized what they were up to and put an end to it.

She nodded at the lad but didn't

answer, her legs suddenly weak.

"Oh! Too high and mighty to talk to us, eh?" sneered the other lad

"No, no," she replied moving to the left to pass them. "My nephew's sick, and I'm fetching a doctor."

"Likely story," replied the boy, moving in front of her once more, preventing her from passing.

She chanced a quick look behind to see if there was anyone coming along the path to whom she could shout for help, but she was alone. If there'd been one of them, she might have attempted to punch him in the stomach, or at least kick him in the shins. Her brother had lost a fair number of those fights. But she wouldn't try that, not with two of them.

"Please move out of my way."

"Or else what?" the taller boy moved closer, reaching out and stroking her hair.

She jerked backward.

"Pretty and feisty, eh?" He leered closer, and she smelled his stale breath. "Hey, be a good girl. Give us your purse and we'll be on our way." He shot a look at his friend.

Her heart was beating too fast, and the question of how far these two were prepared to go to get what they wanted flicked through her mind. She balled her fists so tight her nails dug into her palms. "Hey! Hey!" she shouted, waving as if she was addressing someone coming up behind them. "Monsieur! Get the police!"

The two youths turned to see who she was calling. It didn't take them a second to realize she'd tricked them and no one was there.

But in the instant they looked away, she dodged around them and ran. Not far ahead she could see where the path through the park joined the main boulevard. Please, dear God, she prayed as she ran, let there be someone nearby. She didn't dare look behind but concentrated on the ground in front so she wouldn't trip, trying to ignore the flap of her skirts against her legs as she ran. It wasn't long before she heard their pounding footsteps and jagged breathing as they closed the gap.

Desperation lent her the speed she needed, and she exited the woods ahead of her pursuers. Unfortunately, she was running too fast and, unable to slow down, collided with a gentleman striding along swinging his cane. He staggered sideways with the force of her impact, barely managing to stay upright, too surprised to prevent her from tumbling to the ground. His cane went flying.

"Help me, Monsieur!" She pleaded, attempting to rise from where she'd fallen. She stared in shocked surprise. The man, clearly annoyed at her sudden intrusion upon his person and who stood frowning at her, was Luc Marteille.

"Hélène!" Luc said. "What the devil are you doing here?" He gazed at her in astonishment.

"There were two men," she gasped looking back toward the path.

He glanced up the path as he bent, helping her to stand. "Yes, I see them. They're running away."

"They tried to—" Tears ran down her face. She couldn't continue.

"There, there," he said, pulling her to his chest, patting her back with soothing motions as if she were a child.

The protectiveness of his arm around

her shoulders felt natural. She rested her head, taking comfort from his presence, wanting to stay there listening to his heartbeat quicken. As she regained some composure, she tried to step back, but he seemed unwilling to release his hold.

"Are you hurt? Did they...?" He left the question unfinished as he scrutinized her face and clothes.

"No, no. I managed to get away from them."

"Are you hurt in any way?"

"No. Nothing's broken." She looked up at him. "Oh, thank you. Thank you."

A hint of mischief flickered in his eyes. "Thank me for what? Taking a walk in the evening? But why on earth are you alone in the park? Surely Louise...?"

"I was looking for you. Louise sent me."

He frowned at her.

"Benoît is sick with a fever. She said to ask you for help."

He stared at her, baffled, taking a moment for her words to register, as if he couldn't understand what she required of him.

"We need a doctor for Benoît," she added quietly, "it's urgent."

He galvanized into action, the spell of her sudden arrival broken. He retrieved his cane. "My house isn't far. From there we can take the carriage to the doctor's house."

"Merci a Dieu! Thank you, Monsieur Marteille."

"Luc," he said. "Call me Luc." He took hold of her elbow, hurrying her along, and learned Madame La Grange had told her of the shortcut through the woods. He cursed her for putting Hélène in danger.

The houses gradually became less grandiose and smaller, but still set in individual plots with well-tended gardens. Luc finally stopped. "I'll arrange for the carriage and let Émilie know what is happening." He released his hold on her arm and opened the gate.

She felt an odd sensation of loss without his touch.

He ushered her through the front door. "Her health has not been good since our last child was stillborn."

Ah, Hélène thought, instantly everything made sense: why he would hire her as a model without seeing her; why he would pay for Collette; his many kindnesses toward Louise. She'd never doubted Louise's love and faithfulness to Pierre, but had wondered why Luc had been so concerned about Louise that he'd paid for a midwife, and why her cousin had turned to him for help.

Inside the house, he escorted her into a front parlor.

As soon as she was safe, her fears for Benoît returned with force, and she paced restlessly around the room. In spite of her anxieties, she couldn't help noticing the tasteful and clearly expensive furniture and décor of the room. She would never enjoy the pleasures of luxury such as this, but she didn't envy Luc or his life. You accepted your lot and made the best of it. How you dealt with what came your way in life enabled you to find joy and happiness, not the trappings of luxury. Thinking of the devastation Louise and Pierre would suffer if any harm came to Benoît, she prayed for his protection.

Less than five minutes after arriving at his house, Luc assisted her up into the serviceable brown vehicle that was the Marteille family carriage.

She sat opposite Luc, her hands clasped tightly together, staring out into the night as they drove off to fetch the doctor. The clattering of the horse's hooves complemented the creaking of the carriage in a bizarre night medley. She was thankful she'd stumbled, literally, into Luc, and felt indebted to him for saving her from the attempted robbery or worse. If he hadn't been on his way home when she chanced upon him, she might even now be trekking through the city as night descended, trying to find him in the cafes of Montmartre. She shuddered, wondering how long she might have had to search, and indeed might not have tracked him down if he'd gone to a friend's studio or house. Nonetheless, she had located him. She brushed aside the feeling that a line had been crossed between them.

"Are you quite recovered?" he asked.

"Yes, thank you." She met his gaze. He wasn't looking at her in the same professional way he had during the sitting earlier that day. He was pleading with her. Confused, she looked away. She knew he wanted more from her, but he was married and she was engaged. What did he think was possible? Didn't he understand the rules? Or did he assume they didn't apply to him because he was an artist?

"Benoît will be fine. Babies often have fevers and Dr. Brasson is excellent. He's treated my two little ones and they've come through quite a few childhood illnesses." Luc reached over and clasped her hands. "Don't worry."

His hands on hers were hot. Her attention narrowed to that one point where his skin touched hers. She wished she could tell him to stop, that he was making her forget she was betrothed, but she said nothing, hardly daring to breathe, avoiding his gaze.

He removed his hands and sat back.

"Thank you," she said. She was separating, becoming detached from her moorings: the line anchoring her to her life was disappearing.

As soon as they pulled up at the doctor's house. Luc leaped out. "Stay there," he ordered before running up the drive.

She sagged into the seat, weak with relief, but she didn't know if it was because Benoit would receive the help he needed, or because Luc's presence left her in such turmoil. He returned within minutes carrying the good doctor's bag and chivvying a small, bald, portly man down the drive. She was surprised when Luc clambered back into the carriage as she thought he'd leave after he'd secured the doctor's help.

He leaned out of the window urging the driver to make greater speed.

As the carriage clattered through the darkening streets, Hélène sent silent prayers for little Benoît. She kept seeing his flushed face and hearing his tiny cries. Please, please, she begged, let him be no worse than when I left.

They turned into Rue Theloze and spotted Pierre standing outside his apartment building, looking fretfully up and down the road. His agitated expression lessened a fraction as the coach stopped and Luc climbed out, turning and helping the Doctor from the carriage.

"Thank God you came. I think his fever is getting worse," Pierre threw over his shoulder as he led the way, taking the stairs two at a time and constantly looking back to make sure they were behind him. They heard Benoît's piteous cries long before they reached the door.

The doctor, Luc, and Hélène crammed into the room behind Pierre, filling the space.

"Merde!" exclaimed the doctor bending over the infant and unwrapping the blankets. "He has a fever and you wrap him up! What are you trying to do? Boil him alive?"

Louise looked stricken.

"Fetch me cold water and a cloth. Quick!"

Louise ran to the kitchen, grabbing a bowl, and filling it with water.

Hélène followed. "Oh, he doesn't really mean that." She attempted to comfort Louise.

"But what if I have made him worse? What if he...?" Louise wiped her tears away with the back of her hand.

Hélène snatched up a towel. "Come on! Who are you going to listen to? Me, who you practically brought up? Or a grumpy old Doctor?" Hélène put her arms around her cousin, hugging her tight. "Benoit is going to be fine," she whispered in Louise's ear.

When they returned to the living room, Doctor Brasson had removed most of Benoît's clothes except the cloth diaper. The baby was on his back in the middle of the couch, squalling and waving his little arms and legs in frustration.

The doctor took the towel from Louise, and dipping it into the water, began to wipe down the infant. "I've given him one dose of medicine. I'll leave you several more and I've explained to your husband that you must keep the child cool." He dipped the end of the towel into the bowl, and barely squeezing it, wiped Benoît's face, body, arms, and legs. The child's cries diminished.

"Do this for half an hour, then another dose of the medicine to sort out the fever." Dr. Brasson addressed both parents. "He'll be fine, but you must lower his temperature by keeping him cool. Listen and pay close attention. The second the fever drops, when his skin is cooler, you must dress him. Immediately. You don't want him to catch a chill." He glared at Louise, who appeared genuinely fearful of the little round man.

She nodded, and he appeared satisfied she understood his instructions.

He pulled another paper sachet from

his bag and added it to the one in Louise's hand. "Here's one more dose for the morning. That should be enough. Despite his fever, it's not serious."

"Thank you, doctor. Thank you, Monsieur Marteille." Pierre's voice trembled as he reached out and shook Luc's hand. "I don't know how I can repay you for saving my son's life." His voice cracked with emotion.

"I am finished here. We can go." The doctor's businesslike attitude dispelled the last of the parents' distress.

"How can we show our appreciation, Monsieur Marteille?" Pierre looked at Luc, gratitude in his eyes.

"Seeing little Benoit recover his good health is enough for me."

Hélène thought of his dead child. She shouldn't judge him too harshly.

"Bon nuit, Louise," He bowed, short

and quick. "Hélène, I'll see you tomorrow."

Exhaustion hit Hélène after Luc and the doctor departed. Benoit's fever had abated. The crisis was over. Tomorrow everything would be back to normal. Tonight she'd seen a different, kinder, side of Luc. He had saved her from being assaulted, and more crucially, saved Benoit. What would they have done without him? She remembered the beat of his heart close to her ear. Tomorrow she would have to contend with what was becoming an increasingly complicated relationship with Luc, but for the moment she was happy and thankful that her nephew was alive and healthy.

Chapter Eleven

Crisis, trauma, and distress distort our perspective of events. Small details, generally not noticed, spring into focus; and of the major incident, we retain one or two images which condense and summarize the whole experience for us.

Paris, July 2007

"François! François!" Anna shouted, her voice rising. "Help! Thief! Thief!" She looked around, frantic to get someone's attention but the other diners stared uncomprehendingly at her.

Suddenly François was at her side. "Anna, I'm here. What's wrong? Are you okay?"

She struggled to catch her breath

and couldn't seem to suck in any air.

He pushed her gently back onto the chair. "Slowly. Breathe. That's it."

"My handbag's been stolen," she gasped. She searched the street desperate to point out the young man, but he'd long since disappeared.

"Do you remember what he looked like?" François pulled out his mobile. "What was he wearing?"

Anna kept wheezing. "A paper bag. I need a paper bag."

François stared at her for a second as if she'd gone mad before he understood. He dashed back into the restaurant while Anna sat wheezing and trying to breathe. Then he was back out and thrusting a brown paper bag into her hands.

Minutes later, her breathing under control, she gave the briefest of descriptions–male, jeans, short brown hair–the few details she'd observed of the thief as he fled. She hadn't noticed the color of his T-shirt.

François questioned the people at the nearby tables. They apologized— they hadn't understood Madame's problem. One couple had seen the young man, but from the back, as he absconded. Someone noticed he'd worn a dark blue top. Was the lady all right? They were sympathetic.

As François dialed the police, bombarding them with a stream of rapid French, she kept seeing the photo of Jeremy she'd kept in her card wallet. The picture was one of her favorites and she'd never made a copy.

Jeremy had been ten years of age and playing a solo on the guitar at an end of term school concert. His dark hair was short and neat with his curls shorn off as she'd taken him to the hairdresser the previous day. He wore his school uniform, crisp white shirt, red school jumper, and gray trousers, and stood in the center of the stage searching the assembled parents with his guitar clutched to his chest. When he spotted them, he relaxed. There were two high spots of color on his cheeks. Anna couldn't tell who was more nervous, Jeremy or her.

He looked out at the audience, and in a serious voice announced he was going to play a Spanish piece called *Cuchama*. Anna, Ingrid, and Greg also knew the piece off by heart, as he'd practiced assiduously every night the previous week. Some sections were easy and there were other parts where his fingers didn't press the strings hard enough to produce the correct note. Jeremy bent his head over the guitar so he could see precisely where to position his fingers. It wasn't till Ingrid jumped to her feet and started clapping after the performance was finished that she released the breath she'd been holding. He'd played the piece from beginning to end without a single mistake. Jeremy gave a small bow before leaving the stage.

Eventually, other studies and interests occupied his after-school hours, and he'd stopped having guitar lessons. But he'd kept his guitar, playing purely for pleasure, and taken it with him when he left for uni.

The photograph had been a school one and there wasn't a negative. The joy of the day dimmed: she didn't want to remember how little was left of Jeremy; a few possessions in one room. The photo had been her connection to that particular memory. She wondered if other memories of him would fade with time. But there would be no more new ones.

François was all business. He got the name of her bank, started pressing buttons, and when he had them on the line, handed her his phone so she could cancel her cards.

"Your passport?" he asked.

"No, no." A tiny sigh of relief. She supposed it fortunate that she'd forgotten to carry some form of ID, but she would never have thought to leave the photo. Now it was gone forever. "I left that in the drawer at the hotel." She picked up her phone. "At least. I've got my mobile."

"And the Musée has your letter, that's three good things," he said. "Come. A short trip to the police station and that'll be it."

Without François's insistence, she wouldn't have bothered to go to the authorities as she'd done the most important thing, canceled her cards. However, none of her muttered protestations swayed his decision, and so, shaken, but without any idea of what else to do, she trudged along with him.

Two weary hours later, Anna lay on her bed gazing at the same patch of blue sky she'd seen upon waking that morning. They postponed the visit to the museum to look at Luc's letters till tomorrow as by the time they'd finished the required paperwork, the archive section had closed.

She did appreciate François's endeavors on her behalf, but the effort of spending time with someone new, someone outside her circle of friends and acquaintances with their established, proven relationships, was a struggle.

On the positive side, he was familiar with Montmartre and French history, understood art and today he'd been kind and considerate. He'd turned what might have been a very awkward situation into something bearable. But she hadn't been able to relax. She was continuously aware of him—his scent, his hands touching her arm, and her reactions to him. His presence was complicating her life.

Yet nothing had been too much bother for him. She pictured Greg in the same circumstances. Nothing she could have said would have stopped him blaming her. Not openly. No, nothing so obvious. But he'd have made it clear her carelessness had caused the problem. After all, she'd placed the bag in a position where it could be stolen. He would have made sure everyone was aware of her mistake.

Mentally she placed Greg beside François and compared them. One was like a pair of old slippers that you were so used to that you didn't notice how uncomfortable they'd become. She couldn't help but make the comparison. The other appeared to be a classical style shoe in good condition, even fit for dancing.

Anna knew she was being cruel toward Greg, but the growing gap between them, more apparent since Jeremy's death, couldn't be glossed over anymore. She resented him and couldn't forgive the 'let's move on' attitude he presented to the world. First, she had to come to terms with her loss, after that she would move on, attempt to resume some semblance of her former life.

One of the biggest obstacles was

they hadn't shared the burden of grief. At least not after the first week. Greg grieved in his own private way, but he was supposed to be her rock, her support, the love of her life. Giving up a promising career to bring up their children was a decision she didn't regret. She'd willingly agreed with his proposal because the children were her priority. His salary gave them more than enough money, and it was what he wanted.

But how many of her years were lived through his successes? Sometimes she felt like a shadow, someone or something without substance. In comparison, where were her achievements? Apart from the children, what did she have? Shiny surfaces? Did that mean she had to agree with everything? How much did she owe Greg?

Exhausted and tormented by her thoughts, Anna dozed off. She woke to Ingrid's infectious laughter and Jean-Paul's deeper voice. Then silence. Maternal suspicion kicked in, and moving faster than she thought she could, she was over at the door, opening it with a whoosh. The pair were exactly as she'd suspected, their bodies entwined in a tight embrace. At the sound of the door, they moved apart, at least having the grace to look embarrassed. Jean-Paul stared at a spot on the carpet.

"See you at seven? Ciao, chérie." Ingrid reached up, giving Jean-Paul a peck on the cheek.

"And you also, Anna. You will come too?"

Anna looked blank.

"For dinner with my uncle and you and Ingrid and me? Yes?"

"Bien sûr. A bientôt!" Ingrid answered for her, half turning to blow a kiss at Jean-Paul as she entered the room. "I bags the shower first, Mum," and with that Ingrid vanished into the bathroom.

Anna was tired. The morning climb, the museum, and the afternoon's drama had left her short on enthusiasm. She was sure the wine had fueled some very erratic thoughts but right this minute she yearned for room service, a hot bath, bed, and her book. Instead, she was stuck with another evening of tête-à-tête with François as Ingrid and Jean-Paul drooled over each other

As Ingrid showered, Anna remembered she'd not phoned Greg. She should have phoned him last night and told him they'd arrived safely, but somehow among the mix of

Montmartre, and the thrill of being here, she'd postponed the call. So far today, there hadn't been time. When she got her phone out, she saw he'd left three messages. Needless to say, if you mute the thing, that's what happens, she groaned. She had turned the volume off yesterday evening so as not to disturb the meal and forgotten to turn it back up.

"Well, I'm glad you're both enjoying yourselves," Greg said after she explained why she'd not answered his calls. Yes, he was fine. No problems at home or at work to report. Typical of him, she thought, irrespective of how serious a problem might be, he'd keep quiet and find a solution without ever informing her. He saw admitting to difficulty as a weakness, to be combated and defeated by sheer will power.

Anna didn't mention her stolen handbag. And, ignoring that wisp of desire, that barest feather-light trace of something she couldn't put in concrete terms lying at the edge of her consciousness, she didn't mention François. To be honest, she couldn't think how to tell her husband why she was spending time with a stranger whose nephew had stolen his daughter's heart in less time than it took to choose a painting. So she changed the subject.

Ingrid emerged, fresh and fragrant, from the bathroom. "Let me speak with Dad a sec," she said.

Anna didn't have much time to think as Ingrid was tapping her wrist and making circular motions indicating she should finish talking. Anna wound up the conversation with both of them mumbling how much they looked forward to being together soon, but as she thrust the phone into Ingrid's outstretched hand, she wondered how they were going to bear each other's company for the rest of the holiday in Biarritz. She hurried into the bathroom, listening to Ingrid praise Paris, its culture, lifestyle, and the entire French nation.

Anna wanted to have a serious talk with her daughter about her disappearance with Jean-Paul earlier that day, but they took so long to finish primping, there wasn't time or they'd be well past what was considered fashionably late.

In the lift, Anna made it clear there was a midnight curfew in place, and she counted on it being respected. Her daughter eyed her speculatively but didn't argue. Anna decided to give Ingrid 'the talk' later, and, unless Ingrid noticed, she wasn't going to tell her about the handbag incident.

Anna was surprised, and disquieted, at how natural walking as a foursome was becoming part of their new routine. She and François walked ahead: he pointing out places of interest and she nodding her head in agreement, and taking everything in, while Ingrid and Jean-Paul walked behind with their heads bent close together. They chose a different restaurant where, through a mixture of wheedling and blackmail by Ingrid, and thoughtful ordering by François, the four of them ate another satisfyingly delightful meal of vegetarian food.

"If I feel the need for flesh and blood, watch out!" joked François filling their glasses with red wine as they tucked into couscous, roasted aubergine, potato salad with a Dijon mustard dressing, and garlic bread with the crispiest crust Anna had ever tasted.

"That was marvelous," Anna commented as she sat back.

"Jean-Paul and I are going for a walk. Ok?" Ingrid's directness, as usual, got her what she wanted.

Anna, bewitched by Montmartre's nightlife, felt too replete and contented to voice any objections. "Remember to be back on time," she managed to say as the couple stood to leave.

"I promise," said Jean-Paul looking directly at her.

"Thank you." Anna's smile held genuine warmth. She did like the young man. He had a goal in life and enough determination and talent to achieve it, but this wasn't personal. Ingrid was her daughter–her one remaining child–and, if needed, she would be fierce in her protection.

François ordered coffee and brandy to finish the meal.

"May I ask you something?" Anna was hesitant.

"Anything. Within reason, of course."

Ignoring what she assumed was an attempt at humor she plunged in with her question, wanting to know what he thought, seeing as how he'd been brought up in a different culture to her.

"Do you believe in re-incarnation?" she asked.

He raised his eyebrows, clearly thrown for an instant by her question. "Ah, do I believe that a soul can take birth again in another body? I'm not sure how that works in practice."

He leaned back. She tried to ignore the way he was studying her. The waiter returned with their drinks, and she waited till the man had deposited their drinks on the table and left.

"Yes, that when the body dies, the soul which is separate from the body—"

"I apologize. You've lost me," he interrupted her.

She sipped the brandy, a smooth, aged liquor hiding a powerful punch, letting it slide down her throat, before replying. "Think of the soul as a driver and our bodies as the car. The driver directs the car so he can reach whatever destination he wants. He looks after the car, maintains it, checks the wheels, the engine and so on. But when the car gets old and broken and beyond repair, the driver gets out and gets a new car," she continued, earnestly expounding the concept to him.

"Put that way it sounds possible. Of course, this won't work if you don't believe people have souls in the first place. Forgive me; I've seen what people do in the name of religion, and I'm a bit of a skeptic."

She had read so much in the months after Jeremy's death, seeking answers, and not finding them. Certainly, no religion had been able to explain why a God, who was said to be the embodiment of perfection, punished good human beings. But in a book on Hindu beliefs she read that if two people had strong enough links, there existed the possibility of renewing the connection when the departed soul was reborn. She'd latched onto this.

Anna was determined to make her point. "You're reincarnating right this second, aren't you? The cells in your body are renewed every seven years? Right? So in theory, it's possible to say that the soul, that awareness we have of being an individual, of being you, has already incarnated several times in this lifetime." She laughed triumphant at the logic. "See. It's not so difficult is it?"

"Well since you put it so scientifically," he teased, "but how do you recognize the people you love? If they have another body, or another car, as you so eloquently phrase it, how do you recognize them? Did your book, by the way, what's the name, tell you that? And if they're in a different body, they wouldn't have the personality of the person you loved, would they?"

"Oh, François, I don't know the answer. The book was called the Bhagavad Gita–it means The Song of God–but it didn't say anything regarding that aspect of it. Perhaps there'd be a sense of familiarity, of déjà vu, with the person. It's possible you might have an immediate bond. I mean, don't you wish you could see Lucie?"

She realized loss and desperation had driven her to latch onto this belief, but if, if, a person did have a soul, and if the soul did change bodies in the same way we change clothes, the book said, there was a possibility that she might meet her beloved son once more. To her way of thinking, when, or if, she met Jeremy, it was irrelevant that he wouldn't be her beloved son anymore. Sometimes her mind went around and around in circles, knotting itself up in an effort to figure it out, but she couldn't relinquish the idea.

"Everyone deals with loss in separate ways, chérie." François took hold of her hand and squeezed gently. "What I have learned is that when you lose someone you love, it hurts for a long time. But what they say is true. Life does go on."

Neither spoke; both too caught up in their separate thoughts. She felt the heat from his hand as it gripped hers until he let go. She felt the absence of his touch.

"Here's to loved ones, present and past." He held up his brandy glass. Anna looked at him, raising hers. He understood her pain as well as her need to talk about her son. She touched her glass to his, and they chimed like tiny bells.

*

Ingrid came in ten minutes late.

Anna had tried not to notice midnight approaching—and passing. She'd relaxed, forgetting the trauma of the early afternoon, and had been writing up notes on Luc Marteille after seeing his paintings. She'd decided to give Ingrid an extra fifteen minutes before freaking out.

"Sorry," Ingrid said plonking down on her mother's bed.

"I missed you today." Anna put her notebook down and reached out, smoothing Ingrid's wild curls.

"You knew where I was." Ingrid's voice turned sullen.

"No, Ingrid. I knew who you were with but not where you had gone."

Ingrid went over to the wardrobe, raking through her clothes, mumbling under her breath as several fell off their hangers.

"Please, Ingrid. Don't ignore me."

"Look, Mum. After this summer I'm off to Edinburgh. You won't know where I am or who I'm with, and you won't be able to keep tabs on me either."

"I will know where you are, more or

less, and I will know what you're doing, more or less. Ok, I won't have the details." Ingrid made a snorting sound which Anna ignored, "but today you were in a city you're unfamiliar with, traipsing around with a young man who seems okay, but...."

"Well, I'm delighted he has your approval."

"I was worried, and naturally so."

Ingrid took a deep breath before answering, the resentment on her face giving way to stubborn determination. "No, Mum. It's because Jeremy died, and you're so worried that something will happen to me that you obsess about where I am all the time. Remember Jenny's party? The school dance? The camping weekend? Shall I go on? You're driving me nuts. Stop being such a control freak!"

Anna sat unmoving as the blood

drained from her face. How had their relationship degenerated to this squabbling? Her heart was thumping so loud she was surprised Ingrid couldn't hear it.

But Ingrid continued to open and bang shut the drawers, ignoring Anna.

Anna looked at her daughter. Had she been so caught up with Jeremy and Greg that she'd not noticed her sweet girl turning into this willful young woman?

Ingrid snatched up her nightclothes, and before entering the bathroom, turned around, staring straight at her mother. "What I want to ask," she said, "is why didn't you mention François when you were on the phone to Dad this afternoon?"

Chapter Twelve

When people go for a walk, they have a destination, a purpose, in mind. Dancing, on the other hand, is an action which has no goal, other than joy in the activity for its own sake. After the dreary defeat of a war with Prussia, people from Paris rushed off to Montmartre in droves to the Moulin de la Gallette for entertainment and dancing.

Paris, July 1873

Hélène studied her reflection in the full-length mirror kept in Louise's bedroom. The dress was gorgeous: a confection of pink and white striped organza with rows of white lace trimmings at the ruffled neck, wrists, and hem. It was a perfect fit around the bust with yards of material flaring out from the waist, underpinned with layers of snowy petticoat. Hélène had protested when Louise started taking her measurements, but Louise would hear none of it. She insisted on adapting the dress to fit Hélène's more slender figure, declaring she couldn't wear a lot of her clothes because she'd put on too much weight carrying Benoît. Hélène could consider it an early wedding gift.

"No more country bumpkin, for you," Louise said smoothing a few escaped hairs back into the elaborate coil of hair at the nape of Hélène's neck. "There." She pulled out and curled a few tendrils to frame Hélène's face. "What do you think?"

Her cousin was right. Yes, she did

recognize herself, but she was looking at a more grown-up sophisticated version. She was surprised at how elegant she appeared. A lady. That's what she looked like—a young lady from Paris.

Tomorrow, though, she would be on her way home. Louise was up and about, back to full health, and her help was no longer needed. Benoît had recovered from his fever and the sittings for Luc ended yesterday. She'd written Claude and her family about arrangements for her return and received a reply. Claude would meet her in Bordeaux.

She attempted to ignore the loud knocking of her heart against her ribs at the possibility of seeing Luc this afternoon unless he was spending the day at the studio. It was hard to believe, but soon she'd be home, and this interlude as a Parisian artist's model would be a dream in the past; nothing more than a memory. As new experiences came her way, this one would fade. Maybe she'd occasionally take it out and dust it off. This was not a path she could ever have taken, but merely to look back and know that she'd experienced something different from her parents and those around her; something other than what was expected of her. "Thank you! Thank you!" Hélène hugged Louise and gave her a resounding kiss on the cheek.

Louise dragged Hélène into the living room where Pierre dozed on the couch, one hand on Benoit's back as he slumbered on his father's chest.

"Look!"

Pierre opened his eyes at the disturbance, watching Louise spin Hélène around, before putting a finger to his mouth and shushing them.

"Ah, if the love-struck Claude could see you how beautiful you look!. He'd die from wanting you," Louise teased with a smile. "Do you remember how you used to follow me around everywhere? Who'd have thought that a scrawny little brat like you would grow into such a charming creature? Oh, the women will envy you and the men will admire you!"

Hélène blushed.

Louise had been babbling about the Moulin de la Galette for days. It had become her sole topic of conversation since she decided she'd made a good recovery from childbirth and it was time for an outing. Before falling pregnant, she, Pierre and their friends had gone dancing regularly at the Moulin on a Sunday afternoon; she was dying for Hélène to see this aspect of Paris life before she went home.

Louise tenderly lifted Benoit off her husband's chest, settling him on her shoulder, patting and soothing his back. Hélène marveled at the ease with which Louise had taken to motherhood. She bloomed with love.

Pierre stretched. He adored his wife and son and felt utterly content with life. He smiled up at the two women. "Well, many a man will be jealous of me with you two beauties by my side," he laughed.

"It's good you're leaving tomorrow because if you stayed in Paris any longer, well, M'sieur Marteille would have to fight the other artists off," said Louise, dotting the baby's head with kisses.

Hélène reached out and took Benoît into her arms to hide the heat in her face. The tension between her and Luc had eased since the night of Benoit's illness and he'd shown her nothing but the utmost respect, yet echoes of his previous outburst lingered between them, a faint pale ghost refusing to leave.

During her recent sittings, the two of them appeared to have reached a tacit agreement; both behaving with perfect decorum, as if nothing had happened, as if he'd never spoken of his feelings or stared at her with eyes of burning intensity. But he had revealed himself to her. As she sat facing him each day, she compared her memory of those looks to the clinical expression he wore as he painted her during the current sittings.

Hélène tried not to admit it, but his declaration had played havoc with her feelings. She waited, tight with anticipation, for those brief seconds when he touched her skin as he arranged her hair. Sometimes it was a brief brushing of his fingers on her shoulder, at other times, his hand rested, unmoving, longer than necessary. At those moments she held her breath, sitting motionless with her eyes closed.

Lately, when she tried to picture Claude, she couldn't remember his face clearly. The image which came to mind was a tall, fair-haired, open-faced young man standing in the distance, his features unclear as he waved at her. More and more often images of Luc, the way he stood, the way his lips lifted as if about to smile, the ritual dropping of coins into her hand at the end of the session, came unbidden into her mind. Afterward, on the way home, she'd go over and over their little exchanges, examining, weighing up the details to see if there were any hidden meanings.

"I can guarantee you that there's nowhere outside of Paris to compare with the Moulin, and, believe me, you will turn heads. Mmm... maybe it is better Claude isn't here." Louise chattered on, her irrepressible volubility more than compensating for the quieter natures of the other two.

Hélène envied Louise the new rhythms the baby had created in her life. She frequently took Benoit out into the fresh air, saying how important it was, but what she enjoyed, alongside the health benefits, was showing him off and lapping up the admiration over her darling from the neighbors and local shopkeepers. Yes, Hélène thought, she and Claude would have lots of babies.

Walking up the hill of Montmartre that afternoon turned out to be a most delightful experience. The trees were in leaf, apples were rounding under the summer sun into balls of red and green, and colorful wildflowers in full bloom bordered the lanes. Above, the sky was blue and the air a soft sigh on the skin.

They merged into the many groups heading toward the Moulin. Some visitors came by train, but the poorer people walked the hour's journey from Paris, decked out in their Sunday finery. Hélène took everything in: the families with young children skipping along; couples in love with eyes only for each other; young dandies showing off the latest fashion to the admiring eyes of the equally bedazzling young ladies, whose eyes slid sideways when they espied someone who caught their fancy. The atmosphere was infectious as laughter and good humored bantering spilled out along the lanes on the sun-filled summer afternoon.

As they approached the top of the hill, Hélène stopped, taking in the sight that greeted her. Louise hadn't exaggerated. They had nothing to match this in Bordeaux. The mill housed a restaurant on the ground floor, with a large area in front for dancing. Trees bordered the dancing space, providing plenty of shade. Several decorative chandeliers, swaying in the breeze, glistened as stray shafts of sunshine bounced off them catching her eye. Later, as evening drew in, the chandeliers would be lit.

The crowd thickened nearer the entrance and she caught the strains of dance music over the chatter of conversations and brief glimpses of couples twirling.

"Come on," Louise called from

ahead. "Are you going to stand and watch or join in the fun?"

As they entered the Moulin de la Galette, Hélène tried not to gawk at the dancing couples or at the crowded benches, tables, and chairs where fashionably dressed people were talking, laughing, eating and drinking. She scanned the crowd, and, despite a rising wave of excitement at being in this exotic environment, felt an undercurrent of disappointment that Luc was nowhere to be seen.

*

Luc lay slumped on the back veranda of his house, staring bleakly out at the garden. The summer heat encouraged the burgeoning lush growth; the buzz of insects and birds chirping from the trees, their wings making tiny flapping sounds as they flitted from tree to tree completed the idyllic picture.

Since Émilie and the children had left for her father's country estate, he hardly spent any time at home. He disliked the empty feel of the house and couldn't stand to be there without Guy and Giselle's chatter and laughter. While they were away he preferred to stay at the studio, where he put everything out of his mind but his painting. Unfortunately, he'd run out of clean clothes.

He wasn't thinking of the children, though, he was preoccupied with Hélène's portrait. Painting her had been effortless, and he'd captured more than the beauty of her youth and innocence. He'd caught the directness and lack of artifice in her gaze.

Yesterday had been her last sitting. The background needed some touching up, and he could finish that without her, but he was reluctant to complete the work, wanting to delay the final moment as long as possible. Guiseppe had dropped in last night. They'd drunk wine and discussed inspiration, muses and the struggle for recognition till the early hours of the morning.

Why had Hélène mentioned she'd be at the Moulin this afternoon? Was it the prattle of a country girl impressed with the goings on in the big city, or had she let it slip because she wanted him to know? He took out his watch and checked the time. He had time enough to make the one o'clock train, but what was the point in going? He'd sensed a certain intensity in her this last week— nothing he could define—and hadn't responded in any way or said one word to her which might be misinterpreted. Everything else aside, he had needed her present to finish the painting, and he hadn't wanted to frighten her away.

Last night Giuseppe had convinced him that falling in love with models was an accepted hazard of the profession but in the light of day he knew his fixation with Hélène was out of control. His feelings for her weren't fading one bit; was it possible she had feelings for him? She sat so quietly, an air of expectancy about her, as he arranged her hair. The satin of her skin under his fingers, he knew he was taking advantage, but had been incapable of restraining himself. Occasionally he made a few weak attempts to persuade himself it was for the painting, but the attempt at self-deception failed. He touched her because he wanted her, and this was as much contact as he would ever have. At times, keeping the barrier he'd erected between them was almost intolerable.

He sat brooding until the last minute before grabbing his coat and rushing out. His feet automatically took control as he strode along, his mind turning over various ways to open a conversation with her—assuming he bumped into her. Of course, she'd be there with Louise—and the baby. Probably the husband too. What was the man's name?

He was so absorbed in thinking of Hélène, he'd walked halfway down the Rue de la Pépinière before he saw the way was blocked. There'd been an accident and a crowd had instantly gathered, a few to help, but most to gawp. He pushed forward, but people eager to see the mishap were jammed so tightly together he wondered if it would be quicker to go back and find another route rather than continue. He decided he was too far into the crowd and it would be easier to keep going.

A horse had taken fright when a horseless carriage, with its noise and smoke, came charging toward it. Terrified, the animal had reared, and the driver lost control of the reins. The carriage overturned, with the driver trapped underneath, and the horse dragged both some distance before a bystander had the wit to grab the horse's bridle, and stop its frantic distress. Someone was screaming for a doctor.

As he reached the spot where the accident had happened, he paused—his eye drawn for a second by the drama— but he was too driven by his desire for Hélène to spare the scene more than a cursory glance. He continued to wiggle and, when necessary, push and shove his way through the packed crowd. The more obstructions he met, the more pressing became his need to catch the train. If Hélène was there, arriving after they'd left would be pointless. At one time Louise might have stayed late to dance, but not since she'd had the baby.

After a frantic effort where time stretched till he wondered if he'd ever break free of the moving crush of people, he exited the mass of onlookers. Like someone chased by demons, he ran for every breath he was worth. He didn't bother about how much time he had before the train departed; he knew it would be close. Familiar with central Paris, he took as many shortcuts as he could, dashing along and nearly twisting his ankle on the ancient cobblestones of one narrow alley. One thought possessed him: Hélène.

By the time the station came in sight, sweat ran down his back, his handkerchief was soaked from mopping his face, he'd undone half of his shirt buttons and was carrying his jacket. The long queue at the ticket office gave him time to cool down, but the shuffling forward, the waiting, the checking his watch every two seconds was unbearable. He caught sight of the train belching steam as light-hearted groups of passengers boarded.

Feverish thoughts, glimmerings of ideas chased through his brain, but he pushed them aside. He had to get to the Moulin. He had to be on that train.

"I have to get to Montmartre. It's a family emergency," he muttered, elbowing and pleading his way to the front of the queue, oblivious to the complaints and disbelieving looks thrown at him. He arrived at the front, and was reaching for his ticket from the painstakingly slow clerk when he heard one long piercing blast on a whistle as the train signaled its departure.

Chapter Thirteen

When you're young and in love, you are unaware that precious moments of sweet bliss may not appear often in life, and that when they do, there is no guarantee they will last. But because of them, and regardless of the frequently later occurring heartaches, life is always richer.

Paris, July 2007

Before they left home, Ingrid had extracted a promise from her mother that they would visit a few designer shops when they were in Paris. She had her birthday money and was intent on buying at least one designer item—

even if that item was the tiniest of handkerchiefs.

"Rue du Faubourg, St. Honoré!" Ingrid's voice was that of a pilgrim who had located the Holy Grail. "This is Paradise!"

Anna smiled. The simple pleasure of being alone with Ingrid was enough. Her daughter's gaze fastened first on one shop, then another and another, and she let Ingrid take the lead as they meandered among the chic shoppers on Paris's most exclusive street. Anna did her best to ignore being treated like an oversized accessory.

"There's one thing more I need." Ingrid linked her arm through her mother's, a wistful 'please Mummy I want' expression on her face. "A credit card with a balance the size of Paris Hilton's."

"Possibly in your next incarnation,

eh?" But Ingrid didn't hear. She had stopped in front of a shop window, her jaw dropping lower by the second.

The previous night's argument had ended with Ingrid hugging her mother and apologizing for being such a brat. That was Ingrid, volatile and passionate, everything near the surface but over and forgotten in a flash. They'd hugged tight and gone to sleep friends. Jeremy and Ingrid. Chalk and cheese. She had felt complete with her two children but when Jeremy died a part of her heart had been amputated.

Anna had woken that morning with her pillow wet. She'd lain there, without moving, eyes closed, holding onto the fleeting picture of Jeremy, trying to stay in the dream-memory as it faded.

It had been cold and raining, and Jeremy had been at his new secondary school for a month. He, with the other boys of his year, looked small and frail compared to the gigantic fifth and sixth formers.

The minute he climbed into the car she saw something was wrong. He wasn't as clever as Ingrid when it came to dissembling.

"I'm not well. I don't want to go to football tonight."

"What's wrong?"

"I have a stomach ache."

"Okay." Her gut instinct told her that wasn't the problem, but as it was rare for Jeremy to complain about being sick, she accepted his excuse—for the moment.

As soon as they got home, he dug a crumpled envelope out of his backpack, dropping it on the table. "I'm going upstairs. You've got to sign that."

"Okay. I'll be up shortly. Are you well enough to have some soup?"

"Yes, please." He climbed the stairs, his footsteps heavy and slow.

She opened the letter.

To: Mr. and Mrs. Seeger.

This is to inform you that your child, Jeremy Seeger, will be in detention for the next week due to misbehavior in the playground.

Please sign below and return the slip to the school office.

Mr. Loksley.

What kind of misbehavior in the playground warranted a letter and detention? When she brought him up the soup and bread, she couldn't believe he'd changed into his pajamas and lay reading a book in bed. Whatever had occurred must be serious.

He put the book aside and sat up, waiting for the inevitable questioning. "Sorry, Mum."

"Tell me what this is about." She laid the tray on his lap.

"I punched someone."

She waited to see if he'd say more but he started eating. Whatever the problem, it hadn't affected his appetite. She waited till the bowl was empty. Growing boys were in better moods on full stomachs.

"Thanks, Mum."

"I'm not angry but I do want you to tell me what happened."

Jeremy tightened his lips.

"How can I help if I don't understand why you hit that boy?"

He sighed. "You're not going to stop till I tell you, are you?"

Anna smiled. "That's because I love you and care for you and need to know you're safe."

He proceeded to relate how a boy from the year above had been picking on him and his new friends since the very first day. The boy, Brian, big for his age and aggressive, had started out pushing them when they went to the toilet or when he saw them in the lunch queue. Within days this had progressed to following them around at break times, calling them names, shoving them into walls, and demanding money—the worst offense. Alex, who was smaller than Jeremy, had been punched in the stomach and collapsed wheezing on the floor when he stood up for himself.

So Jeremy had hatched a plan, persuading his friends to follow his lead. He'd lured Brian into the toilets, and when he accosted Jeremy ordering him to hand over his money, Alex and Charlie, who'd sneaked up behind Brian, kicked him hard in the backs of his knees. As he collapsed, lurching forward, Jeremy had punched him right on the nose. Brian had fallen sideways and hit his head on the side of the stall. The three boys had told their side of the story, being honest as to the reasons for the incident, and they'd been given detention for a week.

"Jeremy, when things like that start to happen, you have to tell someone. Anyone. Parents, teachers, any adult you trust. That's what we're here for. To help when things go wrong."

He looked at her, his chin tilted up, a mischievous glint in his eye. "We sort this stuff out ourselves."

"Jeremy... promise me."

"Okay, next time, I will. Promise. But Brian won't be bothering us or anyone else for a long time."

She knew he shouldn't have taken matters into his own hands, but she was glad he'd stood up for himself and his friends. After that, she thought of him as her little knight in shining armor.

Ingrid's fingers squeezed Anna's arm. "Oooh! Those names! Gucci! Chanel! Lanvin, Givenchy, Yves Saint Laurent, Christian Lacroix, and Dior! Oooh! It's not Paradise. I've died and gone to Heaven." Ingrid rolled her eyes at her mother. "You know, I don't mind that we've no time for Versailles or the Louvre. I'm happy with Montmartre," she gestured along the street, "and this."

"I wonder how much different this street would have looked in Luc's day?"

"Luc?" Ingrid raised her eyebrows.

"Luc Marteille. The reason we're here."

"Oh, that Luc." Ingrid dismissed him.

Anna thought that right now Jean-Paul might be in second place if Ingrid had to choose between love and shopping.

"Yes, I need to do more research. Find some photos." She peered up at an ornate metal balcony. "I'm positive a number of the older buildings around here are from that period."

"François will be able to tell you," Ingrid said. "Ask him."

Anna continued to be annoyed at being obliged to spend time with François, despite certain images—the frank assessing stares he continued to give her when he thought she wasn't looking, how laughter at one of Jean-Paul's jokes took years off him—intruding at odd moments.

They had arranged to meet outside their hotel after lunch and would pass the afternoon at the Musée. The archivist was going to bring out Luc's letters, at least those in the musuem's possession, and François would translate them for her. She would focus on the letters and do her best to disregard his unwanted presence which, although she wasn't sure how it had happened, now appeared necessary to her research.

"Mum, stop! In here!"

Anna had wandered ahead, lost in contemplation of ideas for paintings she might undertake when home, completely ignoring the shop windows, but Ingrid was a guided missile, homing in on her target. Nothing deterred her. She towed her mother into the Dior shop. Anna's back ached and her legs hurt, but she didn't protest. There was no point. To refuse Ingrid at this point would result in a nuclear explosion. She followed Ingrid, wondering if Luc Marteille's daughter had wound him around her little finger as easily.

"But you don't wear powder!" Anna hissed in Ingrid's ear as her daughter examined an exquisite small powder compact.

"No, but Grandma does," Ingrid hissed back. The sales assistant informed them of the price in a haughty voice as her gaze lingered on Ingrid's curls.

Half an hour later, back on the bustling street, Ingrid was ecstatic with her purchase. Nestling in its exclusive box and elegantly designed wrapping paper, she'd tucked her purchase away in the depths of her bag.

Anna was touched at Ingrid's kind-heartedness in remembering her grandmother. This child of hers was full of surprises. When at last the shopping was finished, Ingrid had bought a skimpy hand-knitted jumper and matching scarf in bright rainbow colors, after begging the last fifty euros off her mother.

They lunched at a small bistro after wandering down a side street and getting lost. This time, with Ingrid by her side, Anna was happy to explore.

Ingrid moaned over the lack of choice for vegetarians and dropped a comment on how useful it was to have François around to order for them; but in the end, they sat outside sipping coffee, people watching and eating cheese sandwiches made with fresh crusty French batons and salad.

After they'd finished, Ingrid began glancing at her watch at regular intervals.

"Thank you, darling," Anna said, trying not to smile.

"Why? What have I done wrong?" Ingrid eyed her suspiciously.

"For spending time with me when

I'm fully aware you'd rather be enjoying Jean-Paul's company. You really like him, don't you?"

Ingrid looked at her mother, her features softening. "Like? Mum, I think I'm in love." She bent toward her mother, lowering her voice. "This might be it. I've never had feelings like this for anyone. I mean I love you and Dad. Of course I love Grandma and Granddad, but this, Mum, this is something else."

Anna said nothing of Jeremy's absence from the list. It wasn't the time or the place to remind Ingrid that she had lost a brother whom she also loved.

"Mum, can I ask you something?" Ingrid asked.

"Anything you want, darling. This morning, I'm yours."

Ingrid paused, obviously thinking

how to phrase her question. "Would you ever have an affair?"

Anna gaped openmouthed at her daughter before she burst out laughing.

"I'm serious, Mum," Ingrid repeated the question with more confidence this time. "Would you ever have an affair?"

"And who on earth would I have this affair with?" She stared at Ingrid in puzzlement. Her mouth dropped open as it dawned. "Are you asking me what I think you're asking me? Do you honestly think I'd have an affair with François? Someone I've known for barely more than a day?"

Ingrid dropped her gaze under her mother's scrutiny. "Well, why didn't you tell Dad about him on the phone yesterday?"

"Ingrid, you're eighteen, and I'm your mother. My life is not a soap opera to be discussed over lunch." She huffed, offended at her daughter's question. Honestly! What on earth went on inside Ingrid's head? Did the girl not know the difference between what she saw on television and reality?

"I'm sorry Mum." Ingrid reached out taking hold of her mother's hand. "I didn't mean to upset you, but it's that I think you're, well, happier since we got here..." She left the sentence unfinished.

Anna relented. Her daughter had a lot of growing up left to do. "And do you think I'd tell you if I was?" she joked, but Ingrid was too busy checking her watch and Anna's remark went unheard.

"Can we go, Mum? We're supposed to meet them at the hotel at 1.30 and Jean-Paul might think I'm not coming."

Anna felt a surge of warmth toward her daughter. Ingrid had always been an independent child, racing to catch up with her older brother. Since she'd hit puberty, she guarded her privacy, rejecting Anna's advice, shutting her out and ignoring her attempts to find out what was going on at school, or with her friends. She hoped this pouring out of an intimate confidence marked a change. Their relationship was no longer that of parent and dependent child; Anna realized Ingrid wanted to be treated as an equal, a friend.

"Well, we wouldn't want to keep Jean-Paul waiting on tenterhooks for you, would we?" She reached over and kissed her daughter on the cheek. "But I insist that you come to the museum, Ingrid. You have to see the other Marteille paintings, especially Hélène's portrait."

"Sure, Mum."

Anna was suspicious of the speed and ease with which Ingrid agreed, but she had no intention of disrupting the mood. The morning had been exactly how she'd envisioned this trip with her daughter, though she'd thought Luc Marteille and not Dior would be the object of research.

They had to rush and barely made it back on time. Jean-Paul was pacing outside the hotel, but there was no sign of François.

A sudden surge of resentment hit Anna at having to share Ingrid with people she considered strangers.

"Mon oncle have business 'e must do," Jean-Paul looked anxiously at Anna, "but 'e phone me and 'e will be 'ere soon."

"Well, he's not here now, is he?" That morning when he'd been absent, she'd found herself thinking of him, but at the moment he was a disruption to her plans.

"Mum, it's not Jean-Paul's fault!" Ingrid was indignant.

"I'll take the packages up to the room and hopefully he'll be here when I get back." Anna took Ingrid's packages and marched off into the hotel. Damn man, she grumbled under her breath as she waited for the elevator. Wasn't it enough she endured the intrusion of this man into her personal quest? And to top it off she had to wait for him when he knew they were expecting him. It was too much.

He still hadn't appeared when she returned, even after taking plenty of time to freshen up and change her blouse, wondering why she was bothering to do so because it certainly wasn't to impress anyone. Ingrid and Jean-Paul were talking animatedly but their conversation petered out when she appeared and the three of them stood in awkward silence.

"There 'e is," Jean-Paul exclaimed, his relief obvious as he pointed to where François was making his way through groups of tourists sauntering along, cluttering up the pavements.

"My apologies," François said, slightly out of breath. He tried to catch Anna's eye, but she looked away.

"Finally, you're here. Let's go." She gave him a tight smile.

"Bien sûr."

At that point, Jean-Paul burst into a rapid flow of French. Ingrid stood next to Jean-Paul watching him, making no secret she thought him fascinating; being French definitely added a layer of exoticism to the appeal.

Anna watched the facial expressions and body language of the two men.

François didn't appear happy, and it was clear Jean-Paul was pleading, but the exchange was rapid and she barely caught a word or two.

At last François, his tone a mixture of exasperation and apology turned to her. "Jean-Paul is asking me to beg for permission to escort the beautiful Ingrid to the Louvre museum."

Anna glanced at Jean-Paul, who couldn't have done a better imitation of a puppy begging for a treat if he'd graduated from drama school. She didn't need to look at Ingrid to know her expression mirrored Jean-Paul's.

"I told him I do not approve of this idea," François continued, "but I said I will pass on his request."

"Please, Mum. We did discuss the Louvre and remember you said you wanted to take me if we could fit it in. This way," Ingrid finished in a triumphant tone, "I can go with Jean-Paul and you can go with François. In any case, he'll be able to help you better than I can."

Anna wanted to ignore her growing anger. Did Ingrid think that because they'd spent the morning together, she'd paid her dues? Of course, she should have known her daughter would try something along this line. She'd have to be alone with François. Again. The anger bubbled. She wanted to scream, *what about me? Don't I get anything I want? Why am I always the one maneuvered into a position, not of my choice?*

Sucking in a deep breath, she held it for a second before letting it out as slow as possible. Ingrid's words from last night crossed her mind. She couldn't keep her daughter on a leash. "That's fine." Her words were clipped.

"I understand."

Ingrid and Jean-Paul had the grace not to crow at their triumph.

François fixed Jean-Paul with a stare. "We'll meet back here and go for dinner. Together."

"We'll be here on time. Promise." Ingrid said. "Don't worry. We'll be fine. You two, go and research to your heart's content. Remember, this is our last full day here." She gave her mother a quick hug before she and Jean-Paul took off for the Louvre.

François and Anna stood watching the young couple as they left with their hands intertwined, bodies leaning toward each other, the way people the whole world over do when they are in love. The older couple stood silently watching the youngsters as they disappeared into the crowd before heading off in the opposite direction.

"This is a first for Jean-Paul." François shrugged with Gallic eloquence attempting to make conversation as they walked.

Anna grunted. Her mood of the morning was gone, and she was boiling with resentment. What choice did she have? She was stuck with him, just because his translation skills would be useful at the museum. She wished he wouldn't walk so close.

"Yes, he's had girlfriends, he's nineteen, but I haven't noticed that particular look when he's talked about other girls," he continued, apparently determined to overlook Anna's fractious mood.

"What look?"

"Oh, what is the word? Enchanted? Is that how you say it? I can tell when he's thinking of Ingrid because he gets a special softness in his eyes, stares out of the window, and doesn't hear a word I say." He gave a loud sigh and gazed up at the sky with an exaggerated love-lorn expression.

Anna's antipathy toward François thawed the tiniest bit. Perhaps she should have pity on the man. He wasn't the one manipulating this situation; he was giving his time to help. "Oh, I'm sure it's reciprocated." She attempted to sound civil although she wasn't sure she succeeded. "Jean-Paul is the first young man I've seen Ingrid so enamored with, and so quickly as well." She restrained a smile, deciding she wasn't going to tell him she'd observed Ingrid in a similar trance-like state.

"Shall we?" He offered her his arm and waited for her to link with him.

She thought of the hardness of his muscles underneath her hand. For goodness sake, she was more than capable of making her way to a destination on her own two feet. Hadn't she managed to walk unaided for most of her life? And she didn't want to send him the wrong message.

"I'm fine, thank you. I don't need a walking aid." She stalked off wondering how he managed to bring out the worst in her.

"Where are you going?" he called after her, "the Musée is this way."

She stopped, her face flaming with embarrassment.

He was pointing in the direction of a nearby side street. "Ah, a shame you English are so stiff," he mocked, "because everything would be so much smoother if you relaxed."

Anna was so incensed by the disdain in his voice that she didn't speak for fear of what she might say. She hardly noticed the route they took as her antagonism toward everyone and everything—him, Jean-Paul, Ingrid, Greg, Fate—spewed out from every pore. Her emotions were raging out of control and calming down was out of the question at this point. The best tactic was for her to shut up and say nothing.

François walked fast and made no attempt at conversation.

Bit by bit, her anger cooled. If she was honest, she would admit she was enjoying Paris, in a different way to Ingrid, but her existence was no longer an unending stream of bleak granite gray days. She was gratified by how soon she was at home in Montmartre with its cobbled streets, small green spaces, and glimpses into courtyards ringed with terracotta pots filled with plants. Although she'd visited the place no more than a couple of times, already the route felt familiar. By the time they reached their destination, her remaining grumpiness had dissipated.

"Madame, M'sieur." The curator recognized them from yesterday and welcomed them with a nod of pleasure.

"M'sieur Battingnon," François replied for both of them.

Anna frowned. The man obviously thought them a couple, but she couldn't be bothered to correct him. She had more important matters to think about; she wanted François to translate accurately.

"A colleague of mine is examining your letter. When do you need it back?" he inquired.

"I leave early tomorrow afternoon. But I have several photocopies at home if you need more time," she answered promptly. This was her affair. She didn't need François answering for her.

"No, no, that won't be necessary," the curator protested. "If you can come back tomorrow morning, I should have news for you."

They followed his short rotund figure through a side door and along a corridor into the archives. The room was well lit, lined with tall dark brown wooden cabinets filled with drawers, a large empty table in the center, and the slightly musty smell of a room not often aired.

Anna shivered with anticipation as the curator opened a drawer and pulled out a slim hardback gray book. Holding the book with great care, he placed it on the table, opening it with no less reverence than a priest toward the Holy Eucharist.

"This is the total collection of correspondence we have to and from Luc Marteille. It is not very much of a record as there are not many letters, but," he paused, giving them a smile, "they do reveal some interesting facts about his life." He trudged out of the room leaving them alone.

Anna stood, looking at the book for a moment, listening to the curator's footsteps fade. She moved forward. Her hand trembled as she opened the book. This was why she had come; here she might uncover something, anything, about Luc's love for Hélène. She leaned forward to read the first letter, smiling at the sight of Luc's familiar handwriting.

"This" François pointed at the list of numbers in the middle of the page, preceded by the old sign for francs, "is asking for payment for these items."

"What does this mean?" she asked François, pointing at a word.

"Debt," he replied.

She turned the page and the following ones carefully. These letters were unmistakably business ones appearing to ask for or demand payment for goods taken or agreeing to delays in payment. Luc didn't appear to be managing his finances too well.

"These are dated from before he achieved any level of success." She turned several more pages of the book before finding the first personal letter. "Would you translate? I want to be sure I understand."

François read for a minute. "It's from his mother and expresses her sadness at receiving the news of their stillborn child."

"Yes, she was a widow. Luc's father died when he was young and she never remarried," Anna explained. "They were poor relatives on the outer fringe of a distinguished family."

"I know what that's like," muttered François, his lips thinning and his eyes narrowing.

Anna paused in her study and looked at him.

"My father was a proud man descended from a family that had, in the past, been powerful: we can trace our ancestry back to the fifteenth century. My grandfather drummed the importance of this link to the past into my father, and he made sure I grasped its importance. But this meant nothing to anyone I grew up with in France."

She had a flash of him as Saladin in flowing robes and was piqued by the image. Maybe that's how she'd paint him.

"So, he never approved of Lucie because, first she wasn't a Lebanese Maronite, and second, her family could trace their roots back no further than the French Revolution." François grimaced, "He let me know, constantly, what a source of disappointment I was to him."

Anna nodded. Greg's family were similar in that they had also dropped down the social ladder. In the 18th century, one family member had accumulated a fortune in manufacturing of some kind, but the generations since either dissipated or lost it through bad investments, and nothing was left. Greg's father had continued to behave as if he was descended from aristocracy, looking down on her father who had risen by the power of his intelligence and hard work from working class privation to middle-class comfort.

"That can't have been easy to live with," she sympathized. Family histories were complicated.

She returned to Luc's letters. The first few pages, except for the one letter from his mother, dealt with business. François translated a phrase here or there when she needed it but otherwise was content to stand back and watch her search.

She scanned the next few pages before stopping at a letter to his wife. "Could you translate this one for me? It's the personal side I'm more interested in, and I don't want to misunderstand something vital."

"My dearest Émilie," François translated. In the letter, Luc expressed his desire to join his family in Le Conquet. "Where is that?" He pointed at the name.

"In Normandy, on Capelle-les-Grands. It's a hamlet near Brest where her father was a wealthy landowner, and where his mother's family lived.

That's where they met. Luc would take Émilie walking along the Normandy coast when he was courting her. But wait a minute, I want to check something." She took out another photocopy of her letter from her bag and examined it. "See," she indicated the date on the letter in front of them, "this is around the same time–almost to the day–that my letter is dated."

"May I?" He held out his hand for her letter.

She hesitated. This was her treasure. "Be careful, please."

"Naturally."

Was he being sarcastic? She stiffened and restrained from snatching it back. Both pairs of eyes moved from the book to the letter.

"So he tells his family he wants to be with them, but he doesn't go. He stays in Paris and writes to Hélène?" François said as he handed back the letter. "Many French people have a different attitude to marriage and sex than you British."

Anna glared at him. It annoyed her she was unable to tell whether he was joking or not, because, to be exact, he wasn't French.

"They are more pragmatic," he said not looking up from the letter.

He's right, Anna reflected. We Brits pretend to have one standard which we disregard whenever we're inclined. Does that make us more deceitful? She kept those thoughts to herself. As far as she was concerned the relationship between François and her, whatever relationship they had, was based solely on the fact that he wanted to keep an eye on his nephew in the same way as she wanted to keep an eye on her daughter. That was it. She certainly didn't want any more intimacy with him than she already had because that would create a dilemma for her. One she didn't want to tackle. With a sigh, she returned to the book, trying not to think of the two of them poring over details of a life long gone.

"And artists, well, Manet, Degas, Lautrec, any number of artists were besotted, and married sitters who were their mistresses. Absinthe, actresses, and ballet dancers were part of an artist's lifestyle," François said lightly.

"Ooh! What's this?" Anna exclaimed. "Look, it's a note from Monet to Luc." She studied the words. "It's offering congratulations for his success at their second exhibition and what does this phrase mean?"

François smiled at her as he finished reading. "He's congratulating him on the birth of a healthy baby boy."

"I knew he had three children but…"

"And the date," François, pointed at the top of the letter. "That means the child would have been conceived near the end of the previous summer—when he was painting Hélène."

Anna made a few quick calculations. "So he must have been sleeping with his sick wife and having a torrid affair with Hélène?"

She struggled to reconcile the disparate images of the artist. Stuck in a marriage with a wife whose health, according to research, left her more or less an invalid; then getting her pregnant at the same time he was having sex with another woman. She'd not pictured him as licentious and it jarred.

"Maybe Émilie was getting better. What does torrid mean?"

"Very passionate, intense. His work

gained quite a degree of popularity in the following years," she went on, "and his paintings sold well. But he died at the age of fifty-eight."

"So he lived happily ever after, eh?"

"Oh, what's this?" It was the last letter and was addressed to Sauvet & Hugo, followed by the words Société d'Advocats. "Is this his will?"

"No," said François reading over her shoulder. "It's a letter to his lawyers stating he doesn't want the painting of Hélène or the one of the vase of flowers–your painting–to be sold."

She could feel his breath on her neck as he leaned forward; she breathed in his scent.

"I wonder if Émilie knew about Hélène. If she did, maybe she didn't want to be reminded after his death? None of his biographies have more than a sentence or two on Hélène at most, and they only mention her as a model. Nothing more. Maybe in the end, the painting of flowers was sold."

They were both silent, pondering the mysterious intricacies of past lives.

"Who knows?" François shrugged. "It may be that the family fortunes declined, and they needed the money. It's possible the affair may have been brief, but who knows how long he carried a flame in his heart."

Anna looked at him. He was standing too near. Before she could move away, he pulled her close and kissed her.

Chapter Fourteen

People say that a great artist, writer or musician may, on occasion, be forgiven faults and mistakes not overlooked in less gifted men. The justification for this selfishness, as when someone places their needs foremost above everything else, is that nothing should take precedence over the call of the Muse.

Paris, July 1873

Luc did not often question his motives. Too absorbed by his compulsion to transpose the world onto canvas, he was often impulsive and gave no consideration to the consequences of his actions. He could latch onto an idea and follow it wholeheartedly wherever it took him, for his nature was such that a zealous tide gripped him when he was under the sway of a fresh passion. However, his character also possessed a certain stubbornness and tenacity, enabling him to follow that obsession to its conclusion.

The fever which gripped him when trying to catch the train had somewhat receded. The hour's walk to Montmartre in the hot afternoon sun offered plenty of time to think. Luc mulled over his plan, hoping Hélène hadn't left before he arrived. He could go to Louise's apartment if need be, but, restless and impatient, he wanted arrangements settled and the sooner the better.

Moulin de la Galette was packed with the Sunday afternoon crowd of locals and visitors. The atmosphere, as well as the conversations, epitomized the best of Paris life, with young and old taking pleasure in the Moulin's exquisite pastries and wine. People put the war behind them and took their pleasures in the moment, dancing to the band and enjoying themselves.

Luc scanned the crowd looking for Hélène, but it was his friends he spotted first. Manet, his pupil Eva Gonzales, Giuseppe and Degas sat around a table, deep in conversation. He watched them from a distance, knowing exactly what topics they were discussing. How to capture the texture of the land, the movement and light of the ever-changing sky? These were the real questions, their real passions in life. Luc watched as Manet made an amusing remark and the group laughed.

Today Luc's turmoil didn't allow him to pass an afternoon of animated intellectual discussions, at least not till he'd settled a particular matter first. Circling around the outer tables, he exchanged a few words here and there, nodding to friends and acquaintances, but not stopping. He was about to give up, deciding that either Hélène had already left or she hadn't arrived, when he caught a glimpse of her. She sat at a table, smiling up at Louise and Pierre, clearly returning from dancing. Louise's face was flushed and she was out of breath as she sat down, laughing. Pierre held out his hand to Hélène, who looked uncertainly at Louise. Louise nodded, smiling and kissing Benoit on the forehead as Hélène passed him over.

Luc stepped behind a tree where he could see her without being seen himself. His breath caught at how lovely, how innocent and fresh she looked. A bitter envy blocked his throat as Pierre led Hélène onto the dance floor, placed one hand on her back, took hold of her other hand and they began dancing.

He had the strangest experience. He felt divided in two, with one half detached and completely removed from any feeling whatsoever, noting details as if he were studying and making sketches for a painting. This half also observed another part of himself enduring agonies of possessiveness as the object of his desire enjoyed dancing with another man. It meant nothing that the exchange was innocent. He burned with jealousy: he should be holding her in his arms, leading her through the dance, amusing her, having her gaze at him as if he was her entire world.

The minute the music stopped and

he saw Hélène and Pierre making their way back through the dancers, he marched up to their table.

"Madame Louise," he made a small bow. "Mademoiselle," he bowed in Hélène's direction, as she and Pierre approached. "M'sieur. How pleasant to meet you here," he addressed Pierre, taking care not to pay Hélène too much attention.

"Ah, Monsieur Luc!" Louise smiled up at him, "And as you can see, Benoît is completely well." She turned her pride and joy around to face Luc, "and everyone says he's growing exceptionally fast. I will never forget how you helped us."

Luc smiled, somewhat embarrassed to be so praised in public, but he covered his discomfort by leaning forward and lightly stroking Benoit's cheek. The baby gurgled up at him. "He is an angel," he said to Louise after giving Benoît due consideration. "Fortune has smiled on you. You have much joy ahead of you and many sleepless nights too."

"Well, you would know, wouldn't you? You must have plenty of experience with your two."

Luc gave a forced laugh and focused on Hélène. "And are you looking forward to having a large family with many children, Mam'selle?"

"I haven't given the matter a lot of thought," replied Hélène, thrown off balance by Luc's sudden appearance and blurting out the first words that popped into her mind. She couldn't look at him, staring instead at her hands clasped tight together in her lap.

"Oh, what a fibber," cried Louise. "I know for a fact she wants at least half a dozen."

Hélène felt the heat rise to her face.

"Louise, stop!" Pierre chided. "You're embarrassing her."

"I won't keep you long. May I sit?" Luc put his hand on the back of the fourth chair at the table, looking at Pierre for permission to join them.

"Of course, Monsieur Marteille." Pierre nodded, more than willing to oblige. He felt indebted to Luc and wasn't the type of man to forget what he owed. "Something to drink, M'sieur Luc?"

"No, merci. That's very kind of you but I'm meeting friends soon. Actually, I have a proposition." He hesitated then glanced around the table, adopting his most earnest honest expression. "Seeing you sitting here this minute an idea has struck me." He paused before finishing in a rush. "I wish to paint you and Hélène, with the baby, in a garden scene. Would you consider it?"

He relied on Louise and her husband appreciating the extra money as it couldn't be easy for them with a young baby. After Hélène left, Pierre's wages would be their sole source of income.

"Oh, dear," Louise said with a nod in Hélène's direction, "she's leaving tomorrow, but I'm available."

"The thing is the scene in my mind is more than mother and child. That has religious connotations," he said animated by his vision. "I want my painting to show a normal family interaction. The kind of activity you can see any day in a park or garden."

The band played a slower melody and around them, the hum of conversations rose and fell.

"How long will you need us for?" Louise asked. "If it's not too long," she turned to Hélène "would you stay a day or two more?"

Hélène heard the plea in her cousin's voice.

"Yes, that will do." Luc didn't wait for Hélène's answer before rushing on. "I could sketch the outlines and get the basic color blocks down in maybe two, three days. Is it possible you might delay your journey by that amount?" He gave Hélène an appraising look waiting to see which would win. The waiting fiancé or her cousin's financial needs.

Hélène thought about staying, but Claude expected her to arrive in Bordeaux tomorrow. "But my fiancé—" she started.

Luc spoke across her objection. "I'll pay for a telegram if that helps?" He directed the full charm of his personality at her. "You, your cousin and nephew immortalized..." He let the idea hang in the silence.

"Yes, yes. I could stay two more days," Hélène said, "but not three. Three will create difficulties for others. I have a number of commitments... you understand..."

Louise's eyes lit up.

"Wonderful!" Luc spread the attraction of his smile equally between the two women. "Two days will be enough. Tomorrow at eleven o'clock I will meet you at the Porte Maillot entrance to the Bois de Boulogne. Don't worry; there'll be shade for the little one." Abruptly he stood, his tone that of brisk business. "A pleasure. M'sieur, Madame Louise, and au revoir Mademoiselle." He bowed to Louise and Hélène, holding the bow to Hélène a fraction longer. Making his way toward the exit, he was soon lost to sight among the revelers.

It wasn't until Luc returned home, and noticed the dining room table was laid, smelled the aroma of food being prepared, and heard Annette's frenzied activities from the kitchen, that he remembered his family was due home that afternoon. He quickly bathed and was pulling a fresh shirt from the closet when the clatter of hooves outside and the squeals of children's voices announced their arrival. Two minutes later, Luc straightened his shoulders, smoothed his hair, opened the front door and went to greet his family.

As soon as Guy and Giselle caught sight of their father, they flew up the garden path and threw themselves at him. "Papa! Papa!"

He gathered them both up, arms around their waists and held them close, smelling first Guy's hair, then Giselle's before swinging them around till they squealed. "I must help your mother," he said putting them down and kissing both heads.

At the carriage, Émilie stretched out her hand for him to help her descend. They exchanged kisses on both cheeks.

Luc took a step back and studied her. "You look well," he said, "I mean it, you appear," he stopped, searching for the right word, "recovered. Are you yourself once more?"

Émilie, pale from the journey, with faint smudges under her eyes, her face framed with fine blonde curls escaping from her bonnet, gazed at him with bright blue eyes. Luc realized he had forgotten how much in love they had been when they married.

"Yes," she smiled up at him, "I am much better."

Marie gathered up the bits and pieces the children had left strewn around the carriage and chivvied the children inside as the servants fussed about unloading bags.

"Would you like to take a rest straight away?" he asked Émilie, taking her arm as they turned toward the house.

"Yes, Luc, thank you, I will. It's been a long journey."

"I shall have Cook bring tea and something light for you to eat to your room."

"You're so considerate of me."

For a minute he thought she might cry, but she maintained her composure. "I'm happy to be home with you."

He put his arm under her elbow to make sure she was steady on her feet as they climbed the few steps to the house.

The children ran off to their rooms, their excited cries filling the house as they rediscovered favorite toys.

As evening drew in and the house quietened, Luc went up to Émilie's bedroom.

She sat at her writing desk wearing the lavender Chinese silk dressing gown he'd given her as a gift last Christmas. Her face lit up when he entered. "What do you see?" She pointed at the empty tray on the chest of drawers waiting for Marie to collect.

"Nothing. I don't see anything." Luc was puzzled. Then he understood. The sea air had done its work and her appetite had returned. "I'm sorry I didn't come." Apologies had never been his strong point.

"You wrote. I got your letters."

"Do you forgive me?" He swallowed.

"Forgive you for what? Not wanting to spend time with my cantankerous father?" She gave a little laugh. "He sends you his regards and wishes you well, and he has promised me he will come to your next exhibition."

Luc looked at her, his eyebrows rising. "I'm so glad I have that to look forward to."

They laughed and sat in companionable silence.

"How goes your painting?"

Émilie's support since their marriage had helped him fulfill his ambitions. Her assistance was more than financial; she was knowledgeable about art and made an excellent critic.

"Well, I've nearly completed one which I'm pretty sure I'll be submitting to the new salon this year." Hélène's smooth peach-gold cheeks had required quite a bit of detailed work, but the painting needed no more than a few minor touches before he declared it finished.

"A new salon?"

"Yes, we, Monet, Renoir and a whole host of us are staging our own exhibition. So far, we've not got a name, but it's not a Salon des Refusés. You'll see how we shall thumb our noses at the Académie." He hoped she wouldn't ask too many more questions about his work.

"Well, tell me, I'm eager to know what you're working on at the moment?" In the past, Émilie's advice and encouragement had, in some cases, made crucial differences to his finished work.

"Oh, it's a portrait." He attempted to keep his tone casual.

She persisted. "Are you pleased with it?"

"Yes." What else could he say? *I've enjoyed painting this young girl with her incredible vibrancy for life so much that I've fallen in love with her when I'm supposed to be in love with you.* Luc thought about the new painting he was starting tomorrow. He'd decided how he intended to arrange the two women and the baby. Hélène would sit...

"That's wonderful. I miss seeing your work."

Luc was genuinely happy that Émilie's good health was returning–she had been poorly for almost a year–yet he couldn't help but compare her to Hélène. His wife was older, with her fine bone structure and blondeness adding an air of fragility, although anyone who was well acquainted with her soon discovered the strength of her love and devotion to her family. In spite of her less than robust health, she had carried three babies to full term.

"I'm tired. That's enough for today."

She put down her pen and reached for the green tablet lying next to a glass of water on her desk. "I'll finish this letter to Papa tomorrow." She downed the tablet and looked at Luc.

The trust in her eyes brought a stab of guilt. Émilie, his wife, and companion, was the mother of his children for God's sake! Why did he have such a powerful longing, an almost physical ache, for another? "I'm truly happy you're home, chérie. I've missed you." He meant it, even as he recognized his angst over Hélène had rendered Émilie invisible.

She rose, moving over to where he sat, and kissed the top of his head. "Good night, my love."

Each knew the other so well; the tenderness in her tone caught at his heart. Yet instead of turning his face up so she could kiss him on the lips, he reached out, squeezing her fingers lightly. He stood to leave "Good night. Sleep well."

Luc wasn't tired, and the thought of tossing and turning in bed held no attraction. He paced back and forth on the back porch, finding relief in the cool of the late evening and watching the sunset colors change from peach to crimson as night fell. The air was velvet and a luminous full moon broke through the trees.

Montmartre's nightlife didn't appeal, and tonight he preferred to stay home. Thoughts of Hélène fevered his brain. He couldn't concentrate on anything. Neither did he want to draw. Images of Hélène would emerge on the paper, no matter what he started out intending to sketch, and Émilie was too attentive to miss so conspicuous an indication of his state of mind.

Luc fetched a bottle of brandy, hoping it might help him sleep, and a large glass, making himself comfortable on the veranda. He filled the glass, and took a couple of sips, before downing the rest in one gulp. He enjoyed the harsh tang as the liquid hit the back of his throat; slumping back, he waited for the alcohol to take effect.

Night crept on and Hélène, not the sleep he sought, kept him company. Luc went inside, bringing the bottle of brandy with him. He threw back the fiery spirit hoping to quench his torment. It was too much—this intense ache of wanting. He uttered a growl of anguish. His heart was cracking and there was no reprieve. No release.

He paced faster. Visiting Brigitte or Marie-Claire, two prostitutes he'd made use of since Émilie became too sick to perform her wifely role, held no attraction for him anymore.

Why did he feel this way about Hélène? Especially if he acknowledged it was becoming more and more unlikely she would ever succumb to his advances? Different models had sat for him over the years, many of whom were far more striking than Hélène, and he never felt any attraction for them. He'd decided early on that this road was one he refused to travel; married to a beautiful woman he was in love with, he wanted nothing to come between them. Why, and how, had this changed? Why this obsession with Hélène? Not having her was transforming him into a crazed demented stranger. Maybe because he'd not slept with Émilie in a long time? He was a vigorous man and having sexual relations with his wife was his prerogative.

No sooner had the thoughts flickered through his agitated brain than he was up and moving. Luc stumbled through the darkened house, tripping up the stairs, not bothering to quieten his footsteps; whether he disturbed the other occupants of the house, his children, and the servants, wasn't a concern. He was burning. Luc approached Émilie's room with the same lack of consideration.

She didn't stir when he entered.

"Émilie! Émilie!" he whispered loudly as he stripped. "Wake up, chérie!"

She stirred but didn't wake as he lifted the covers, crawling into bed beside her.

He shook her shoulders as he climbed on top of her pulling at her nightdress.

Émilie, heavy with medicated sleep, struggled against him, bewildered by what was happening.

"Chérie, it's me," Luc whispered in her ear.

As understanding dawned, she tried to rouse herself.

"Relax," insisted Luc, pushing her back onto the bed. "It's okay." He understood his wife's body; she would carry out her duty.

The next morning Luc woke with a start, flinching as the pale dawn light struck his eyes. His head hurt, and it took him a minute to remember his actions of last night; what he had done. He propped himself up on his elbow, gazing at Émilie. She slept deeply, her breathing regular. He reached out, stroking the fine gold filaments of hair spread out on the pillow. She would always be faithful to him, in mind and in body.

He'd never, ever, used Émilie in this

manner, and a wave of emotion swept over him. Guilt. A crawling flush of shame. The night before he'd been desperate and drunk, his lovemaking an attempt to expunge Hélène from his soul one way or another. It hadn't worked; it had been Hélène's face he saw and her body he imagined underneath him. But surely he had the right to demand his wife satisfy his need?

He listened to Annette raking the coals in the kitchen, but the rest of the house remained quiet, with Giselle and Guy still asleep. He pulled on his trousers and shirt, picking up the rest of his hastily thrown clothes from the floor, and tiptoed back to his room.

Chapter Fifteen

Suppressed emotions do not dissolve; they simmer and fester in our subconscious until they bubble to the surface forcing us to act—in ways we are generally not able to foresee.

Paris, July 2007

A soft gentle pressing of his lips on hers. That was all. He stepped back, and she gasped openmouthed before instinct kicked in and she swung her hand at his face. But he was ready and his hand locked around her wrist. The blood rushed to her cheeks. As if summoned, an image of Greg, a little drunk and smiling at her as they celebrated their last anniversary, sprang to mind. Greg embodied safety and comfort; the familiar. She'd be glad to see him. No, she had no wish to go dancing; she preferred to stay at home in her comfy slippers. Leave the dancing to the young.

"Let me go!" Anna's voice shook. He released her hand, turned and without a word walked out. She stood transfixed. Had she unconsciously given off signals that made him think she would enjoy such conduct? Or at any point behaved in an improper way for a married woman away from her husband? Up till this point in time, there had never been any opportunity or desire to be unfaithful to her husband. To kiss or sleep with another man was something people like her didn't do.

People like her. The phrase jolted her. Who were these 'people like her'?

Were they set apart from humanity with a special dispensation protecting them from troubling urges? Could she honestly say she'd never entertained the whisper of a flirtation at any time in her twenty-three years of marriage? Had there never been one dinner party, dance, company event or holiday where a flicker of lust had momentarily flamed as her eyes met another's? If it had, she would have brushed it aside immediately. Anna huffed. People like her possessed standards and adhered to them.

She stared at the letter in front of her. At the end of his life, Luc's will specifically mentioned the paintings connected with Hélène. Theirs must have been a powerful relationship. No, she wasn't a Luc Marteille having her cake and eating it. Well, a relief to have that clarified. Thanks to François, she understood more clearly what kind of man Luc had been.

Anna remained looking over the book of letters trying to focus on Luc's life, not on hers, and certainly not on François. She revisited the gallery and, gazing at Hélène's fresh-faced beauty, she softened. Maybe she'd thought of him purely as an artist, forgetting he was human, with everything that encompasses. Who knows precisely what goes on between a husband and a wife? There are many ways to inflict suffering on those to whom you're tightly bound.

She looked at her watch. It was getting late. She'd better get back to the hotel. Doubtless François had left. Should she try to get out of the evening meal? Plead a headache? But then she'd miss the last evening in Paris with Ingrid. Her daughter was growing up too fast and developing interests which lay elsewhere. When the summer ended... she swallowed hard. Soon she would have to face an empty nest. As for François, well, she would show him.

She stepped out of the museum, bolstered by a life of carefully cultivated habits to find François waiting for her.

"I'm so sorry. Please," he looked distressed. "I don't know what came over me."

"Well, it's obvious to me." She was composed. "You thought you were Luc, and I was Hélène." She saw a spark of amusement on his face for a second, but then it was gone, and he was full of apologies once more.

"What can I say? We were investigating a sweet sad love story. You, you...," he trailed off.

"Yes," she prompted, assuming the role of inquisitor. "What about me?"

He shrugged.

"Stop shrugging!" She exaggerated his gesture. "What is it with everyone over here and the shrugging?" She mimicked him a second time.

He narrowed his eyes as if ready to challenge her but thought better of it. Blinking a few times, he took a deep breath and looked straight at her. "I have to be totally honest with you. I find you desirable, and I refuse to say I'm sorry."

She looked away, unable to bear the frankness of his look and glad he didn't trot out an excuse to do with being alone since his wife died. That she wouldn't accept. She was flattered though she certainly wasn't going to tell him. He considered her attractive enough to do more than think about it. He'd actually kissed her!

Anna remembered little Billy Preston

grabbing her in Class 1, plonking a kiss on her mouth and telling her he wanted to marry her. Thrilled to be the chosen one, she had said nothing to the teacher. The following week he picked another wife.

"I apologize for my action but not for the reason I acted."

She ignored him, afraid that whatever she said would be misconstrued, and set off for the hotel.

Anna dressed with extra care that evening. She rejected the persistent thoughts of François and the kiss. When the memory stole into her mind, the touch of his lips on hers, firm, pliable, his hand on her back pulling her close, she distracted herself with plans of what she would do in Biarritz, or of the paintings she would do when she returned home. Perhaps she could redecorate? Not Jeremy's room, not yet, if ever. She recognized that today, for the first time in a long time, she had lived in the present, caught up so strongly in the now that there had been no room for the past. She had let it go. That was important.

"Ooh, Mum! Who do you want to impress?" exclaimed Ingrid, coming out of the bathroom and stopping at the sight of her mother.

Anna looked stunning. She'd swept her hair up into a smooth French coil, and kept it in place with an antique jeweled comb, applied her makeup with a subtle hand to eyes and lips, and dressed in a jade green silk suit, bought a number of years ago, but which didn't often get an outing. The below the knee pencil skirt and flared short jacket made the most of her long legs and slim figure. She looked and felt elegant when wearing it.

"Don't be silly, Ingrid. We're merely having dinner with Jean-Paul and François." She turned away and started fishing in her purse to hide the sudden heat in her cheeks.

"Exactly, Mum. Exactly!"

"Chérie—"

"Ooh! Français pour François?"

"Listen, darling. Tonight is our last night in this wonderful city, and I'm not letting anyone spoil it."

Ingrid watched her mother's face in the mirror. "You know, Mum, you seem more the way the old you used to be before... before Jeremy died." She became solemn, the teasing gone. "In fact, I think you're more like your old self than you've been for a long time. Does that sound absurd?"

Anna hesitated, lipstick in hand. "Of course," she applied the final coat of lipstick, blotted her mouth with a tissue, and turned around, a wide grin spreading across her face, "but it's entirely possible that it's you who is seeing everything from a new viewpoint."

"Okay, okay." Ingrid laughed, blushing bright red. "Let's both enjoy tonight, eh?"

During dinner Ingrid and Jean-Paul spent most of the meal absorbed in each other, coming up for air and sporadically contributing to the general conversation. Anna and François made polite noises, the chill between them unnoticed by the younger couple.

Anna avoided looking at him. She didn't want eye contact. The kiss and his stated interest in her that afternoon had cut through her defenses more than she was prepared to admit. She was moving on from the overwhelming grief of Jeremy's loss but where was she going? This wasn't a crossroad, it was more a perception that different paths were opening up, and she had other choices. Normally she was a cautious decision maker—coming here to research Luc Marteille had been an unusually impulsive act. She wasn't sure she knew what she was capable of anymore.

"Ah," said François as they finished dinner. "More deliciously different ways to be a vegetarian in France. You've almost persuaded me, and I'm a hundred percent sure Jean-Paul is a convert."

Ingrid's eyes sparkled at him. Everyone, except Jean-Paul, recognized his fountain of new sentiment concerning animals was solely aimed at impressing Ingrid.

The two youngsters had plans. Jean-Paul wanted to take Ingrid to a club.

"Oh no, it's not a nightclub," he added as Anna prepared to object, "it's a dance club."

"All right, but you must be back by midnight. Or else, you will find," François left no doubt as to the intent behind his words, "there will be consequences." He looked at Anna who nodded her assent.

The young couple agreed with enthusiasm, and Ingrid planted a loud kiss on her mother's cheek. "Don't worry, Mum. I'll be back before the coach turns into a pumpkin."

Anna watched as the two departed. The look on Ingrid's face said everything. Love, lust, infatuation, whatever you called it, Anna knew how magical it was to be so delighted by and filled with desire for another person. The sweetness of loving exchanges, the hurt when disagreements occurred, the aching want and need to be with that other, dominated your thoughts and emotions during your waking moments. She didn't envy Ingrid; she was pleased her daughter was experiencing one of life's gifts.

"Pumpkin? Why a pumpkin?" François's amused voice broke her reverie.

"A child's fairy tale. Are you familiar with the story of Cinderella?"

"Ah, yes. But Ingrid is no Cinderella. She's a princess already. Yes?"

"Oh, yes. That she is. But she has a kind heart."

Despite his earlier action, Anna was unable to hold her grudge throughout the whole meal and she relaxed as they sipped the last of the wine. And, if she was honest, she'd admit she had dressed for him this evening. Her peace of mind had vanished when her son died and she should have been able to find solace with Greg, but they'd built walls, creating barriers that were easier to keep in place than dismantle. Accepting how comfortable she felt with François was another matter. That he wanted her and had told her so, made him dangerous. It was good she was leaving tomorrow.

"Tell me about the first time you fell in love?" François's voice, subdued, neutral, broke the silence. He waited, saying nothing when she didn't answer straight away.

"Why on earth do you want to talk about that?" Why did he have to throw that into the conversation, just when she thought she was at ease with him? Her first love? It had been half a lifetime since she'd shared that memory with anyone but close friends at the time. Why should she reveal her past mistakes to him?

"Why not? Tomorrow you leave. We won't be meeting anymore. On occasion, it is easier to share with a stranger, n'est-ce pas?"

She'd already shared more with him than she had with anyone else, and he was right, airing an old memory couldn't do any harm. "Anthony Cowlen." The name came out in a rush. "And you?"

He smiled. "That's easy. A very beautiful nightclub singer called Francine. What was your Anthony like?" The way he pronounced Anthony, with his strong French accent, made the name exotic and fascinating.

"Oh, Anthony was very handsome. Do you think glamour lasts? I doubt we'd think the same if we saw them today."

"I'm intrigued."

"Okay." She took a deep breath. "I was in my first year at university; he was an art student in my year and we shared a few classes. He was an Adonis and most of the girls in my year had crushes on him. When he asked me out, there was only one answer." What an innocent view she'd had of life back then. "That's enough for a start. Okay, your turn." Anna studied François picturing him as a young, naïve student. He must have been incredibly good looking.

The corners of his lips curled in a small smile. "When I came to Paris, like most students away from home for the first time, we were desperate to do something our parents disapproved of. We thought it daring to visit nightclubs. Francine sang at a club we often visited. As you can imagine, she had many fans—mostly students. We were in heaven if she bothered to glance our way." He laughed. "We didn't care if she was tone deaf. So what happened with this Adonis?"

She tried to picture Anthony's face but she could barely dredge up any memories, just a few frozen images. He had taken her virginity one week after they'd become a couple. At the time–drunk after a party–it hadn't been a conscious decision. Other memories rose: of rolling around naked in bed laughing hysterically after making love; walking through the campus, his arm around her waist, the envy of her friends.

"We were together for roughly eight months, till after the summer break and the next batch of students joined. He dropped me for a stunning blonde. I watched him swan around with her on his arm, and whenever he saw me, he'd smile and ask how I was as if we'd never shared anything."

"Life can be cruel," François empathized.

"I was devastated. The public aspect—everybody knew. It did take time but you move on fast when you're young. I fell in and out of love a number of times before I met my husband. And, by that time, I was over Anthony's rejection." She gave the smallest of sighs as the memories washed over her. She was enjoying this. Time had made these events, so life changing when they happened, feel as if they'd taken place to someone else. Opening up to François, who had no part in her normal life, meant there were no judgments. "And la belle Francine? Do tell."

"To start with, she was a mixture of

Brigitte Bardot and Marylyn Monroe." François smiled at the memory, "You can understand, as an impressionable young man, I didn't stand a chance. One night she came and sat at our table. Next to me." He made a fanning motion with his hand. "The memory of that night stayed with me for many years. Such passionate madness! And everyone assumed I was making it up."

"So why did she dump you?"

"You are so sure I didn't dump her?" he joked, "but you're right, there was certainly no question of my ending it. It lasted ten days. One evening before it was her turn to sing, she came over and told me we were finished because her fiancé had returned."

Anna laughed out loud.

"Please, don't mock my youthful passions." François pretended to be offended. "I thought my life was ruined.

My friends laughed at how stupid I'd been. I was young and thought she'd broken my heart." He paused reliving that moment. "I'm sure it'll be no surprise to hear I never had the courage to return to the nightclub."

"Oh, I think you got off lightly," she bantered. "It's a good job we've become mature adults who can laugh at these encounters."

She thought of Jean-Paul and Ingrid. Long-distance relationships took a lot of work and they would part after having had no more than a couple of days together, though that was enough if you believed in Romeo and Juliet. At university, a whole new community awaited exploration.

"But falling in love doesn't end because you get older, Anna." He leaned toward her.

She stiffened. Oh, no! He certainly

knew how to spoil the mood. She'd enjoyed this looking back at her youthful indiscretions with the benefits granted by age. Jeremy would never enjoy this gift. He'd been too young to want a serious relationship; he'd wanted to do so many things—finish university, travel the world and have adventures before he settled down to marriage and children.

She remembered one holiday at her parents' in Kent. As often happened, Greg was working and hadn't accompanied them. Ingrid was with her grandmother learning how to make gooseberry preserve. Anna, her father, and Jeremy sat out in the back garden chatting, enjoying the weather and each other's company. Jeremy, fifteen years old, thin as a rake, awkward and gangly at five feet nine, was stretching into his adult body. His dark hair had grown longer over the summer and fell into his eyes

"So, what do you want to be when you grow up, Jeremy?" Anna's father, John, had asked the question.

"A pilot."

Her father smiled, pleased at Jeremy's choice but Anna had been surprised. This was the first time she'd heard Jeremy express any particular ambition.

The next morning over breakfast, Jeremy announced, "Granddad, I've been thinking. I'm not going to be a pilot. I want to be a doctor."

She and her father had exchanged glances. "That's an excellent choice too, Jeremy," her father said.

For the rest of the week, they nodded patiently as Jeremy changed his mind, listing in progression every profession from explorer through to scientist. Each time Jeremy's face lit up when his grandfather had shown his approval. She'd never known her father to be so patient.

When Jeremy left for university, he chose to follow in his father's footsteps and study law—the one profession he'd not named in his list that week with her parents.

"It's Jeremy, isn't it? You're thinking of him?"

She wondered how it was possible for François to read her moods when they barely knew each other. Greg would either not have noticed or ignored it and attributed it to her depression.

"It pains me that he won't experience the joy and suffering that love brings." She choked back her emotions, pushing them down, struggling to contain them.

François topped up their glasses with more of the sweet red liquid.

She didn't want any more wine because she would start bawling if she continued drinking. Nevertheless, she kept sipping; she needed something to occupy her, to help her get a grip.

François waited as if he had all the time in the world. "But life remains an adventure for you? Yes?"

Not trusting herself to speak, she nodded. She couldn't say, *no, my life feels empty despite having a faithful husband who works hard, and a beautiful, intelligent daughter who has a great future ahead of her. From the outside it looks as if I lack nothing; my material needs are taken care of. I think of people who have so much less and, in spite of difficulties, struggle on. But my son, a part of me, died and things aren't fine anymore.*

"Are you satisfied with what you've uncovered about your impressionist artist?"

She was thankful to him for changing the subject. Greg would have.... Why did she keep comparing him to Greg? For goodness sake, she told herself, stop it because nothing is going to happen between you and this man sitting here just because he's giving you the attention and support you've been looking for. He has his motives, the same as everyone else.

"Anna?"

"Sorry. My research? Yes, I think I am content. No one can ever know the complete inside story. What was the real reason Hélène left? Did he have any other mistresses? Yet seeing Hélène's portrait and reading his letters have given me some perspective on how my letter fits into his life. Yes, considering what I've learned about him since finding the letter, I do have more insight into him."

"Maybe you should write his biography someday?" François smiled, his gaze moving from her eyes to her mouth.

"Yes, that's a proposition I might consider." she replied, "I'm finding this research very satisfying." It was an idea and her letter did have new information. There was the possibility that Luc, and maybe Hélène, might be mentioned in other artists' letters of the time. Or was getting involved in another's life a way for her to escape her own?

"You'd have to come to Paris, wouldn't you?"

"François, stop flirting!" Had she said that? She couldn't believe they'd become so casual that she had tossed a comment like that at him. It was a throwaway remark, but this thing, whatever it was between them, didn't feel light any more.

"Why?" He challenged her.

"We've been polite and friendly, more or less, since circumstances threw us together. Please, I'd prefer to keep it that way." She lifted her chin but refused to look at him. This was new, alien territory.

"And what of tonight?" He reached for her hand. "We can make what we want of this time. We have that choice." He held her hand, his thumb lightly stroking her palm.

She wanted to scream let go of my hand because I'm vulnerable and you're taking advantage. But she didn't answer because, underneath everything, an awareness surfaced that she more than liked him; she might actually want him, and not as a platonic friend. François's touch had woken her to the fact Greg never initiated physical contact with her in any way. No coming up behind her, putting his arms around her waist and squeezing tight till she laughingly begged for breath as he'd done in the early days of their relationship; no hugs, or pecks on the cheek. Except for when they had sex— these days she refused to call it making love. They lived parallel lives with Ingrid as the one link gluing them together.

"I can't," she told him. "I want to be honest with you, François. Meeting and spending time with you has been, well, different, unusual, for me. But that's not who I am. I'm not a person who has sex outside marriage." She was intensely conscious of the pressure of his fingers as they moved up her wrist and pressed on her pulse.

"Anna, you are researching a dead painter's love for a mysterious girl. You are also a mother who has lost one of the greatest loves of your life, your son. You're in Paris. This is the city of love. Wake up! Don't live in the past!" He kept a firm hold of her hand, turning it over.

She jerked her hand back "Don't you dare tell me what I should or shouldn't do." Her raised voice attracted looks from people sitting nearby, and conversations halted as they listened, but she didn't care. "This is who I am. A mother and a faithful wife!"

"In an unhappy marriage?"

"But I can't throw away my principles. For what? A one-night stand?"

François expression changed; a door clamping shut. Neither of them spoke.

The other diners lost interest and the hum of conversation resumed around them.

Wanting to ease the sharpness of her remarks, she rested her hand lightly on top of his. "Be honest with me, wouldn't you have tried everything within your power to save your marriage to Lucie if you were in my position? And possibly there's time to repair my relationship with my husband. Whereas if you and I take this further... I might be saying my marriage is finished. But it may not be."

He moved his hand away from under hers.

Strange that this small gesture should leave her so alone. "In another time and place...." She left the sentence unfinished. The tide of rising emotion threatened to drown her. She desired him but couldn't have him. She wouldn't ever have him.

"Or in another life," he said, his voice soft.

The waiter approached their table and as François waved him away, the raucous laughter of a group of passing pedestrians intruded, shattering the intimacy of the moment.

Anna stood up abruptly, knocking over her glass. The remnants of her wine spilled out, a plum stain spreading across the white tablecloth.

He looked up at her in bewilderment.

"I'm fine," she snapped, holding up her hand, indicating he should stay. She left, walking as fast as possible, choking back the tears running down her face.

Chapter Sixteen

The purpose of a promise is to encourage trust and cooperation. A promise establishes the parameters of certain behaviors to which all parties agree. But who hasn't, at some point in their lives, given their word and for one reason or another, intentional or otherwise, broken it?

Paris, July 1873

Hélène and Louise sat in an open grassy area of the Bois de Boulogne, holding the parasols Luc had brought for them and posing as ladies of leisure. A small copse behind them provided the woodland greenery he wanted for the background. He'd liked Hélène's hat with the splash of red from the flower and had instructed her to wear it for the sitting. Benoît lay on a blanket between them—a perfect model who slept the whole day, apart from waking to be fed and changed. The two women appeared to be cooing over the baby and leaning forward as if engaged in exchanging confidences.

This was the second, and final, day of the sitting. The day before he'd painted with intense concentration, hardly speaking to either Hélène or Louise as they lunched on the food he provided.

On the way home yesterday, Louise commented on Luc's behavior saying she'd never seen him so silent and focused. She considered him a chatty artist, wanting to find out the gossip from his competition and giving her his news. She jokingly asked Hélène what she'd done to have this effect on him.

Several times during the morning, Hélène caught Louise studying her with a calculating look in her eye. Not much escaped her cousin's notice. Hélène hoped Louise wouldn't ask any awkward questions. Tomorrow, it wouldn't matter anymore, because she'd be on the train to Bordeaux.

Today they'd eaten another lunch in silence. Thankfully, the noontime heat had lessened, cooled by an afternoon breeze. Benoît woke, his low whimpering alerting Louise to his needs.

"Give me a minute, please," Louise dusted off the last few crumbs of the bread and cheese, and picked up Benoît before his crying escalated. She soothed him with a lullaby, cradling him and rocking back and forth in rhythm to the song.

Luc and Hélène watched her moving slowly toward the copse on the edge of the clearing.

Hélène thought about starting a conversation, but hesitated, not wanting to disturb him. She hadn't lost her initial awe of him, especially when he painted, irrespective of what had passed between them.

"I'll be finished here shortly," he said. "Will you accompany me to the studio?"

"What for?" she asked in surprise.

"I need to do one more check on the portrait." He sounded distracted, "Will you come?" Luc had been distant these past two days, but his undeclared emotions hung heavy in the space between them.

Hélène recognized being alone with him wasn't a good idea. She had Claude and her future, but yet they diminished in importance when he required something of her.

"Louise can accompany us and view the painting," he stated.

Hélène knew he mentioned Louise to add the subtle pressure of making her appear ungracious if she refused. That she would be safer with someone else present so that nothing might happen between them, was understood. "Of course. It won't take long, will it? I still have some packing to do."

"No, a couple of details and that will be it."

When Louise returned, he counted out their payment, handing it to her and inviting her to come along and see Hélène's portrait. However, it turned out she'd promised Irene to look after her three youngest for a couple of hours so she was unable to go.

Louise wasn't happy with Luc's

request. She trusted Hélène, and she usually trusted Luc, but something didn't seem right, though she couldn't put her finger on anything in particular. She would need the money from the modeling Luc sent her way after Hélène left. Having little choice in the matter, she let it pass.

Luc stood up, meticulously brushing his trousers and waistcoat before marching back to his painting. He didn't wait for Louise to settle Benoît before starting to paint, and he continued without stopping for another hour.

"Okay, that's it." He called out, moving back and scrutinizing his work before beckoning them over. "Come and look."

"You go," said Louise.

Benoit had begun fretting, waving his arms and legs, his face screwed into a grimace, his mouth opening ready to inform the world of his requirements.

"There, there, little one." She picked up the squirming baby and headed for the shrubbery.

Hélène folded the blanket they'd sat on, gathered up the parasols and lunch basket, before walking over to study the painting. She could see various details, the wisps of cloud, shimmering greenery, the sleeping infant, were unfinished, but Luc had captured the naturalness of the outdoors as well as depicting the women's protectiveness toward the infant. "It's beautiful."

He gave no indication that he noticed the admiration in her voice and continued packing up his paraphernalia.

Louise emerged after feeding Benoit, who'd fallen asleep in her arms and came over to examine the painting. "M'sieur Luc, it's wonderful. Merci beaucoup."

"Ah, no. It is I who should be thanking you."

Hélène was startled to see Luc smiling at Louise with genuine pleasure. For whatever reason, he did have a soft spot for her cousin.

"A bientôt." With a deftness born of practice, Luc tucked his paints into his shoulder bag, hoisted his easel under one arm, holding the painting with the other.

"Don't keep her late," Louise called after his retreating figure. There was no doubting the edge in her tone.

"I'll be fine," Hélène hugged Louise and dropped a quick kiss on Benoît's head before running after the artist.

Luc set a fast pace. He'd disciplined his emotions throughout the day, understanding himself well enough to realize that if he started a conversation, something might slip out, and the feelings he struggled so hard to contain would spill out beyond his control. He pictured the result: Hélène distraught, Louise outraged. He'd be the laughing stock of Montmartre, and the gossips would make sure Émilie heard of the incident. He required at least one person in the world to look at him with absolute adoration. It was essential he retain the high estimation in which his wife held him.

Hélène trailed behind, hot and gasping for breath, unable to keep up with him. Her heart thudded against her ribs, but she couldn't tell whether it was fear or anticipation. Louise was right; you couldn't figure out artists; they were beyond comprehension.

He slowed as they turned into Rue Gabrielle and upon reaching his building, held the door open, waiting for her to enter.

She sensed his gaze burning into her back and attempted to move up the stairs faster, but the day's heat, plus the effort she'd expended trying to match his pace, left her drained of energy.

"Sit," he instructed as they entered his studio. "The usual pose."

Dabbing at the sweat on her forehead, she followed him into the familiar disarray. "Where's the chair?"

"Sit on the couch. It'll do," he said.

She crossed the room, sitting down and watching Luc as he fussed with brushes and paints.

"Hair," he instructed, moving over to her portrait on his main easel and choosing a brush.

She removed her hat and loosened her hair, attempting to arrange it as it had been for the sitting. He was making it clear this was purely business. She wondered why that disappointed her. Wasn't it better if this was her last impression of him?

"No." He didn't scream or shout, but his harsh tone made her wince. He walked across and stood over her. "I didn't mean to scare you." He said, his manner softening.

When she glanced up his eyes were kind. Encouraged, she smiled up at him. "I'm not that easily frightened. Besides, you're an artist," she said as if that explained everything.

"I wish that were the problem," he said lifting her hair.

She sat as motionless as possible as his hands brushed her shoulder. They were different from Claude's hands, toughened by farm work, but neither were they weak. Luc's hands were his instrument, the fingertips a little roughened, but they were the tools of his art. She blushed as the unbidden thought of what it would be like to kiss them wandered into her mind.

Luc breathed in her fragrance. He was aware he should move away from her; this close, she intoxicated him. But he didn't. He knelt and took hold of her hands. His fingers rested on her wrist and he felt the butterfly of her pulse beating under his touch. He didn't look up but examined her hands, turning them this way and that. He caressed her palms, long gentle strokes, heard her intake of breath.

"I'm in love with you." He experienced an immense release as he said it and slumped down, laying his head on her knees. "Please, Hélène," he raised his head and stared at her, "You say you love Claude but you also have feelings for me. I know it here." He placed a hand on his heart.

He reminded her of a child hankering for a favorite toy. She stroked his head, the thick curls springing around her fingers as she pushed them through his hair. An irritating voice whispered, you realize he won't leave his family for you, don't you? What about Claude? This isn't real. She didn't call this thing between them love although she admitted he fascinated her. What was so wrong with this attraction? Today was her last day. When she left Paris, this temptation would become a faded memory, and she and Claude would live the life they'd planned.

He reached up, and pulling her toward him, kissed her.

Her body responded, it seemed natural, and she wanted this. For that instant, for both of them, nothing existed except the other. The yielding touch of the other's lips completed them; the closeness of the other, the point of contact where hand brushed over the other's skin was complete satisfaction. No other time or place was real. Only he and she existed in this moment.

He rose, put his hand under her head, moved her onto her back, and shifted alongside her.

For a minute she acquiesced, but as he began exploring her body, the nagging voice resumed. You're a virgin. You should be doing this with Claude. Luc continued to kiss her, his lips moving down her throat, but all she could see was the look Claude had given her when she set off for Paris. You won't be the same when you return, he'd told her. That's true, she'd laughed. I'll be grown up and sophisticated.

"No." She attempted to push Luc off

her. "Stop! Please stop."

But Luc was deaf. He'd been consumed by thoughts of Hélène for weeks. The fact that she was leaving drove him insane. What was it about this girl that she'd been able to take over his every waking moment in this manner? He leaned into kiss her. She'd responded to him moments ago; she couldn't have gone cold on him from one second to the next.

Hélène panicked. She wrenched her mouth away, pushing his head back.

But he kept pressing down on her. It wasn't until she started hitting him on the head and shoulders with her fists that he grasped what was happening. When he saw her eyes, fierce, fighting back the tears, he released his hold on her and sank face downward.

She jumped up, straightening her clothes.

"I'm sorry. I'm truly sorry." He twisted around, staring up at her, mortified; his expression one of abject misery. "I—" Guilt froze his tongue, he could hardly speak.

"No... no... I shouldn't have... it's as much my fault." She grabbed her hairpins from where they'd fallen on the floor, jabbing them in into her hair with far more force than necessary as she pinned it up again. With her hat settled back on her head, a facade of composure in place, her voice betrayed nothing of her inner turmoil. "I have to go." Her shoes rapped a staccato across the floor. She didn't turn around, simply opened the door and left.

Luc lay unmoving, drowning in shame. He heard the studio door close, her light quick footsteps on the stairs, and the finality of the front door banging shut.

*

By the time Hélène arrived home, Louise was bustling in the kitchen preparing the evening meal, and Pierre was walking around the sitting room with Benoît in his arms. The baby gurgled up at his father when he brought his smiling face close. The tears she'd been holding back nudged nearer to falling.

"How's the painting?" Louise popped out from the kitchen, hair in disarray and flour on her nose and chin.

Hélène focused on putting her hat carefully in its place on the stand turning aside and hiding her tears from Louise. "It's fine. He just wanted one final check."

"Here," said Pierre. "You'd better

take the opportunity while you're here." He winked as he handed the baby over to her.

She kissed the creamy skin on the top of Benoît's head, the fine baby hair tickling her chin. "How will I cope without seeing you every day?" Her tears, cool wet drops, fell onto the baby's head making him cry.

"Are you upset?" asked Pierre, looking distinctly uncomfortable.

Louise dried her hands, came straight over and put her arms around Hélène's shaking shoulders. "Here, take the baby." Louise made a clucking irritated noise and lifted the sniffling Benoît out of Hélène's arms, giving her husband a cross look as she returned the baby to him.

Benoît was set to let rip but quietened as his father's face came into view.

Louise led Hélène into the bedroom, sat on the bed and patted the space beside her. "Come," she ordered. "Tell me what happened. What did that bastard do to you?"

"Oh no, Louise," protested Hélène, "it's not him." How could she say she was so attracted to Luc that when he kissed her, she'd kissed him back? That if she hadn't been leaving the next day with a fiancé waiting for her, the outcome might have been very different.

Louise had sat for many artists to supplement her income as a laundress when she'd first arrived in Paris, and received many offers, she'd confided to Hélène on one of her sporadic visits home. She'd accepted none of them.

"No, it's seeing you and Benoît and Pierre. You're so happy. I hope I'll be as content as you are."

"Oh, I see. Well, as long as that's it." She pulled Hélène into her arms. "You wait. Your turn will come. Remember we don't stand around gazing into each other's eyes the whole day either. I'll finish cooking, you finish your packing, and we'll go for a stroll after dinner."

Hélène closed her small suitcase—she didn't have a lot of clothes—but the single image haunting her was Luc's expression when he realized how he'd behaved. Guilt and shame. Remembering the feel of his body pressing down on hers brought heat to her cheeks. She couldn't believe how near she'd been to letting go. A wave of dizziness hit her, and she sat down before she fell.

Her thoughts were drawn to what might have happened next if she hadn't pulled back from the brink. Her skin tingled with expectancy. No. This daydreaming about him had to end. Women of her class didn't get away with making those kinds of choices. Men such as Luc Marteille had mistresses; he'd probably had a dozen. Nobody would blame him with an invalid for a wife, but a country girl from a farm had one chance. She was lucky. She had Claude, and they would work, live, have a family and grow old together. To have someone who loved you, and would care for you no matter what, wasn't something to be tossed aside; you didn't abandon the prospect of a lifetime of marriage for momentary gratification. Not in her world.

Early next morning Hélène and Louise, with Benoit in her arms, jolted along the route to the station. Pierre had hired a horse-drawn cab for the journey as it was too far for Louise to walk.

Hélène had said goodbye to him before he left for work, extracting a promise to come for her wedding. Soon she would be gone from this city with its grand buildings and crowds of people. She made an effort to fix these last moments in her memory. Who knew if she would ever return?

The Gare d'Austerlitz was crowded, and they pushed their way through the early morning crowds of hurrying Parisians. Flower sellers, beggars, and hawkers of all sorts called out, trying to sell their wares in and around the station entrance.

"The farm is going to be quiet after this," said Hélène as they hugged.

"Oh, you'll be busy enough with your wedding preparations," Louise said as Benoît started to fuss "I hate rushing goodbyes but you understand, don't you?" Benoît's thin cry rose to a wail.

"No, it's fine. I'll see you in a month. I'm going to miss you so much." She dabbed the tears from her eyes. "Thank you. It's been wonderful."

Louise drew Hélène to her and kissed her. "Write me a long letter full of news from home. I'm so looking forward to your wedding."

Hélène stood watching her cousin leave, waving every time Louise turned. Then she was gone in the crowd. Hélène envied Louise. She had everything she desired. Hélène could but hope and pray her future held the same.

She picked up her small case, hoping she'd find a seat. As she turned, preparing to climb into the carriage, she caught a flicker of movement out of the corner of her eye. She looked for a second time to see what had attracted her attention.

A man, his face partially hidden by a straw hat, was climbing into a carriage further along the platform. In his hand, he carried a brown portmanteau.

There was no doubt about it—the man was Luc.

Chapter Seventeen

"He that is without sin among you, let him first cast a stone...." St. John 8:7

Paris, July 2007

Anna focused on the needle hot jets of water hitting her back and shoulders. Turning around, she let the heat penetrate and ease the tightness in her muscles. She'd made it to the hotel without running and, more importantly, without losing control in public. Small steps, she repeated, lots of small steps and before you know it, you've made a big step.

When she'd first heard the news of Jeremy's accident—a policeman and a policewoman knocking at the door asking for permission to enter, compassion in their eyes as they performed their duty—days and weeks followed when the smallest thing triggered a crying jag. One time the sight of a silver spoon in the cutlery drawer, a christening present from a grandparent, left her broken and huddled on the kitchen floor as the dinner burnt. Jeremy loved to use it when young and it had become a family joke that he was born with a silver spoon in his mouth. Unexpected episodes like this left her bereft and weeping for hours.

Jeremy was dead. No new memories of him were possible from the moment she'd received the news. He would never have anything new to celebrate. Yet, she was here, alive. Abruptly changing the shower temperature to cold supplied her version of shock therapy and set her gasping as the water struck her skin. She tolerated the freezing blast for as long as she could before she reached for the tap.

As she prepared for bed, her thoughts kept circling back to François. Why had his proposition upset her so much? She tried to figure out why his behavior provoked her to the extent it did. Maybe he was breaking through her barriers? Had spending time with him these last couple of days made her more conscious of the widening distance between her and Greg?

She stared at her reflection in the bathroom mirror, and as the memory of his lips on hers came to mind, she watched her skin flush right up to the roots of her hair. Was she such a fool she didn't recognize how tempted she was by the promise he presented? But what was the purpose of such a temporary liaison? Did there have to be a reason for everything, she wondered. Why should enjoyment of the moment, accepting what life offered her, be wrong? "To have and to hold" echoed in her mind. She'd made vows. Vows she wasn't sure meant a lot to her anymore.

Anna felt as if she was engaged in a schizophrenic war. One part of her longed to throw off restraints, to live without caring what other people thought. The other half battled to keep the principles of loyalty and faithfulness she'd valued the whole of her married life. She sighed, certain of which one would win. She didn't think of herself as a coward, but fear of stepping out of line, of repercussions, maintained the status quo. Tomorrow it wouldn't matter. She and Ingrid would meet up with Greg at the airport and the dilemma triggered by François's presence wouldn't be an issue. He'd be out of her life.

Nonetheless, this expedition to Paris had been good for her. Her pallor had gone, and her eyes no longer looked haunted. Was Ingrid right? Had her old self returned with something different added? She looked vibrant, alive. How much of this was the result of researching her story here in Montmartre, and how much was due to François? She decided both had contributed to the change.

Maybe she was finally coming to terms with her grief and moving on; something she'd not been able to envision before coming here. In one sense she'd never move on from her firstborn, but she wasn't stuck in that emotionally frozen place she'd inhabited since he died.

Anna climbed into bed with her notebook, intending to write a few observations on this afternoon's visit to the Musée. She'd discovered more than she expected when researching the history of a love affair between an artist and his model. *Merci, Luc,* she whispered to the artist, picturing Luc standing in his studio painting Hélène's portrait. Tomorrow morning she'd make one last visit. Her eyelids drooped, and she dozed.

Waking with a start, she looked over at Ingrid's bed. Empty. She glanced at her watch on the bedside table. Two o'clock! Suddenly she was reliving that night. Life repeating itself. Waking up, finding him not home, the knock on the door. Breathe, she told herself, as dread of some nameless disaster squeezed fingers tight around her heart.

Her heart beat louder, pa dum pa dum, speeding up. Come on, how often have you done this? Breathe in, one two three four; hold, one two three four; breathe out, one two three four; hold, one two three four. She forced herself to continue till her heart rate had slowed somewhat, and the dreadful thoughts ebbed.

Her imagination had to be reined in, controlled. Because it was late and Ingrid wasn't back, it didn't mean... This wasn't a replay of Jeremy. It couldn't be. She wouldn't allow it. Rustling in her handbag for her mobile phone, she dialed Ingrid's number. Straight to messaging. She rang again.

Keep breathing. Breathe in, and release everything with the out breath. She blocked the tendrils of memory seeking to re-establish themselves. That night had been replayed too many times. Nothing has happened to Ingrid, she recited. Nothing would happen. Everything was going to be fine. Ingrid was with a nice young man, whose uncle had helped in her own research.

François. He'd been so calm and self-controlled when her other purse was stolen, taking charge and sorting out everything. But she didn't have his number. A flash of memory surfaced: Ingrid mentioning Jean-Paul's room was two floors above, number 401. She grabbed her dressing gown, snatched up her phone and keys and hurried out the door.

Anna ran, slippers flapping against her heels, shoving her arms into the dressing gown sleeves as she sped along the corridor. She tapped the lift button non-stop, fidgeting with the keypad on her phone, repeatedly trying to get hold of Ingrid as she waited, without success. Thankfully, when the lift arrived, it was empty, but it rose excruciatingly slowly. As soon as the doors opened onto the fourth floor, she rushed out, checking the door numbers. She spotted François's room, third on the right, straight away.

She hesitated for a minute suddenly nervous about waking him up in the early hours of the morning, and hoping he wouldn't misconstrue her actions. But getting in touch with Ingrid, finding out she was safe, was more important. He could do that for her by phoning Jean-Paul. That was vital.

She knocked. No response. She knocked a second time, with more force. Still nothing. The third time, she rapped hard on the door, not caring if she woke everyone in the whole hotel. She heard movement inside the room. Thank God.

The door opened and François stood there tying the belt of his robe and blinking the sleep out of his eyes.

"It's Ingrid," she blurted out, her voice high and strangled. "She's not back, and she's not answering her phone. I'm going mad with worry." Her face twisted with the effort of not crying. "I need you to ring Jean-Paul. Please."

"Come in, come in." François, solicitousness personified, opened the door wide. "Here, sit down." He led her over to the couch. "What time is it?" He rubbed his chin.

Anna perched on the edge of the couch. "That's the problem." She managed to restrain the whine in her voice. She didn't want him to think she was weak, not capable of standing on her own, always needing others for support. This was a practical matter.

"It's two in the morning."

"Jean-Paul!" exclaimed François.

Anna's eyes widened at the anger lacing his words as he picked up his mobile phone from a table by the couch.

"I told him to be home by midnight." He stabbed the phone. "Wait till I get my hands on him." He held the phone to his ear. His forehead creased in annoyance. "No answer," he said, trying once more. This time, he left a message. "Listen, Jean-Paul. This is François. Anna is here with me and I want you to get back here, with Ingrid, straight away or I promise you'll be on the first train back to Lyons tomorrow." The threat sounded serious. Hopefully, it would work. He faced Anna. "I'm sure they're safe," he reassured her, "but I understand you can't relax till you see Ingrid."

Anna's shoulders started to shake as she struggled to stay calm and in control. Not here, not in front of him, not when she'd been doing so well.

François strode over to the sideboard, pulled out a bottle of brandy and two glasses and poured two generous measures. "No, no, no. Don't worry. Everything will be fine." He sat beside her. "Drink this." He handed her a brandy with one hand and pushed the box of tissues on the table toward her with the other.

Unable to stop herself, Anna began to laugh.

François looked baffled.

"I'm sorry," she wheezed half-laughing, half-crying, as she dabbed at her eyes with a handful of tissues. "You handle everything so gracefully. Brandy and Kleenex! What more could a woman ask?"

"This is not the time to answer that question," he said.

She ignored the hint of mischief as his mouth quirked up at the corners—she was becoming familiar with that look—and took a large sip of her drink. The liquid seared the back of her throat, and she coughed as it slid down into her stomach. "Thank you, François. What would I have done without you?"

"Yes, I must congratulate myself. I think I've done remarkably well seeing as how saving damsels in distress is an occupation at which I'm quite new. But don't forget your daughter wouldn't have gone out if it wasn't for my nephew." As François settled himself next to her, his phone buzzed. He uttered a groan of annoyance as he read the message. "I apologize for my nephew. It appears he has met up with a friend from home and, surprise,

surprise, he and Ingrid have gone onto another club. However, he was in such a rush to leave, he forgot his door key. He's in so much trouble. But it strikes me that Ingrid is someone who knows what she wants, and she's too old for you to control anymore. You are aware of that, aren't you?"

"No." Anna bristled. She knew no such thing. "If she's under our roof and living off our money, she has to respect our wishes." Both she and Greg shared the same view on this.

She'd only ever had one serious screaming argument with Jeremy. The summer holidays were approaching, and in less than a week they were due to leave for their annual vacation in France. Jeremy had finished his end of year exams, and one of his close friends was organizing a group trip to a music festival. Jeremy told her he'd pay for himself, he didn't need any help; and after the festival, he would hop on a plane and join them. He was certainly old enough to travel by himself.

Jeremy had spoken to her first, figuring that if she agreed, and was on his side, it would be easier to persuade his father. To his chagrin, her opinion was that sixteen was too young to traipse off to one of those music festivals with friends. Greg was of the same mind and Jeremy had sulked for days.

The night before they were due to leave, Jeremy came into the kitchen in a final attempt to convince her to change her decision. She could see it galled him to the point of absolute frustration to be unable to do what he wanted. The conversation, repeating the same points, incensed Jeremy, and he accused her of making no effort to understand his viewpoint.

She'd shouted at him that as far as she was concerned he was not an adult, and therefore not free to do as he pleased. He yelled some insult back. She snapped something else at him, telling him to go to his room. He stormed out of the house, slamming the front door behind him. She didn't remember the actual words they said, but what stayed with her long after he walked out was the look of total disgust, almost hatred, he'd given her in that moment.

She'd waited up for him. He came in at eleven-thirty and leaned next to the kitchen door. Physically, he was mature for a sixteen-year-old; tall with his dark hair falling over his forehead, and he'd already begun shaving. He was growing up fast. In a few years he'd leave for university, and after that, he was unlikely to return and live at home. Who knew where his life would take him?

He pushed his hair back off his face. "Sorry, Mum." He walked over to her and kissed the top of her head.

"You'll understand when you have children," she'd told her son.

François topped up her brandy. "You British can be so uptight about the important aspects of life."

She chose not to reply. A tit for tat conversation was one thing she could do without; she let the remark pass.

"Forgive my asking a personal question Anna, but are you planning to have, what do you call it, counseling?"

Her back stiffened. What business was that of his? "Oh, I had a lot of counseling for what good it did me." She took a large sip of brandy. "My shrink even prescribed medication, which I assure you I took religiously." She wished her earlier mood hadn't been so temporary, so fleeting. Moving on didn't seem to be on her agenda at the moment. "It helped, but as I'm sure you've noticed, it doesn't take much to set me off, does it?" Anna swallowed another huge gulp of brandy.

"Letting go is the hardest. Guilt comes when you start to enjoy life because you think if you hang onto your grief, you hang onto them. But if you remember them, they're always alive. That's what memories are for. You never stop loving them, but you do learn to survive without them. From my personal experience, time is the one thing which truly allows healing to take place."

They were silent. Both remembering the one person they could never see again—the one person they would have paid any price to have in their arms.

When François's arm encircled her shoulders, it felt the most natural thing in the world. Her defenses crumbled and dissolved; whatever their purpose, she had no need for them tonight. He shifted closer, and it was the easiest thing to lean in and rest on his chest. She savored the quiet comfort in being close to him. His physicality. She smelled his aftershave. The particular woody tone in its perfume was a favorite. She could feel his heartbeat quicken.

Something inside of her clicked into place and the paradigm shift, which had been set in motion with the discovery of Luc Marteille's letter, completed its realignment. She'd been the pliant agreeable one. Her family, and certainly Greg, took her for granted, but tonight she didn't want to play it safe. Would there be consequences? She didn't care anymore. Comfy slippers no longer appealed. She'd made her decision; she desired to dance. François was right; she was here, he was here, and this time was theirs to seize and enjoy—if they wanted.

Anna shifted, looking up and studying him. He looked vulnerable with his lips in a half smile and his expression uncertain. She should remember him like this so she could paint him when she got home.

"Kiss me," she said.

"Are you sure?"

"Yes." This was her choice. Hers alone. He took the glass out of her hand, and placed both their glasses on the table, before turning to her. Bending down, he kissed her full on the lips. He carried her into the bedroom laying her on the bed as if she were porcelain and might break if he wasn't careful.

"Are you sure?" He asked her a second time.

She smiled up at him before pulling his head down toward her. "I haven't been more sure of anything in a long time."

Some time later, they lay with legs and arms entwined.

Anna was euphoric. Whether it was the brandy or surrendering at last to her attraction for François, she didn't care. She was beyond caring. Never having been, or had the desire to be unfaithful to Greg had made it impossible to admit her feelings. The truth was she had found François desirable from the first moment they met. Remembering Greg, she smiled.

"What are you thinking about?"

François asked, his fingers tracing the line of her jaw.

"That this is the first time I've ever been disloyal to my husband."

He continued his exploration of her lips. "Are you consumed with guilt? You puritanical middle-class English people are notorious for repressing your feelings." His words were mocking, though his tone was gentle. He lifted her hair off her shoulder.

"No, I'm not. Why do you think of the English in stereotypes?" Anna accused him but she couldn't stop smiling.

"What's so funny?" François said propping himself up on his elbow and twisting a strand of her hair around his fingers, holding it up to the light.

"Well, I'm thinking that if he doesn't find out what I've been up to, I have no problem with it."

"I wanted to make love to you from the moment you threw yourself at me."

"I know." She glared balefully at him before collapsing into giggles, as if she were a young girl, light and free. "And, indeed, you have." She walked her fingers down his chest, letting them rest there. Later she would have to consider what tonight, what making love with him, meant to her. But not in this moment.

"What is it you say?" He leaned toward her, his eyes soft, "My pleasure!" He was about to kiss her when an insistent knocking on the outer door startled him. "Oh merde! That must be Jean-Paul!"

Chapter Eighteen

It is important not to lose oneself in the world of 'if only'. Opportunities are lost in life, and it is hard to never think what if I had taken a particular road, or made a different choice? Yet regret can function as a warning, preventing disaster, but to dwell on our disappointments for too long disturbs the balance of day to day living.

Paris, July 1873

"Here, Mademoiselle." An elderly gentleman gestured to a place opposite him as Hélène climbed into the carriage. "You're a little pale. Are you feeling ill?"

"I'm fine." She managed to keep the

tremor out of her voice. "Thank you."

Stowing her suitcase on the rack, she sank onto the seat between a small gentleman with a full mustache and an amply bosomed matron. She clasped her hands together so the other passengers wouldn't see how they shook, grateful for the seat because she wasn't certain how much longer her legs would have held her up. When she'd arrived in Paris, she'd been agog, her head periscoping from one side to the other, soaking in the sights. Today she didn't even notice the train pulling out of the station.

Why was Luc on the train? Should she go and ask him? What would he answer? Her mind stuck, churning over the question. Confronting him and being told he was visiting a friend in the country to do some painting would make her seem mad. No, asking him was out of the question. But her heart refused to stop its loud pounding; she was feverish one minute and chilly the next. Was she scared of him? No, she decided, it wasn't that.

She had a sudden image of walking arm in arm with Luc along the promenade in one of the small towns on the Cote d'Azur that he and his friends often discussed. They smiled at each other with love. Luc had rented a cottage near the sea with a garden where he painted in the mornings. The sun shone in the clear sky above and the sea lapped on the beach below—they were so happy.

The train jolted and the large lady, whose blue muslin covered arms pressed into her side, rocked forward. Don't be so foolish, Hélène scolded herself. Luc's business had nothing to do with her, and she was probably the last person he wanted to bump into, especially after yesterday. What was wrong with her? Had her stay in Paris made her think the world revolved around her wishes? Her parents had brought her up differently, and she knew better.

Hélène gazed out of the carriage at the lush countryside. Paris was behind her and she was going home. By evening she'd be in Bordeaux and tomorrow Claude would be up before dawn to come and fetch her. She worked at conjuring up Claude's face. His smile. The color of his eyes. What would he think of the changes in her? She wasn't the same girl who'd set off for Paris, the one deeply in love with her fiancée. Paris had changed her. Luc had changed her. She wasn't sure anymore if she could give her heart completely to Claude because Luc had stolen a piece of it. The train journey was torture. She couldn't stop thinking of Luc sitting in another carriage close by, and her thoughts kept returning to yesterday.

At Orleans the train stopped for half an hour, so she got out to stretch her legs. Not having the nerve to walk far, she stayed close to her carriage, peering into those on either side. No sign of anyone who resembled him. By the time the train pulled out, she was convinced she must have made a mistake. The man she'd seen wasn't Luc.

When the train pulled into Bordeaux, Luc waited behind, letting the other passengers leave ahead of him. He'd spent the whole journey considering his reckless behavior. Now he was debating whether he should take the next train back to Paris or not. He alternated between envisioning one last passionate plea where Hélène might be persuaded of the depth of his feelings and cold rationality when he knew no matter what happened he'd never leave Émilie and his children.

In the end, it was the memory of Giselle and Guy's laughing faces which assuaged both his guilt and his fever. Their absence had reminded him what life was like without them. He promised himself that soon his life would return to normal as it had been before Hélène.

"Monsieur!" The guard's voice interrupted his reverie. "Everybody must get off the train."

Luc apologized and grabbed his bag. He was the last passenger, and the platform was deserted. Yes, everything was becoming clear. He'd buy a ticket and go back to Paris. This crazed behavior must become a thing of the past–he had to put it behind him–no more constant chewing over his actions. Hélène would be greeting her fiancé; he must focus on paintings for the exhibition and lose himself in his work.

Luc remained calm and resigned, even after the ticket clerk informed him the first train to Paris wasn't leaving till 9.30 tomorrow morning. There was a station hotel if M'sieur needed somewhere for the night, or the clerk could recommend a boarding house if M'sieur preferred that?

Luc chose the station hotel as it was nearest. A receptionist booked him in, allocating him a room on the first floor with a large window facing onto the Place du Saint Jean. The room satisfied Luc with its dark polished wooden floors and serviceable table and chair, chest of drawers, and a wardrobe that had seen better days. It would suffice for one night. Most important, it was near to the station, and this time tomorrow he'd be back in Paris. He'd hardly eaten since breakfast but wasn't hungry. As he looked out over the square, his habitual compulsion to capture life around him surfaced.

Making himself comfortable on the chair by the window, he got out his drawing pad and pencils. Manet had instilled the necessity of always having them with him early on in their acquaintance. He started to draw. As he worked, the fugue which had permeated his existence these last weeks lifted. He sat and sketched, absorbed in catching his impressions of the busy evening square.

Luc felt satiated, at peace; he was moving along the desired course. This was his purpose in life. It wasn't till the warning noises from his stomach broke his concentration that he decided it might be time to find something to eat.

After dining in the hotel restaurant, he sat at the bar sipping a brandy. As the evening deepened, he fancied a stroll around the square, enjoying the sensation that being in a different place gave. Returning to the hotel, he nodded pleasantly as the doorman bowed when he entered. His birth had blessed him with an education and a distinguished ancestry, and despite an upbringing without luxury, he took it for granted that he was one of those for whom others opened doors. This was the way of the world.

He was outside his room, key in hand, when the door to the next room opened and someone bent down, about to place a tray on the floor. For an instant, he didn't breathe as he recognized the hair.

Hélène.

His ruminations of the afternoon fled. He froze. Everything narrowed to this one moment of concentrated observation: a bird's sweet trill wafted in through the open window at one end of the corridor; the formal tick-tock of the grandfather clock at the top of the stairs; an insect thrummed past his ear; the smooth cotton of his shirt against his chest; the pounding of his heart. His breath caught in his throat.

Hélène looked up. Her shock mirrored his. She dropped the tray. It hit the floor with a clatter, bowl and plate rolling to a noisy stop by the door as she stood transfixed. He had followed her. Why was he here? Staying in the room next to her? Her knees buckled, and she collapsed.

Then he was beside her, helping her

to stand. "I thought you'd left Bordeaux." His voice was muted, soft, concerned.

"Claude's coming for me in the morning." She faltered as she registered the warmth from his hand through her sleeve. "But why are you here?" Yet as she spoke, she knew the answer. She leaned against the door frame.

He gathered up the knife and fork from where they'd fallen, replacing them on the tray and pushing it away from the door. Ushering her inside the room, he closed the door.

She allowed him to lead her over to the bed.

"Come," he said sitting down next to her. He stroked her face, his fingers gentle. Tracing the curve of her brow, and along her cheek, he leaned in and kissed her.

She responded eagerly. Images of the sea, the cottage, living with him and seeing him from morning to night returned.

They both wanted this.

"Will you leave your wife and children for me?" she asked.

He pulled back. "Why do you ask?"

"Will you?" she insisted.

He walked over to the window, staring out over the square without answering.

"Look at these." Hélène pointed at the tall vase of flowers on the dresser. The roses, lilies, forget-me-nots, and chrysanthemums were magnificent as they caught the deep gold light of the setting sun. She crossed the room, pulling out one rose, caressing its velvet surface. "For you artists, women are like these flowers. When they are fresh and young, they are beautiful.

But," she plucked first one petal, then a second and a third, tossing them one after another to the floor, "as they age, they lose their bloom till nothing remains." She finished stripping the flower and flung the bare stalk at him. It fell at his feet. "If you won't give up anything for me, how can you expect me to give up everything for you?"

He stared at her torn between desire and despair. He had no answer.

"I think you had better go." She turned her back on him.

As he moved toward the door, his footsteps quiet with slow deliberation, she realized how easy it would be to surrender. She did want him. To have his arms around her, his mouth on hers; his touch on her skin made her feel as if she was on fire. In Paris, she'd been flattered and overwhelmed by the attentions of a famous artist. But back here in Bordeaux, ready to start a new chapter in her life, she recognized that if he had been less than honest—at least he'd been that—she would have risked her future for him. As the door closed, she threw herself on the bed, burying her sobs in the pillow, so that no one, especially not him, would hear.

Luc returned to his room. His earlier sketches lay strewn on the bed. Almost without any conscious control over his movements, he picked up his pad and pastels and returned to his seat overlooking the square. Deep shadows had gathered in the corners and small pools of yellow light shone under the gas lamps. There were a few people out, couples and groups sauntering out for late evening strolls or on the way to visit friends, but that sense of needing to get somewhere was absent. Snippets of conversations drifted up accompanied by the heady scent of jasmine from the potted plants outside the hotel entrance.

Seeing Hélène highlighted the precariousness of his state of mind. A finality tinged his thinking. Not that deadness which comes with callous endings because Hélène would forever be utterly and completely alive to him. It was the acceptance that whatever lived in his imagination with regard to Hélène would never manifest other than in his inner world.

He needed to do something which would stop his fixation on Hélène from consuming him. He drew, letting the sheets of paper fall off the table as he finished, not noticing that darkness had fallen until he could barely see. At last, he stopped, and with great care gathered up his drawings, placing them in a neat pile on the table. From time to time, the plaintive bark of a dog at the rising moon was taken up and bounced around the town, disturbing the night before silence fell once more.

Without bothering to undress, he lay fully clothed on the bed and surveyed the ceiling. He couldn't sleep but nervous exhaustion left him unable to move. Whatever he tried to think of— his circle of friends, his family, his painting, nothing made any difference; his thoughts traveled back to Hélène. Finally, he surrendered, allowing his mind to wander where it willed.

He relived their relationship from the very minute she'd walked in the door, taking Louise's place as a model. He recalled his impressions when he'd seen her for the first time. She'd been a mixture of timidity—scared, not knowing what to expect—and courage because her fears hadn't prevented her coming alone to his studio so her cousin didn't lose the income. It was more than being a country girl in the city, it was the fresh way she viewed the world, full of interest and innocence. He went over every sitting, every look, every gesture, and every conversation. From this moment on, memories would be all he had of her.

Toward dawn, he rose and splashed his face with water. He studied the drawings he'd made last night. Most were of Hélène: a profile, a hand, full face with eyes cast downward; one was of the rose, half stripped of its petals, but several were of the vase of flowers from her room. He liked these, and an idea for a painting struck him, partly because the sketches were good, but partly because of what she'd said to him.

He listened to the early morning

workers calling out greetings to friends from across the square. Doors opening and closing, footsteps on the hotel stairs, and the sounds of people waking told him time was short. Hélène would soon be leaving. He understood he'd never see or speak to her again. What was the point in creating more misery for either of them? But he had one final thing he wanted to say to her. Picking up a pencil and paper, he began scribbling down his thoughts.

My dear Hélène,

I realize we have parted for the last time, but I must tell you that knowing you has changed me. My golden hearted Hélène, I would have given you everything that I possibly could, though we are both aware it is not enough to win you. But remember this, I did, and still do, love you. With every beat of my heart. You have shown me my world afresh, and I know you love me because I have seen it in your eyes.

I am broken into a thousand hard useless pieces and my days will be empty without you. I cannot ask you to be with me, but I shall keep my sweet love for you locked away in a secret place deep inside my soul where I shall cherish it. When dark clouds descend, for my life will become bleak without your presence, I will take out these precious memories of our time together, and they will comfort me.

Your distraught admirer,

Luc.

Reading it through, he was satisfied with what he'd written. He thought of her sleeping. She would find the letter when she woke. He was about to push it under her door when the rattle of cartwheels and the slow clop of a horse's hooves outside caught his attention. He stiffened as he heard Hélène's voice. He ran to the window, peeked out—he didn't want her to catch him spying on her—and glimpsed a fair-haired young man sweeping her up in his arms. The young man swung her around before putting her down and kissing her. They laughed, examined each other and kissed for a second time.

Claude, for it could be no other, took her small case, placing it with care in the back of the cart. She waited, smiling at him as he put his hands on her waist and lifted her up onto the front seat. He strode around to the other side of the cart and climbed up, seating himself with quick, graceful movements. With a flick of the reins, the horse and cart lumbered into motion. As they drove away, Luc leaned out and saw Hélène lean her head on

Claude's shoulder and his head incline toward her. He watched till they disappeared, oblivious of the tears rolling down his face.

Chapter Nineteen

Our perception of time changes as we age. When we are young, the days are endless and we cannot see how we will ever get old. But when you are older, you realize how quickly the years pass. This is a 'spot' life, short in the grand scale of planets, stars, and the universe. Yet allowing fear to prevent living life to the full should be deeply regretted.

Paris, July 2007

Anna flew off the bed with the grace and speed of a high jump champion going for gold. One knock on the door and romance was gone.

"Tidy the bed," she hissed at

François, looking for her clothes "then go and let them in."

"Are you sure you've never done this? And why are you whispering? They can't hear us," he hissed back at her.

"I'll tidy myself and be straight out."

"Use the other door—it leads into the sitting room."

Anna swept up her nightclothes from where they'd been tossed, sprinting for the bathroom as François ran around smoothing the sheets and flicking the coverlet straight. Neither of them paid any attention to the fact they were stark naked.

"Come with me to find out about the letter, and for one last viewing of Hélène's portrait in the morning," she said before closing the bedroom door.

In the bathroom, Anna jerked her nightdress over her head, shoving her arms into her dressing gown with an odd sense of fast forwarding through the motions. What could be more embarrassing than being found in a compromising situation with a man–who wasn't your husband–by your daughter? She giggled. In retrospect, Ingrid's question that morning about having an affair appeared prophetic.

A generous splash of cold water refreshed her, and she checked her appearance in the mirror, smiling at the unaccustomed flush on her cheeks and bright shiny eyes. Finding a hairbrush, she dragged it through the tangles, deciding to wait till Ingrid and Jean-Paul were in the room before making her appearance. She stared at her reflection a bit longer, grinning at this new exhilarated self looking back brazenly at her.

She cracked open the door to the

sitting room and watched François stash the two empty brandy glasses in the sideboard, tightening his belt before reaching for the door handle. The knocking stopped, and she smiled as he put his ear to the door, watching him take a deep breath before opening it. She glimpsed Jean-Paul and Ingrid jumping apart, two startled rabbits caught in the headlights.

"Is my mother here?" Ingrid inquired, recovering her poise and walking past François, flicking her hair back as she entered the room.

"She's in the bathroom."

"You took your time opening the door, oncle."

The unrepentant couple exchanged a look.

"Ah, there you are at last." Anna swept out of the bathroom, glaring at the youngsters with a frosty expression. She hoped it was enough to hide the fact that all she really wanted to do was dance across the room. She took the position that the best type of defense is attack. "You pair are late." She hoped any oddities which the young couple might have noticed would be forgotten as they explained their tardiness.

François eyed Ingrid. "And your mother is not happy with you."

Ingrid's attention flickered back and forth between the two adults, and her shoulders slumped a fraction.

"Come on, Ingrid, bed. Thank you, François, I see you were right. They are fine."

Ingrid followed her mother meekly, turning and blowing kisses at Jean-Paul, before scurrying along the corridor to keep up with Anna's forced march. "Mum?"

Anna didn't answer. Chaotic, euphoric thoughts chased around and around. *I've made love with François; I've had sex with a man who isn't my husband. I shouldn't but I did. I feel terrible. I feel great.*

"Mum, are you okay?"

Anna couldn't trust herself to speak. Greg's wounded expression, alternated with vivid pictures of François, flushed with exertion, as they'd relaxed in that one, far too brief, moment before Ingrid and Jean-Paul returned. The lift hummed to a stop, and the doors slid open.

"Mum, answer me. Are you okay?" Ingrid repeated. "You're not behaving like your usual self."

"I'm more myself than I've been for a long time," Anna replied as she pressed the button for their floor.

As Ingrid finished in the bathroom,

Anna sat up in bed waiting to talk with her daughter, but it was hard to stay focused. She longed to close her eyes and relive the night's experience. Did she have any regrets? At this moment, the answer was no. But tomorrow? She'd have to wait and see.

As Ingrid emerged with her makeup scrubbed off, hair brushed and glowing with health, Anna was aware the ties of attachment were stretching, loosening. She knew this was natural, but it tore at her because one child had been ripped from her so abruptly, and her remaining child strained for release from the restrictive bonds of maternal love.

Ingrid sat on the end of Anna's bed and tucked her knees up under her chin. "I'm sorry, Mum."

Anna didn't want a confrontation. Coming to Paris had transformed her, allowing her to acknowledge the changes in her daughter. "Are you?" Her eyebrows rose. She pushed aside the memory of François's lips on her skin: she'd never betrayed her husband before.

"Look at this." Ingrid was off the bed and retrieving her phone from her bag. She tapped a couple of times and thrust the phone at her mother. "It's a drawing Jean-Paul made of me."

Anna took the phone and studied the photo. Jean-Paul had captured Ingrid's vivacity with a few deft lines.

"Here, press this button. There's more."

Jean-Paul had made half a dozen sketches of Ingrid from different angles. Some were, like the first, merely a few lines, others he'd taken more time over, shading and delineating Ingrid's eyes and eyebrows, her hair corkscrew wild.

"Wow! They're really, really good, Ingrid."

"He's going to use them for a portrait. He says it'll make him feel as if he's with me."

"Can you send them to my phone?"

Ingrid looked askance at her mother. "Ooo! Who's thoroughly modern now? Of course, I can. But should I?" Ingrid arched an eyebrow. She took back her phone and pressed a few buttons. "There, sent you the photos," she said, gazing at the sketches. "I think of him constantly. Sometimes it feels as if we're one person." Ingrid gazed at her mother with the earnest honesty of youth.

"And in the first flush of love, you'll feel that way, whether it's your first or fiftieth love," Anna replied.

"I love everything about him: the

way he squints when he's focusing on something in the distance; the way he runs his hands through his hair before he asks me what I think of his work. Does that sound stupid?"

"No, it doesn't." Anna's voice was quiet. "But people do change, Ingrid. If love seems a bed of sweet roses, remember, roses have thorns."

"I know," Ingrid sighed. "It hasn't been easy for you and Dad since Jeremy died, has it?"

"No." Anna considered how it wasn't her and Greg alone who'd suffered; Ingrid had also paid a price for their inability to cope with Jeremy's loss. Had Jeremy's death exposed the gaps in their marriage previously hidden behind the habits of daily life? But she couldn't, she wouldn't be sad. Jeremy would have wanted their lives to be filled with loving and giving: and

François was showing her that she could live in this world and move past her pain. "I'm sorry if that made things more difficult for you."

But Ingrid had already returned to the present. "And since arriving in Paris, I have two new loves in my life."

"Two?" Anna thought of Greg and François. She thought of Émilie and Hélène. Paris had a lot to answer for.

Ingrid held up her fingers and counted. "Yes." She ticked off one finger. "First, Jean-Paul, and two," she ticked the second finger, "Paris. I've fallen in love with Paris. I might come back after Biarritz. I do have a few weeks before starting university." She let the statement dangle, but Anna refused to take the bait.

The battle to control Ingrid was lost, indeed had been for a while. Anna just hadn't known it. From here on she had to trust Ingrid's choices.

Anna's phone rang silencing her retort but as she stretched over to pick it up from the bedside table, she grabbed one of her pillows, throwing it at Ingrid. The pillow caught Ingrid by surprise, smacking her lightly in the chest.

"Mum!" Ingrid pretended outrage. She laughed and raised the pillow to throw it back.

Anna checked her mobile. Five messages from Greg.

"Give me a minute, I'd better read these, they're from your father." Anna flicked through the texts. The first one confirmed the time his plane would arrive at Charles de Gaulle airport the following day. Next, he asked her to confirm she'd received the first. The third, fourth and fifth messages repeated the second one, but each time an increasingly desperate comment was added. The fifth message ended with 'Please, please answer no matter what time. I'm genuinely worried.' This was followed by an uncharacteristically long row of x's. Most unlike Greg. Another ring delivered the photos of Jean-Paul's sketches of Ingrid.

"What did Dad say? You look like you've seen a ghost. It'll be good to see Dad, won't it Mum?"

"Of course it will."

Ingrid picked up a pillow. "Lean forward," she instructed, plumping the pillow and propping it behind Anna. "There. You answer Dad. I need my beauty sleep. I don't want Jean-Paul to remember me with bags under my eyes!" She kissed Anna on the cheek and gave her a quick tight hug. "I love you, Mum."

"I love you too, darling."

As Anna texted a reassuring reply to Greg, she remembered François. He'd given her the gift of living in the present once more. Maybe it's not the first or second love that truly counts she reflected, pressing the send button, it's the current one. Nonetheless, her bonds with Greg were tied tight. Tomorrow, as far as external appearances went, her life would resume its normal rhythms; the annual holiday, sleeping beside her husband, talking with him. He'd mentioned some spectacular subterranean caves up in the Pyrenees he wanted them to visit. Greg was attentive in ways like that. He was a good man and a good husband.

Till the death of their son, they had traveled a very smooth path in life together, and she wasn't sure if it was possible to find the exact moment she'd fallen out of love with him. The few days apart had revealed a fresh perspective on their relationship. She wondered if they could find their way back. Or was the love they'd had gone forever? She didn't know, despite tonight, if she could picture life without him. Would it take more courage to continue in her marriage or if there was nothing retrievable between them, separate and be on her own? Had she betrayed him tonight or had she been betraying herself for years.

Chapter Twenty

Success is a validation; a confirmation that you have opened the eyes of others to a new way of looking at the world, and people appreciate your vision. Artists of all varieties seek this reciprocation, which is why they put their work into the public arena.

Paris, April 1874

Luc waited outside the front gate by the carriage, tapping his foot, checking his watch and constantly glancing at the house.

Émilie stood by the front door. "Vite, Vite! Come on, children."

Giselle and Guy bounded down the stairs, followed by a flustered Marie waving a sailor's hat.

"Guy, wait. Put your hat on," she called, her hand outstretched without a hope of catching the silver-quick child.

"Guy," Émilie's quiet voice brought him up short.

As Émilie and Marie finished the final adjustments to Guy's hat, completing his crisp blue and white sailor outfit, Giselle skipped out the door, turning and sticking out her tongue at her brother before running ahead.

Today was the opening of the first independent exhibition of the Société Anonyme des Peintures, Artistes et Graveurs, and three of Luc's submissions had been accepted by the committee. He was proud and terrified to have his art on show alongside that of Monet, Renoir, and others whom he considered to be the greatest artists of his day. His nerves were stretched to breaking point. At last, with the four of them seated in the carriage, Émilie by his side and the children sitting opposite, they were ready to leave.

"Are you all right?" Luc glanced at his wife's swollen belly.

"I'm fine, and I wouldn't miss this for the world." She patted her stomach. "This one is as stubborn as you, and won't arrive till after the exhibition is over."

Luc stuck his head out of the window. "Let's go," he shouted at the driver.

The children waved madly, shouting their goodbyes as they departed.

"Bon chance!" Marie's voice floated after them.

The carriage rolled along at a smart pace, the clip-clop of the horse's hooves accompanying the creaking of the carriage. As they left Rue Murillo and turned onto the more major roads leading to their destination the carriage slowed, merging into the traffic. The children were agog at the trams, horseless carriages and the pedestrians on the streets. They pointed and exclaimed over the sights with breathless excitement.

"I'm hot, maman!" Guy tugged at his collar and took off his hat.

"Guy, do as your mother tells you." Luc was rarely, if ever, harsh with his children but today he was unable to control his temper.

Guy sulkily obeyed Luc's reprimand

Émilie placed her lavender-gloved hand on Luc's arm, letting it rest there for a minute. She understood today could be a pivotal moment in Luc's career. Whether those who had important positions in the Paris art world came or not, the critics would put in an appearance to view the exhibition. A lambasting in a prestigious newspaper could leave an artist the laughing stock of the nation.

Nadar, a prominent photographer who supported the artists, had given his studio over to the group. Many promises of help had been given, but no one else turned up yesterday evening and Luc had spent half the night in the gallery helping Renoir hang the pictures in their allocated spaces. The more established artists had first choice of placement for their pieces and the newer, younger artists, like Luc, had to be content with hanging theirs in the less prominent positions. Luc had selected one larger painting, plus two smaller ones, and his work hung in the middle of the left wall. Although not the first ones that drew the attention as visitors entered the room, they were well positioned.

He'd slept little when he finally arrived home in the early hours of the morning and now he had the strangest sense of being both too wound up, and at the same time exhausted and disconnected from himself. As they approached Boulevard des Capucines, Luc's eyes glittered as he searched for familiar faces. His fingers jerked, and he tapped his knees non-stop until Émilie reached out a second time.

"Everything will be fine. You'll see," she told him, stilling his twitching fingers.

He blew his lips out with a loud sigh. "This is important for me."

Guy copied his father, blowing his lips out and making a louder sound.

The tension broke as Luc and Émilie burst out laughing.

Luc pulled off his son's cap, ruffling

his hair before plonking it back on sideways.

"Papa!" Guy was indignant.

Émilie leaned forward, fixing her son's hat as the carriage came to a stop. The crush of carriages and new-fangled motor vehicles parked outside Nadar's meant they had to leave the carriage and walk two blocks to the gallery.

Luc tucked Émilie's hand under his arm and they joined the steady crowd, moving along the busy promenade. Giselle clasped his other hand, while Guy walked by his mother's side, for once sedate and behaving in the manner expected by his parents.

Outside Nadar's a queue had formed waiting to enter the exhibition.

"Follow me, children. Stay close." Luc led the way up the stairs to the second floor muttering apologies as they squeezed past the queue.

When they finally reached the studio at the top, the door attendant, Renoir's half-brother, greeted him with a smile motioning for Luc and his family to enter.

"Over there," Luc spoke in an undertone, "see the man with the straw hat and cane?"

Émilie turned casually in the direction he indicated.

"That's the critic, Louis Leroy." Luc's eyes narrowed as he noticed the man evaluating one of Monet's exhibits and scribbling notes on a small writing pad.

The large room was packed with people, and the loud conversations indicated the paintings on show were eliciting a definite response.

Luc had the feeling the reactions weren't necessarily going to be ones the artists appreciated. "Oh, no!" Luc muttered under his breath.

"What is it?" Émilie asked.

"There's another one. Cardon. Emile Cardon. He hates us."

"Well, you know there are always people who hate change. And this," she waved her arm indicating the whole room, "is change. Art won't be the same after this exhibition. Try to relax, Luc. You know I'm right."

"Which ones are yours, Papa?" Giselle tugged on her father's hand.

"Yes," echoed Émilie. "These are the first paintings you're exhibiting that I've never seen—not one sketch did you show me. So I want to view yours first, and after that, I'll see the others."

Luc guided them through the throng of people crowding the room. Émilie followed him keeping a firm grip on Giselle's hand on one side, and Guy's on the other. They could hear voices raised in argument as they passed. The old guard faces down the new, thought Luc, hearing derogatory comments about Pissarro's painting of Pontoise.

He stopped and spoke quietly in Émilie's ear. "Be honest. Examine all three before you make your judgment." His mouth thinned to a line as he stared at her. "The truth. I need to know the truth." She was his biggest supporter and he trusted her to be frank with him.

As soon as she saw them, she knew which three were his. She stopped, standing a little distance away before moving closer to scrutinize them.

Luc looked, not at his artwork, but at Émilie's face. Her expression would tell him her real opinion.

The first, and largest, was a rural scene painted on a summer day with cotton clouds wisping across a blue sky.

Two women holding parasols sat opposite each other with a baby lying on a blanket between them and various picnic items on the side. One woman, dark hair, and lively eyes, leaned in toward the baby, full of maternal softness as she gazed at her child. In response, the baby stared back up at its mother, looking almost alive as it appeared to wave its arms and legs. The second woman, younger, complexion and hair more golden, smiled at the other two. Effective brush strokes gave the impression of leaves and grass rippling in a light breeze. The title was *Les femmes et le bébé.*

Émilie studied the large painting for several moments.

Luc paced back and forth behind them, frowning, waiting to hear his wife's opinion.

Giselle imitated her mother and

stared with fixed attention at her father's accomplishments "Who's the pretty girl, Papa?"

Luc stopped pacing and looked intently at his daughter.

Émilie moved along to join Giselle surveying the second painting. This was the portrait of Hélène. Émilie could see it was one of the young women from the picnic but here she sat nearer to the artist, with her features shown more clearly than in the first picture.

Luc had captured the woman's frank appraisal as she stared out at the viewer. He'd painted her with her head tilted back a fraction, making her look as if she challenged whoever had the temerity to observe her. She gleamed with youth and in contrast to her pose, her eyes had a humorous expression, and her lips were full, curling up at the corners, making it seem as if she was enjoying a private joke.

Émilie moved closer, scrutinizing details. "She's lovely. You've captured her freshness and innocence. *Hélène*, a simple title, suits the painting. I take it that's her name? Is she going to be here today?"

Artists' models often came to openings, keen to see themselves immortalized on canvas.

"Will we meet her?" She turned but Luc had vanished. "Where's Papa?" she asked Guy who stood with his hands behind his back, imitating his father's pose.

"He left." Guy pointed in the general direction of the entrance.

Émilie searched the crowd in time to catch sight of Luc's head as he disappeared out the door.

"The flowers, maman! The flowers!" Giselle was eager to look at the last painting and tugged her mother's hand. "Maman!"

The last, and smallest, of Luc's exhibits, showed a still life of a vase of flowers with a background of fields fading into the distance. He'd used strong colors on the flowers as most were in full bloom and the painting epitomized summer.

"Of course, chérie." Émilie allowed her daughter to drag her in front of the third picture, but her gaze kept returning to the image of Hélène.

Luc stood on the Boulevard des Capucines. The spring leaves gifted the street with a lushness lacking throughout the winter months. Ladies out shopping mingled with businessmen, and hawkers' cries echoed along the road. In the distance, Luc heard the sound of a musician playing an accordion. He breathed deep.

After returning from Bordeaux the previous summer, he'd put Hélène's portrait at the back of the studio hoping to lessen the ache of her absence. He'd tackled his next painting, the flowers from Hélène's hotel room, in an agitated, maniacal frenzy. After completing it to his satisfaction, he lay in a despondent smog of absinthe during which his mood alternated between self-loathing, guilt, wretchedness, and endless resolutions to be satisfied with his life. He was doing the one thing he was born for, fulfilling his one purpose in life— painting. He adored his family. He lived in an elegant home. What did he lack? Nothing.

For months afterward, Hélène had remained a dull ache on the edge of his consciousness, but eventually, his passion for her had diminished. Hélène had married and lived with her husband in her new life. He accepted it was a life that did not and could not ever include him.

One question which disturbed him greatly, and to which he had no answer, was that if he truly loved Émilie, his wife, the mother of his children and intellectual companion to boot, how had these feelings for Hélène arisen? How had his desire for her flared with such suddenness? And what if this problem resurfaced in the future?

Many of his artist friends slept with their models, but for the most part, it happened when they and the women were young. Several, including Manet and Cezanne, had married their muses, settling down to enjoy marriage and family life. Luc, on the other hand, had married and had a family first, losing his sanity later.

These days the whole affair seemed a mirage, a dream. He'd seen the painting in the studio and chosen to exhibit it, but when Émilie looked at it, he'd forgotten she was the one person who understood his art. As one of his best pieces, it had to be shown, but if Émilie ever caught the tiniest glimpse of how obsessed he'd been with Hélène for that brief period, she might never forgive him. Surely this nervousness stemmed from anxiety about the reception of his work? He had to remain calm.

"Hey, Luc!" A hand slapped him on the back.

"Ah, De Nittis!"

"Are you preparing for the lion's den?"

"No, I've been in already. I needed a little fresh air."

"Well, lead on. I shall take courage behind your back!" His friend laughed.

Luc relaxed. He was letting the pressure get to him. He had to keep things in perspective.

When he rejoined Émilie, she was standing in front of Hélène's portrait, talking with Madame Manet. By the bright expression on the woman's face, Luc could tell the topic of conversation was Émilie's pregnancy.

"Congratulations, M'sieur Marteille!" Madame Manet smiled at him, running her gaze over the three exhibits. "Wonderful! Wonderful!" She gestured grandly in the direction of the wall. "I love them."

"Merci, Madame." Luc made her a polite bow. "Coming from you that is indeed a compliment."

"We'll meet later," she murmured to Émilie, sailing off to mingle with the crowd.

"So, did you sleep with her?" Émilie leaned in, speaking softly and pointing to the portrait. Luc felt a rush of adrenaline. His heart sped faster, his breath came quicker. His work had betrayed him, but he respected his wife too much to pretend he misunderstood her meaning.

"No. Émilie! I never sleep with my models." His voice was a jagged uneven whisper. "I've never broken that vow to you." At least he could say that with honesty, he thought. "Émilie, please. I promise you on my life. On the life of my children."

"I believe you, but that doesn't mean you didn't fall in love with her." She looked at him for a long moment, and his stomach sank at the hostile glare she gave him. "This is exquisite," she moved over to inspect the still life.

"Please don't sell it. I will ask Papa to buy it for me. I love it." She spoke as if the preceding conversation had never taken place and returned to surveying Luc's paintings. "I think these are the best you have done so far."

Luc's shoulders relaxed. He wanted to be acknowledged as a painter of worth, to achieve success in his field, but it was Émilie whose opinion he valued above any other. She'd had faith in him as an artist since the first time she'd seen his work.

"Thank you, chérie."

"So, anything sold?"

Luc turned, smiling at the speaker, Renoir. He was flattered when these older, more well-known artists spoke to him as an equal. "Yes. Émilie's father will be buying one."

They laughed. Artists appreciated their rich relatives, especially the generous ones.

"Well, our families are very important to us," Renoir nodded, beaming at Émilie, "but our mistress is more important."

Émilie's eyebrows rose. "You share a mistress?" She cast a sideways glance at Luc who stared transfixed at Renoir. "You must tell me her name so I may call on her."

"Art, my dear lady! Art, the creative impulse, is the most demanding mistress a man can have."

The three of them laughed at his joke. Luc laughed the hardest.

Renoir leaned forward and winked at Émilie. "Surely, my dear, you must be aware by now she's a very jealous demanding mistress who doesn't like to share."

Chapter Twenty-One

In this world, everything tends toward entropy. You have to work hard to stay in the same place, for the fact is, there is no standing still. You may think you are pausing, resting, but everything around you is changing, corrupting, un-becoming. We have this one second in which to live, experience and fulfill our desires. Yet all endings mark a beginning.

Paris, July 2007

Anna stirred the crystals of brown sugar, watching as they merged into the slow whirlpool she was creating on the creamy froth that sat atop her latte. The distant hum of traffic barely registered. She was dreamy, set apart from the early morning crispness that surrounded her as Parisians and tourists alike stepped out to face the new day. Part of her still lay in François's arms. The memory of François, his smell, his touch, being that intimate with someone other than Greg, had set her adrift. She remembered his profile as he lay back on the pillows and the smoothness of his skin. Yes, sex was a powerful urge. No wonder religion and society kept it under strict wraps.

She reflected on what she knew about Luc Marteille, no longer judging him so harshly. Who knew what desires drove him? She hardly understood her own motivations, let alone someone who had been dead for over a hundred years, although human desires remained pretty much the same. She sighed—part satisfaction, part regret— and picked up a croissant, not in the least bit surprised to find it soft, light and melting in her mouth. She was at peace.

Ingrid's broken French and Jean-Paul's fluid responses announced their imminent arrival, their voices louder as they approached. But she didn't turn, not wanting to end her enjoyment of the moment

"Good morning, Madame Anna." Jean-Paul made a modest bow, his sing-song English making her smile.

"Bonjour maman," chimed Ingrid.

Gosh, what a beauty, thought Anna looking at her daughter's glowing skin, slender figure and auburn curls, a flaming halo in the morning sunlight. "Bonjour, mes enfants," she responded, stressing 'enfants'.

"What are your plans for this

morning?" Jean-Paul inquired hesitantly. He studied his feet, penitent and reluctant to meet her gaze.

"I have to collect my letter, Luc's letter that is, from the Musée, and have my last viewing of Hélène's portrait. We're both packed and ready to check out, aren't we Ingrid?" She preferred the pair of them take off by themselves seeing it was their final morning. Plus, she and François could, I don't know, she thought, talk? Be two adults together?

"Yep," Ingrid moved closer to Jean-Paul. "All that's left is to open the door and grab the bags."

"And if I have time, I might take a walk along the Seine." Was she making it too obvious that she would prefer they went off by themselves?

"That's perfect, Mum. Jean-Paul and I will come with you if that's all right?"

Ingrid's eyes flicked from her mother to Jean-Paul seeking confirmation.

"Why wouldn't it be?" The one time she didn't want them around! "Don't you two want to spend time by yourselves?" She hoped she sounded non-committal.

Jean-Paul leaned forward conspiratorially. "We hope to show you we are not irresponsible. That we are truly sorry for upsetting you and returning late."

They nodded, their red-gold and brown-gold heads bobbing vigorously.

"Oh," she replied. "You mean responsible today, don't you?"

The youngsters looked offended at the tartness of her tone, and she could see Ingrid smothering the retort that danced on the edge of her tongue. Anna hid the pleasure she was enjoying at having the upper hand.

"Bonjour, Anna." François's voice broke the silence. "How are you on this beautiful morning?"

Anna turned her attention away from the two youngsters. "I'm fine. Very fine indeed." Oops, that slipped out too quick. She avoided making eye contact with François. "Sit, children."

François spotted a waiter and signaled him over as he sat down next to Anna amid a clattering of chairs scraping and settling as the group arranged itself at the table.

"Ingrid and Jean-Paul were telling me how they're joining us for the whole morning. They're feeling guilty for the inconvenience they put us through last night," Anna informed François, noting what thoughtful brown eyes he had, how they lightened with humor as he spoke.

"How considerate."

Ingrid and Jean-Paul sat facing them, their backs straight and heads slightly bowed as if hauled before two school principals.

During breakfast, François informed the young pair it was more of a punishment than anything else if the four of them had to pass the entire morning together. He gave them half the morning by themselves and gave instructions to meet up at 11 o'clock at the Pont Royal. He teased his nephew there'd be plenty of time to focus on him after Anna and Ingrid left. Love-sick puppies needed a lot of tender loving care.

Jean-Paul and Ingrid tolerated every jibe. Ingrid wanted a quick trip to the boutiques; Jean-Paul wanted to take her to the Eiffel Tower. So they left, arguing in lover's fashion over where to go, simply so they could make up later.

After they disappeared around the corner François leaned toward Anna. "And how are you? I mean, really, how are you?" His tone was hesitant, his eyes questioning.

She understood. He would take his cue from her. As a gentleman, he was assessing her manner toward him before revealing his thoughts. Anna blushed. She tried to control it, raising her hands to cover her confusion.

He reached out and took her hands away from her face, tilting her chin so she had to look up at him. "Last night was a gift. A gift for me because it showed me I can feel after my Lucie's death. But also a gift for you. You've learned you cannot shut off your emotions. I'm well acquainted with that numbness, that empty place where you do not have to suffer. But for you to truly live, that ice must thaw, and melt.

That place of grief, it is not life."

Slow tears trickled down her cheeks. He was right. Whatever had happened between them, whatever the future held, she realized the universe, Fate, whatever you called it, had stepped in. She offered silent thanks to Luc. Without the search for his story, she would never have come to Paris, would never have met François. She would not have been as fully alive as she was now.

"Thank you, François. Thank you."

He folded a napkin and carefully dabbed her face.

She placed her hand over his. "I won't forget you, François." She couldn't say anymore.

They had come together, and whatever was in store for them, their paths in life were separating, but a dam had been breached. She was different.

She'd returned to life. Jeremy's smiling face flickered before her inner eye. He wouldn't have resented her enjoying life.

"Come, chérie." He stood and smiled at her.

She gathered her bag, and hooking her arm through his, smiled back at him. They were good with each other. Nothing complicated; this was understood, and it wasn't a problem. "Allons y," she said liking his peal of laughter at her French.

Arm in arm, two friends, two conspirators, they merged into the pedestrian traffic and set off for the Musée des Impressionists.

"Ah, Madame, Monsieur." Monsieur Battignon, sporting an incongruous red and black striped tie, dabbed at his forehead with a large handkerchief for the day was warming significantly, and inside the museum the air was close. "The letter! Ah, oui! You are correct". He beamed at her. "It has been verified by Monsieur Trochard of the Louvre archives, and, yes, it appears" he expelled his excitement like the air rushing out of a balloon in one exultant burst, "your letter was written by," he paused, milking the moment for impact, "none other than Luc Marteille himself."

Anna's instincts had told her right from the moment Mr. Bentonly had placed his discovery in her hand, that the letter was authentic, but it was tremendous to have it verified. She gave the curator a big smile.

"Congratulations," François said.

"I wonder if I might make a gift of his letter to the Musée? I'll send you the original after I return to England." She heard François's indrawn breath, but she had made her decision. She wanted to give something back to Paris. The city had revived something precious–the wonder of being alive–and reciprocation was more than important, it was necessary. She glanced at François. Surprise and approval.

"Of course, Madame," the curator stuttered, overcome by the heady gift of a new letter. "Um, there are a few forms. And… after you send the original, we will issue a certificate of authenticity. Please… follow me, and you can sign the necessary papers right away." He bustled off as if afraid she'd change her mind if he delayed.

After the official signing over of the letter was complete, they went for one last look at Luc's paintings.

"Whenever I wish to remember you, I can come here and look at your letter and Luc's paintings, can't I?" François joked, "You're my Hélène."

She elbowed him in the ribs. "Are all Frenchman as hopelessly romantic as you?" She grinned at him. "What do you suppose Luc would have thought if he saw the future and knew that strangers would be picking over his life?" she asked.

"Perhaps he'd be pleased because it wouldn't be happening unless he'd achieved the success he sought."

"Well, we've gained more understanding of the man, haven't we?"

François put his arms around her, held her close and kissed the top of her head. He smelled of musky cedarwood; she breathed in deep so she might remember.

Standing in front of the portrait of Hélène, she experienced a closeness to Luc. She hadn't thought it could be so easy to seek something—satisfaction, pleasure, comfort, she wasn't sure what—outside her marriage. All it had taken was a particular set of circumstances, as could happen at any time to anyone, and her moral compass had located a new north.

And the question of Greg remained. Did they have a future? How much was she willing to invest toward that particular future? What she did know was that she hadn't foreseen participating in an episode like last night. If it did mean something, it would affect her relationship with Greg. She stroked François's arm. He smiled. She smiled back. So comfortable, so uncomplicated. No expectations; enough for the moment.

Ingrid and Jean-Paul were leaning over the bridge and watching the river, his arm around her waist, as Anna and

François approached.

Anna peered over the bridge. "What's so fascinating?" she asked.

"We're deciding which houseboat we want to live on. We fancy that one, with the flowers in those crazy pots." Ingrid pointed at the most exuberantly decorated boat, before giving her mother a big hug. "I can't thank you enough for bringing me here, Mum. I've had the best time. Paris is wonderful!" She directed her smile at Jean-Paul.

"Let's walk." said François.

Ingrid and Jean-Paul's quick back and forth banter, punctuated by giggles, drifted back as Anna and François followed the young couple off the bridge. The sky was blue, the air warm on the skin, and the leaves of the trees shimmered and sparkled in the sunlight. The Seine flowed alongside, small choppy waves ruffling its surface.

François walked by her side, attentive yet careful not to touch. "You remember I told you about my life's ambition?" François asked.

"Your boat? I would have thought that as an estate agent, you must have desired to build something grand?"

"No, quite the opposite. The truth is I have planned the route I will sail and changed it many times. First to Gibraltar, the Azores, across the Atlantic—I'd skip Panama—go to Rio, and yes, I promised myself the challenge of Cape Horn, up to Hawaii, over to Tahiti, Samoa, Australia and back via India, and South Africa's Cape of Good Hope."

"Wow!" She watched as his eyes took on a far-away look. He was there already. For one brief second, he carried her with him. On a yacht, what an adventure it would be—wild seas and wild wind. She blinked the images away. No, that wasn't her dream, but she was conscious of the infectious pull such a voyage exerted.

Anna had the urge to reach out and link arms with him, regardless of what Ingrid and Jean-Paul might think. But she didn't. She accepted this was how you conducted an affair. A couple enjoyed intimacy when alone but practiced deceit in front of the world. She didn't think she could tolerate being divided that way for long.

"After Jean-Paul goes home," he continued, "I shall go and stay on *Ma Belle*, and see what happens. I'm keen to start work."

She recognized the anticipation on his face.

"Yes, Anna. We have both benefited. It's not been one-sided."

They strolled, silent companions,

comfortable with not talking as the life of the city continued around them.

After a taxi deposited them back at the Place du Tertre, they headed for the hotel.

François touched Anna's arm slowing her down and letting the young couple go ahead. "I'm no good at goodbyes, Anna." His mouth drew down at the corners; he shrugged.

She smiled at the gesture. "It's okay."

"Jean-Paul is going with you to the airport but..." he trailed off, leaving the sentence unfinished.

Anna gave him a small smile. "Yes, that might be, um, how shall we say, awkward?"

They laughed.

It was easy to laugh with François. How had she ever thought he was standoffish?

He looked ahead. Ingrid and Jean-Paul had disappeared into the hotel. He cupped Anna's face in his hands, bent and kissed her full on the lips.

She leaned into him, resting her head on his chest. Her emotions welled up and she let the tears fall.

He wiped them away with a tender hand. "So this is my real goodbye to you, Anna."

"Au revoir and thank you, François. Thank you for everything."

They were both aware of tides shifting. Finding each other had been an unexpected gift, but the river of life was taking them in different directions. And that was how it had to be. Hand in hand, they walked toward the hotel.

Once they crossed the threshold and were inside, Anna knew that would be it. This, whatever this was, would be in the past: it would be over. She took a deep breath and paused for a second as they arrived at the entrance. They stood close, arms touching, as a group of tourists, chittering like excited parrots, streamed around them. Their fingers loosened and fell softly apart.

In no time, the porter carried out their suitcases and put them into the trunk of the waiting taxi. Anna sat in the front seat while Jean-Paul and Ingrid curled up together in the back. She hardly noticed the noise and hustle of the traffic as their taxi driver, hell-bent on breaking a Guinness book speed record, darted through gaps in the traffic, braking sharply and weaving between lanes as if on skates. Anna was in-between. In-between what had gone before and what would happen next. She was suspended, outside normality, but strangely enough without anxiety. Jeremy smiled at her. She smiled back.

At the airport terminal, Ingrid and Jean-Paul remained entwined until the last second, and parted with promises of the tweets, texts, emails, skypes, and phone calls they'd make.

Greg was standing outside a bookshop, mobile in hand when Ingrid flew at him. He hugged her and looked up at Anna.

He was so familiar. He had been her life's companion, the chosen, the beloved. She read the questions in his eyes, in his demeanor. Had the trip helped her in any way? Was she still marooned in grief? He would always stand by her as he'd promised on their wedding day, but the journey had become more difficult, more burdensome of late than either of them had anticipated.

Greg moved Ingrid aside as Anna reached him. He opened his arms, and she moved into his embrace, feeling the relief in his body. He released her and looked at her. "You must tell me all about it."

THE END

FROM THE AUTHOR

Thank you very much for reading **One Summer in Montmartre**. If you enjoyed the book, please let your friends know, and I'd be very grateful if you could take a few minutes to leave a review (short or long makes no difference) because you'll be giving me something rarer than gold.

Visit https://writingmynovelnoworkingtitleyet.blogspot.co.uk/ and sign up for the author's mailing list to receive your **free** copy of **Hekate's Chalice,** Book One of the *Adept Solutions Series*, information about new releases, discounts, and advanced reading copies.

Other books by Teagan Kearney:

Kala Trilogy
Healer's Magic
Vampire's Bane
Demon's Nemesis

Adept Solutions Series
Hekate's Chalice
Sorcerous Deeds
Ancestral Secrets

The Saoirse Saga
Stars & Ashes
Awakened Defiance

Hidden World Trilogy
Veiled Planet

Gold Dragon Haiku

You'll occasionally find me at the following websites:

https://twitter.com/@teagankearney

https://www.facebook.com/TeaganKearneyWriter/

https://www.wattpad.com/teagankearney

Drop by anytime.

www.ingramcontent.com/pod-product-compliance
Lightning Source LLC
Chambersburg PA
CBHW022234020726

47496CB00004B/897